THE STARS IN THE SKY

A ROMANCE

GIVING YOU ...
BOOK 2

LESLIE MCADAM

Cover design by RJ Creatives.

Editing by L Woods LLC.

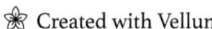 Created with Vellum

THE GIVING YOU ... SERIES

What would you give someone you loved? I would give them

The Sun and the Moon,
The Stars in the Sky,
All the Waters of the Earth,
and
The Ground Beneath Our Feet

This book is dedicated to my children, Joseph and Fiona.
May you always live in a world where people love one another and
see beyond the names we call each other. May you and your children
and your children's children grow up in a world where people care
about the next generation and always want to make it better for the
future.
And may you never read past this page of this book.

"Every atom in your body came from a star that exploded. And, the
atoms in your left hand probably came from a different star than your
right hand. It really is the most poetic thing I know about physics: You
are all stardust."—Lawrence M. Krauss

1

FIRST IMPRESSIONS

GOD, I REALLY HAD to pee.

Only ten more minutes to go until I got there. *Come on, come on, come on.* I willed my car to go faster as I zoomed down a country road out in the middle of nowhere. The last thing I wanted was to have to stop and find a bush. I squeezed my thighs together. Since it was a hot June day and I had on denim short-shorts, this just made me sticky and sweaty. Not helping.

It also didn't help that my body was vibrating with excitement from anticipation for my new adventure this summer. That just made me all the more uncomfortable. Gah! When would I get there?

The time of arrival on my GPS app ticked down to nine more minutes.

I pressed the gas pedal down harder. I drove an old Mercedes sedan that had been converted to biodiesel, so I should probably call it the accelerator rather than the gas pedal. California lacks proper public transit (a perennial item on my crusade list), so you have to drive everywhere. I did my best to cut down on my use of fossil fuels. Leftover vegetable oil from

Chinese restaurants powered my car and I proudly advertised its alternative fuel source on the back window in big green lettering. It always smelled like kitchen grease wherever I went, but I'd do anything for the environment.

This morning, eager and wired, with my car packed up for the summer, I stopped by the new Santa Barbara location of Southwinds Coffee, the local coffee chain owned by Ryan Fielding, the boyfriend of my best friend, Amelia Crowley. He happened to be working there when I stopped in, so I chatted with him while they made me the most unbelievable coffee. Ryan knows that I'm vegan, so I didn't even need to say that my coffee needed to have non-GMO soy milk and organic coffee beans. He just checked the boxes and handed it to the barista, then smiled at me and asked me about my summer internship.

Boy, he was cute. Yes, he was my best friend's surfer hottie, and they were totally devoted to each other, and I'd never get in the way of that, but I also had eyes and it was impossible not to stare. The fact that I was looking at him, though, probably meant that I seriously needed to get laid.

I couldn't think about that at the moment. All I could think about was that I really shouldn't have ordered the ginormous soy latte.

Seven minutes to go. Now I bounced along a dirt road. The ruts and ribs in the road did nothing good for my bladder.

I didn't know if I'd make it. I felt like a little kid. The bushes on the side of the road were starting to look mighty tempting.

I was driving to Headlands Ranch, my temporary home and job site for the summer. For the past year, I'd been going to school at the University of California at Santa Barbara, getting an advanced degree in Counseling Psychology. I wanted to help people, especially kids. I'd gone back to college after graduating ten years ago, keeping my job as a preschool teacher at a progressive school during the day, and going to school at night.

Although I wasn't sure where I wanted to end up, either setting up my own practice or working somewhere, I planned on becoming a therapist.

Hence my interest in this unique counseling job at Headlands.

I'd found Headlands Ranch on the internet after I saw an internship posting on Craigslist. From its website, I learned that Headlands was run by the fourth generation of an old California farming family, with William Charles Thrash, III, now in charge.

Sounded like a stiff old man.

Located on California's Central Coast, about halfway between Los Angeles and San Francisco, north of Santa Barbara near Santa Ynez, it was beautiful. I absolutely loved this part of the world, less than an hour's drive from my apartment in Santa Barbara, where gentle, rolling hills met the Pacific Ocean.

As I drove looking around at the farmland, it felt like a homecoming. My dad had been a migrant farmworker, my mother, an activist. Affected by the progressive politics of César Chávez, my mother, a tall, blonde German, wandered out into the fields one summer to pick grapes to feel how it felt. I get my crusading nature from her.

She met my dad and fell hard, and they worked side by side that summer. Handsome and unusually tall, my father grew up traveling up and down California's Central Valley with his parents, immigrants from Mexico. Unwilling to leave each other, they got married, had me and my siblings, and my mom followed my dad into the fields. They followed the seasons, picking vegetables, fruit, and nuts. Until I was in the third grade, we never stayed in one place for more than three months, and we always lived in agricultural areas like this. I grew up moving from camp to camp, staying in farmworker housing, which was normally utilitarian and small, but clean.

My father had grown up with his head in a book and

despite the constant moving, he cobbled together an education, earning a high school diploma. My grandparents weren't particularly supportive, believing that you needed to work hard and make money—school just got in the way. Nevertheless, he banked the coals of a dream of becoming a teacher. After he was married and had kids, my mom gave oxygen to his dream by talking about it in a way that made him believe he could do it despite his upbringing and despite our circumstances. And after a while, she talked him into getting a college degree from a community college, and later a full degree and a teaching credential. She got one too and became a Spanish teacher. And so eventually he became a high school teacher, working at my mom's rival school and settling down.

But those years of constantly moving, living out of an old army rucksack with my idealistic parents, meant that I never really got to know anyone and I got constantly uprooted. Sure, we'd run into acquaintances as we moved from place to place. There was a community. But I didn't have any consistent friends, at least not as a small child. Like a military kid, I got really good at making friends quickly, the kind of friends for right now, not forever. And as I got older, I learned to be the life of the party. But I never really had any consistent friends until Amelia, who I met in third grade. Even though I'd lived in Santa Barbara since then, I still had the belief that I was going to have to move on at any time.

This latest adventure was another part of this pattern of moving on to the next thing.

While the ranch was a diversified farming operation, with apparently everything from strawberries to blueberries to avocados to citrus to grapes for wine, what interested me was its affiliated nonprofit association where I had my internship. Headlands Ranch ran a therapeutic horsemanship and agricultural program, called the Headlands Program, my new employer.

It had two types of programs. The first was for urban Cali kids, the type who'd never seen a cow. They came to experience ranch life, learn to take care of animals, and do teamwork skills. The other program was for special needs kids, who'd ride therapy horses and spend time in the fresh air. I'd been hired as a glorified camp counselor, to plan and run the activities. It counted for credit for my graduate degree program.

This was going to be so much fun!

But not when I had a full bladder. As the clock on the GPS ticked down to five more minutes until arrival, I passed through a gate with an arch overhead that read HEADLANDS RANCH, ESTABLISHED 1910 in rustic font, very old-fashioned and Western-looking. I continued down an undulating dirt road and pulled up at a collection of farm buildings at the end of the line. I saw a huge, old, white farmhouse, what looked like a bunkhouse, some newer looking ranch houses, and barns, corrals, and other accessory buildings.

I parked my car and got out immediately, hoping against hope that there was a place to go pee, like, now.

A tall, thin woman came out of the bunkhouse to greet me. I'd guess she was around forty with sea green eyes and blonde hair pulled back in a no-nonsense ponytail. "You must be Marie Diaz-Austin. Welcome. I'm Janine Thompson, the head wrangler for the Headlands Program."

I stuck out my hand. "It's nice to meet you." Then I blurted, wide-eyed and pleading, "Can I use the bathroom? It's been a long drive and I'm dying."

She smiled and pointed to the closest building, the farmhouse. "Sure, go in there. Second door on the left down the hall."

I felt embarrassed enough already, so I tried not to run. But I failed miserably, and instead walked really, really fast to the building, like they speed-walk in the Olympics. I ran up the outside stairs, flung open the front door, scooted down the hall at a clip, and opened the second door on the left—

—and literally ran, full body, full bore, into a naked, wet man, who staggered with the impact of my weight against him. My breasts hit his back, my legs straddled the sides of his, and I grabbed onto his soaking nude waist to keep from falling. The front of my shirt, my shorts, and my legs got wet from the water on him.

"The fuck?" he grunted.

"Ohmigod, I'm so sorry," I started, as I jumped back immediately, hands up like I was being arrested, and then I got a look at him. He turned around to look at me, hands on hips, completely unabashed at wearing his birthday suit.

Well, this was interesting.

He was totally naked, as in just stepped out of the shower naked. He had not even had a chance to grab his towel, he was so naked. Did I mention that he was naked? And he was standing there, glaring at me, dripping on a bathmat, with the water that had not rubbed off on me running in rivulets down his legs.

I couldn't tell you what I noticed first about him, except that he was belongs-in-a-naughty-magazine's-centerfold attractive, but I'll give it a shot. I stared at him from his head to his toes.

He was really tall, like at least six inches taller than me, and I'm a not-short five foot ten.

His hair? Longish, wavy, wet (obviously), and a lush, dark brown.

Deep, dark, chocolate brown eyes glared at me, rimmed in enviable thick lashes that curled.

His classically handsome face had strong eyebrows, a straight nose, and high cheekbones, with hollows underneath, and yummy stubble along his square jaw.

His body? Tan everywhere. In other words, although this was a farm, he didn't have a farmer tan. And, since he was naked, as I might have mentioned, I could tell. He had a brawny chest, defined arms, a washboard waist, and strong legs.

And, his junk. Yep. There. Unlike a turtle, it was not hiding in a shell. He stood at half-staff and boy, full-staff would be a treat. His junk was the kind of junk that you used feet rather than inches to measure. As in more than half a foot, unerect. Well beyond.

A fucking gorgeous man.

Totally pissed at me.

I so knew how to make an entrance. I tried to salvage the situation, by mumbling "Janine told me I could use this bathroom," but he interrupted.

"Ever think of knocking?" he snarled, as he reached for a white towel and wrapped it around his waist, now looking like an ad for razor blades.

"I'm sorry," I said, aiming for sincerity. "It's been a long drive and I really have to pee." This last part came out of my mouth desperately.

"Go down the hall, there's another bathroom. I'm using this one." And he pushed me out, by physically pushing my shoulders, and shut the door.

Way to start the interactions with my fellow staff.

I took off running down the hall where I found the bathroom and relief. All was well, finally.

As I headed back down the hallway, his bathroom door opened and he came out, dressed in dark blue Wrangler jeans, with a belt and a huge belt buckle, a tight, faded blue t-shirt, and cowboy boots, hair still messy, curly, and wet.

He looked me up and down. Then he reached into his back pocket and pulled out a can of Copenhagen and stuffed a wad of chew in his cheek, staring at me.

Disgusting.

He turned and started walking away, muttering to himself, "Another fucking liberal."

"Hey!" I yelled. "What's wrong with that?"

My politics were extremely liberal, but so what? How could he tell? I wore normal clothes—my denim short-shorts, Tom's shoes, and a white cami that was probably see-through due to my literal run-in with Mr. Shower. I'd have to change.

Well, I suppose my nonconservative status was obvious, given my tattoos and my eyebrow piercing. I normally dyed my hair in colors that were not found in nature. But right now, it was bleached blonde and would probably stay that way for the summer. Naturally, my medium brown hair matched my medium brown eyes. I was skinny, with long legs (it was genetics, my parents were that way) but I had some boobage going on (again, genetics).

But how dare he judge me so quickly? And what do my politics have to do with my job?

He stopped, turned around and looked at me again, eyes traveling from head to toe and back again. Then he spoke.

"Darlin', life's too short to list all the things that are wrong with being a liberal," he drawled and sauntered out the front door and down the steps of the ranch house.

Oh, now I was pissed at him for being such a gross, judgmental asshole. But I didn't want to get into a fight in the first five minutes of my new job so I kept my mouth shut. For now. But this run-in did nothing good for my first day jitters.

Still, I couldn't help but watch him go. He had a damn sexy walk, almost like he owned the land he was walking on. Now, I'm not one who goes for cowboy hats and big belt buckles—my favorite type of music is *anything but country*—still, I couldn't help but notice that he filled those Wranglers out well. While I was still appreciating the craftsmanship of his jeans, he turned around. "This is Reagan Country, and don't forget it."

He turned back around just as quickly and kept going until he was out of sight.

Reagan Country? Was he kidding? Was he even born during the Reagan years?

Ugh.

Motherfucker!

2

EVEN

"HOME SWEET HOME," I thought, as I dragged my oversized suitcase up to the bunkhouse, behind Janine who led the way, carrying a large duffel bag of mine. I never packed lightly. I liked to feel like I had a home.

Reminiscent of the farmworker housing I lived in as a small child, the large, clapboard-covered building looked like it'd been there for a hundred years. It probably had. Inside, I found bunk bed-outfitted rooms, for girls on the bottom floor and boys on the second. The floorboards creaked and the rooms were small, but it had an aura about it of being well-kept, with swept floors, clean walls and sweet-scented, cool air. Framed black and white photos lined the hallways, with what looked like vintage pictures of the ranch. The building had been retrofitted with handicapped access, including a ramp up to the entrance, and even had an elevator to the second floor. I was impressed.

I was to bunk with the female staff, Janine and another woman, on the first floor towards the end of the building in a medium-sized room with four bunk beds; male staff slept on the second floor. We each got a full bunk to ourselves along with a small chest of drawers.

The bunkhouse had a utility room down the hall with a washer and dryer, a small kitchen with a staff refrigerator, which as a vegan, I'd definitely need, and a lounge, with ratty couches and a decrepit, old television with a DVD player. There was also a small office for me to use to plan programs and research on the internet.

While I was charmed by the vintage surroundings, one thing hit me: there was no privacy. I'd gotten used to living on my own in my apartment. This felt like living in a college dorm again. That said, even though it had been a decade since I lived in a dorm, I'm an extrovert who thrived off being around people. This sounded like fun and I was ready.

After giving me the tour, Janine took off for the stables, leaving me to change and unpack.

I set my suitcase on the floor by my bunk, went out to the car to get my pillow, sleeping bag, and other things, then came in to change into jeans. Janine was going to take me out on a horse, and I needed to be wearing long pants and good shoes. I also needed to take off my damp white cami.

I quickly took off my shirt, which had a shelf-bra, and stripped down to my thong, searching in my duffel bag for a bra.

And then I heard a recognizable, deep, male voice and loud footsteps coming quickly down the hall. Shit. Mr. Conservative Shower Man. I had, literally, nowhere to hide, and I hadn't thought to lock the door, since this was the floor for girls. It stood ajar. I moved toward the door to close it, but was too late. "Janine?" he called, and then knocked on the door frame and walked in, without waiting for a response.

Hi.

Now it was my turn to be caught naked. Well, practically. Amelia often accused me of being an exhibitionist. She's right, I am. But now it felt like Mr. Grouchy Shower Man and I were even.

There I stood, wearing a white lace thong and my tattoos, boobs on full display. Even though I was thin with long legs, I almost filled a C-cup. A cool breeze found its way through the building and made my nipples pucker. But I'm sure he didn't notice.

I also had my tattoos out for his perusal. On my left arm, down the inside, script lettering read *Omnia causa fiunt*, meaning "Everything happens for a reason" in Latin. On my left side waist, a Noah's ark was anchored, with animals, two by two, spilling out onto the front of my waist and the back. My plan? To save them all, if I could. On each hip bone I'd inked a star. I hoped that someday my lover would have matching stars and we could unite them. A dove permanently flew on my collar bone, with an olive branch, for peace. And on my right ass cheek, where he couldn't see it right now, up high near my waist rested a green and blue mother Earth, to protect.

Mr. Handsome Shower Man stood there, staring at me. Then his eyes raked down my body, then up, then down again.

Then he shook himself and turned red, shoving his hands in his jeans. He had to be close to my age, or maybe older, so seeing him act sheepish was kind of cute, and a marked contrast to his earlier asshole behavior.

"Guess it's my turn to be sorry," he said gruffly, and turned to go.

"Wait," I said, still practically naked, not caring, wiggling just to mess with him. And because goddamn he was hot.

"Yeah?" he responded, not turning around.

"What's your name?"

He finally turned to face me and looked me in the eyes. "Will Thrash."

The boss.

It figured. He walked around like he owned the place

because he *did* own the place. Still, everything happened for a reason.

"I'm Marie," I said, reaching out my hand to shake his.

He looked at me like I was crazy, which I probably was. While I should be embarrassed, I wasn't. I thought it was the funniest damn thing. He couldn't figure out whether to shake the hand of the topless, practically naked, female employee or not. It wasn't like we were in a strip club, where this was expected of the employees. He finally decided to shake my hand and did so firmly, averting his eyes and looking to the side, "I'll just go look for Janine," he said and then left.

But not before I saw a bulge the size of California in his Wranglers.

After I heard his footsteps fade down the hall, I collapsed on my bottom bunk in peals of laughter. And then I got dressed and went to go join Janine with the horses.

ANIMAL LOVER

T HIS TRAIL RIDE WASN'T going to be my first time on a horse. I used to ride as a kid. Exposure to animals like horses, as well as our family dogs and cats, made me become the passionate animal lover that I am. I was so happy to have the opportunity to be around horses and animals all summer.

Before we left, Janine took me on a tour of a few buildings on the property and I met some of my fellow staff. One of the wranglers, Hector Torres, was young, slim, and shorter than me, with a gentle smile and an immediately-apparent sweet disposition.

Jimmy Johnson, another wrangler, had to be older than my dad and he'd been at Headlands since before I was born. He had weather-beaten, wrinkled skin, eyes that seemed like they were permanently squinting, and wore jeans and boots like he never took them off. I immediately pegged him to be the one who knew everything there was to know about the ranch—and perhaps life—and I really wanted to drink a beer with him.

Stephanie Wright, the therapeutic animal specialist, was my other roommate. Brown haired, plain, and a little plump, she moved with a grace and confidence that belied her ordinary exterior. She seemed like she could become a real friend, and had a caring and therapeutic demeanor.

Janine assigned me to a horse named Happy, who was a big draft horse, kind of slow. I gave him a carrot in a blatant attempt to bribe him into being my friend.

Once I got on the horse in the corral, my excitement for this job increased. I'd forgotten how much I loved horseback riding. As we started off, riding past the corral and barn to the trail, I turned to Janine, "I'm going to be sore tomorrow. It's been years since I've been on a long, hard ride. This is going to exercise muscles that haven't been used in a while."

I heard a low, male chuckle, and saw Will, standing by the tack room, cover his mouth with his hand, having overheard me.

Dirty motherfucker. Guess I said that too loud.

Still, perhaps he had a sense of humor?

Dirty humor plus attractive body equaled way more interesting in my way of doing math. I wasn't sure those things made up for the fact that he was Republican, however. I mean, hooking up with a conservative? That crossed a line. A party line.

Our horses walked along the hilly trail and Janine told me that the program started because Will's mother needed rehabilitation after a car accident. Will's father had brought in a specialist to teach her how to ride horses as a way of exercising. With facilities in place, they decided to form a nonprofit for disabled kids. Then they expanded to take care of kids who lived in urban environments. Janine ran the day-to-day operations of the nonprofit, while Will oversaw the ranch.

When we got to the top of the hill we stopped, still astride the horses. The wind picked up and blew my hair around. I took in the panoramic view of the Pacific, brown hills to the back of us, and appreciated the beauty of the land around me.

I imagined what it would be like for a kid from Los Angeles

or another big city to see this, nothing but wild nature next to the vast blue-green ocean. Then, I remembered that my first group were visually impaired kids. So I thought about how I could help them to experience what it felt like to ride a horse, guided by a wrangler holding a rope. Besides the movement of the animal, they'd feel the tang of the wind on their cheeks and smell the dry, sagey native plants.

We headed back after an hour or so on the trail, then put away the horses and tack, ensured that all animals had enough food and water, closed up for the evening, and went to the chow hall for dinner.

Now, since I had been a vegan for years, I was used to all the issues that came up about eating differently than everyone else. I didn't push my choices on anyone, but I also didn't want to be force-fed meat or dairy. Normally, wherever I went, there was nothing for me to eat, so I came to Headlands prepared to take care of myself, stocked with canned tofu chili, soups, crackers, cereals, soy milk, and almond milk. I planned on cooking my own meals.

But this first night, I wanted to at least make an appearance in the chow hall. Janine walked me into the large, industrial kitchen and introduced me to Jaime Gonzales, the ranch cook, nicknamed "Cookie." A wide and tall man, with forearms like hams, he grinned and his huge smile showcased gold teeth.

"Any allergies?" he asked.

"Well, I'm vegan," I replied.

He blanched.

"So, no meat? Shit. What do you eat, girl? No wonder you're so skinny." His brows furrowed and he looked concerned.

I smiled. "Don't worry, I can take care of myself. I brought my own food."

Cookie breathed a sigh of relief. "We'll always have peanut butter and jelly sandwiches."

"Good to know," I said.

I went out to the dining room and surveyed the lines of tables and benches, clearly set up for feeding a crowd. Because it was just the staff, everyone gathered at one table, passing bowls of food, family style. Even Will was there. I picked up dishes and silverware and joined the table, sitting at an empty seat on the bench right next to Will. My jean-clad leg brushed his and he flinched. I intentionally ignored him.

Cookie had made pinto beans, Mexican rice, and salsa that were all safe for me, in addition to chicken and cheese for the others to make tacos. I filled up a bowl and looked around.

"Hi, everyone!" I chirped.

"So, what's this about you not eating meat?" asked Jimmy. "You some sort of hippie?"

"Veee-gan!" I sang. "I just don't want to eat animals. I think they should have rights."

The table stared at me, all except Stephanie, who smiled.

"Fucking liberal," I heard Will mutter under his breath. Such an asshole. A tan, handsome, muscular asshole.

If he was going to be this way the whole time, I wasn't sure how I'd make it through the summer. I needed this internship for my program. So, I reminded myself to be polite to the boss, even if he was rude.

I let out a breath. "I understand that you might not want to make my choices," I said, as calmly and diplomatically as I could, "but they are mine to make." Then I couldn't help myself and hissed, lower, "And, seriously? What is your problem?"

Will just stared at me. But I saw something flash in his eyes, perhaps a thrill at egging me on?

Motherfucker. He is not fucking this job up for me. "I'm so excited for this first group of kids to come," I gushed to the rest of the table, ignoring him and his surliness.

After dinner, in the bunkhouse, I picked up my phone,

thinking about the day. Only I could have two naked (or almost naked) run-ins with my hot boss within a matter of minutes. I laughed to myself and checked my messages.

How was your first day of work?

This was Amelia, texting me.

I rode a horse. I saw my sexy but right-wing asshole boss naked. And he saw me topless in a thong.

I thought this was summer camp not a nudist colony.

You don't seem surprised by my misadventures.

I know you. Let me know how he is in bed.

Girlfriend . . .

Legally, you'll need to sign a love contract before you sleep with your boss.

No need for legal advice yet.

Well, it's only your first day.

4

HOW MANY ACRES?

"**G**OODNIGHT, JOHN BOY," I called to Janine, who laughed at *The Waltons* reference. I think she was old enough to have seen that show on TV. I'd never actually seen it. My parents had always said that to me and my siblings before we went to bed. "Goodnight, Ma," I sang to Stephanie, who giggled.

Given the sleepy atmosphere, instead of having a nightcap of the tequila I'd brought with my food stores, I finished unpacking, put on my jammies and crawled into the bottom bed of my bunk. Janine and Stephanie beat me to sleep, Janine sleeping in a long sleep t-shirt and Stephanie sleeping in frumpy granny pajamas.

It was wholesome. Quite. Novel, really, for me to be so wholesome. I normally drank a beer before bed and slept nude if I could pull it off. Not here, though.

As I lay in my bunk bed in the dark, I couldn't help but think of Will and his impressive body. A sexy man? Yes. But not one who respected me or my core beliefs, apparently, given the name-calling. That said, he was serious man candy and thinking of him made me tingle in all the right places on my body. Since there was no privacy, however, I just curled up. I must have been worn out from the day because I fell asleep immediately and did not dream.

The insistent clanging of a triangle—seriously, a fucking metal triangle straight out of the old west—woke us up the next morning, and the wranglers groused and put on jeans and went to take care of the horses. I slipped on shorts and a t-shirt, pulled my hair in a ponytail, splashed water on my face, and headed out. Cookie had set out coffee for us in urns in the chow hall. After eating breakfast and taking a cup of Joe to go, I went to work in the bunkhouse office.

The small, comfortable room featured a large window to look out. I fired up the computer, logged on with the password Janine had given me, and went to work planning sessions for the upcoming weeks. Janine stopped by mid-morning to give me information that I needed to go over with each group, like how to deal with emergencies, such as earthquakes, fires, and animals such as rattlesnakes or mountain lions, in addition to other rules.

The clanging of the triangle, signaling lunchtime, surprised me. I'd spent the entire morning absorbed in planning, and I had no idea how the time had passed. It was the best feeling to be absorbed in your work; I'd just known that I'd love it here.

I stood up to go to the chow hall when I heard footsteps and two male voices passing outside, close by the office window. One was Will's low voice, saying, ". . . Hamilton Development."

"What do those bastards want?" This sounded like Jimmy, the older, wizened wrangler. I peeked out the window. I was right.

"For me to sell so they can develop Headlands into ranchettes. They made me another offer. This one ten percent higher than their last." I heard their feet stop.

"What are you gonna do about it?" asked Jimmy.

"Say no. But with the costs of berries going up and the prices staying where they are, they think they'll get me one of these days. I heard that people have contracts for four grand an acre—without guaranteed water. It's crazy."

"Yeah, it's crazy these days. But they don't have you to run it, Will. This place is in your blood."

"No, they don't," Will agreed. "But with the government taxing the hell out of you and then getting squeezed on labor costs and worker's comp insurance and whatever the fuck else, you never know what's gonna happen."

Listening to them talk, I realized that Will had a lot going on. If a developer was offering him money, maybe he was worried about the future of the ranch. Headlands was such a big operation and had been around for so long, you'd think that it was a self-perpetuating institution, but I could understand why it could be tempting to sell and get out of it. It was a lot of work. That would be a shame though, because the area was so naturally beautiful. I'd hate to see it developed.

And as I heard him talk, I thought that maybe he wasn't the capitalistic conservative I pegged him to be, out to get money however he could. Maybe he was different.

"What're you gonna do about the new one, Will? She's not yer type, but she's a looker."

Then I heard Will's rumble. "Yeah. She's fucking hot. Too bad she's an elitist left-wing."

A smile spread across my face. I already knew that Will hated my politics. I hated his. All the more reason for me to stick my heels in the ground and dig. He didn't have to like what I believed.

More interesting to me was that Will thought *I* was hot. He wasn't boyfriend material, but a summer fling? Maybe. It felt dirty. I mean, how naughty would it be to fuck your political opponent, literally?

I kind of got turned on by that idea, actually. Or maybe it was his junk. Or abs.

Pushing those thoughts to the side, I left for lunch.

At the tables, I made sure to sit next to Will, just to fuck with him. I was acting like I was still in high school but I didn't care. As much as he repelled me with his surliness, he attracted me with his hot body. I made sure to brush up against him as I sat, just to see his reaction, which was to flinch like he did before. His jaw ticked when I reached over him to get the water pitcher and his breath hitched when I leaned down to pick up the napkin I dropped.

As I finished my peanut butter sandwich, which Will looked at in disgust, Janine asked if I wanted to take a tour of the property.

Of course I wanted to. As I nodded and opened my mouth to ask her when, Will interrupted. "I'll show her around."

I looked at him in surprise.

"S'my ranch."

"True," I said with a smile. "I'd love to see your ranch. How many acres do you have?"

He blinked at me and asked, "How big are your jugs?"

What the fuck?

"What?" I censored, but I was still taken aback.

"S'bout as polite to ask a farmer how many acres he has as it is to ask a woman the size of her tits."

I never knew that.

"Sorry," I said. "I didn't know that."

"Now you do." For the first time, I saw him smile, and it was a glorious, full face smile that hit his eyes, gentle and a bit mischievous. I didn't know that he had it in him. Total about-face.

It dazed me, it was so beautiful, and it felt like forgiveness. I thought that I'd do anything to see him smile like that again.

And like that, things shifted slightly. I realized that I hadn't sat next to him just to fuck with him. I sat next to him because I was very much attracted to him, drawn to him like a magnet, even though he was my opponent on issues that mattered very much to me. I couldn't seem to leave him alone in the short period of time I'd known him and whenever he was around he was the only one I paid attention to.

He seemed to be the same way, because I noticed him conscientiously *not* looking at me, but I could have sworn he'd just been watching. We were two galactic bodies orbiting each other, pulled by gravity, but repelled by an equal force.

Okay, I don't know if that exists in physics but that was how I felt.

And I wanted more of him.

He continued, quietly, still smiling, "But you can always ask to see and if they wanna show you, then that's okay."

See what? My breasts? Or his ranch?

Guess I'd find out.

5

CHECK YES OR NO

W ILL PUT TWO FINGERS up to his seductive, full lips, whistled, a loud, piercing whistle, and yelled, "C'mon girl!"

For a second, I thought he was talking to me, and I went to put my hands to my hips and say "Excuse me?" or a whole lot worse, but then a beautiful, white and mottled gray Australian Shepherd dog came bounding up to him, circled around him in excitement, wagging its tail, and then jumped into the back of Will's truck. So he was calling the dog, not me. Serves me right for making assumptions.

"This is Trixie," he said, introducing me to his dog. Then he paused a second, eyebrows closing in on each other, looking at me. "You okay with dogs?"

Was I okay with dogs? I loved dogs! "Hel-lo, gorgeous," I cooed, rubbing behind her ears and putting my face in her ruff. She was fluffy and licked my cheek while I giggled.

Will let out a breath and looked at me, somewhat satisfied, like I'd passed a test.

After lunch, we'd bussed our dirty dishes to the kitchen

window and then I followed Will out to his truck to get my tour of the top secret quantity of acreage of Headlands Ranch.

That cowboy drove the biggest truck I'd ever seen, a brand new, white Ford F-350. I hated to think of its freeway gas mileage, let alone the MPG in town. I'd practically needed a stepladder to get up into it. His truck could eat my car for dinner and still have room to spare. Although it was so new that it didn't have license plates, the sides were covered in mud and the inside had dried clumps of earth from his boots. As he saw me gingerly put on my seatbelt, he gave me a half grin. "You okay with things being a little dirty?"

"Of course," I said, more heartily than I felt. Ignoring the double entendre, I wasn't about to complain and make him think that I was more of an elitist than he already seemed to think. It was strange: part of me could care less what he thought of me because he was an asshole with whom I didn't agree about anything, and part of me told me to be quiet and polite because he was my boss. And there was this other part that felt pulled to him, like I was navigating by his light. Throw in the fact that he was outstandingly good-looking, and I knew what was under his big belt buckle, and it was extremely difficult to know what to do from moment to moment. I figured that I'd continue to wing it, because this was my summer adventure, after all. I liked not knowing what would happen next.

At least that's how I justified not thinking about it for the time being.

He shifted the truck into reverse, turned on country radio— *ugh*—and started down the rough, dirt road.

I'd already figured out that Will wasn't much of a talker. Fortunately, or unfortunately, I was, so I decided to drill him with questions as we drove.

"So. You grew up here, huh?"

"Yep."

He kept his hand on the steering wheel, staring straight ahead, not looking at me.

"Do you have any brothers or sisters?"

"Nope."

After a few more one word answers, I realized that this wasn't working well. Still, I kept on.

"What are we listening to?"

"George Strait."

"It's, uh, not bad." This was a white lie. It was definitely country music, and twangy, so it was not my style, but the song was cute, about a girl passing a guy a note in school to "Check Yes or No" if he liked her.

I felt like that's what I was doing. Did he like me? Did he want to be my friend?

He turned and looked at me hard, and then put his eyes back on the dirt road as we bounced along. "Not bad? He has more number one hits than anyone. More than fifty, I think. *Not bad*." He shook his head. "Christ. What do you listen to?"

"Anything but country."

At this, he let out a chuckle. "Shoulda figured."

As we drove, I watched the landscape change. The compound with the buildings was located west, towards the ocean, sheltered by the hills. We were headed east, going inland, through low plains of strawberries.

Parking the truck and leaving it running, Will got out, boots on the ground, and I hopped down my side of the truck, Trixie at our heels. "We put in strawberries twice a year. Winter crop and summer crop. This crop will be ready to pick soon. They're organic, so we have to paint an organic pesticide on the flowers when they open to keep the bugs away."

I loved that he had organic produce.

"Really? How much effort does that take?"

"It's a lot of labor. That's one of the reasons why you can

charge more for strawberries. On this plain, near the coast, it's cool enough for them. Pretty good growing conditions, although on days like today, it's too hot." He looked at me and I wondered what, exactly, he was thinking was too hot. I stared at his lips just a beat too long and he stared at mine.

We walked up and down the rows, which were covered in black plastic.

"Why do you use all this plastic?"

"Keeps the berries pretty." He stopped at a row. "These were planted a little earlier. Wanna try one?"

I nodded enthusiastically.

He picked me a berry and held it out to me, with a look on his face that if I didn't think that he despised me I'd think he liked me. Then he smiled. "Take a bite."

So he was a flirt.

Okay, I'd flirt with him. I leaned over and bit into the berry as he held it, my lips brushing his fingers, tasting his salt. I'd never eaten a strawberry out of the field. If you were lucky, you could get little strawberries from farmer's markets or smaller grocery stores, which had real flavor unlike the almost wooden ones from the big stores. But this small, red berry that Will gave me? The flavor exploded in my mouth. And it was organic to boot.

"Oh, it's so good," I enthused, a dribble going down my chin. He gave me another look as I wiped the juice off my chin and sucked my finger and he stuck his hands in the pockets of his jeans and adjusted them.

"Some saps call that a country valentine," he muttered.

God, I felt so confused. He was clearly flirting with me. But he didn't like me? Or my politics? And he thought I was hot? What was going on here?

And what did I think? Setting aside his good looks, if this man was my political opposite, that meant that he believed in racism and homophobia. That meant that he was pro-life and anti-gun control. That he hated environmental regulation. That he didn't support equal pay for workers and raising the minimum wage. Right?

All of the things that I cared about.

And that made me feel stupid, because he wasn't a potential country fling. He was someone I couldn't or shouldn't consider. Because if I got together with him, then I was hypocritical. It was okay to believe what I believed out in the open, paint it on the back of my car and shout it to the world. But if I actually did it, I'd be letting down the side and I couldn't do that.

That said, the idea of crossing that boundary felt so hot, like when a CEO is submissive in the bedroom. Shedding my image privately might be freeing. I was entitled to my sexual fantasies. I didn't know what to do. I felt like I should do something, but what, I had no idea.

I broke my gaze away from him and shuffled back to the truck.

We drove past new avocado orchards, then kept going and went to a higher area, with long rows of large metal hoops, most of them covered in plastic. "What's growing here?" I asked.

"Blueberries."

He stopped the truck, again getting out, and this time I totally checked out his ass. Not that I hadn't done it before. I just let myself do it again. Again, he kept the truck running, but this time, he scanned the area and pulled out his cell phone. I wandered down the rows and fingered the leafy plants, Trixie at my heels. I could hear him talking.

"Guillermo?" He waited for a response.

"Hace falta cubrir las moras." The berries needed to be covered. Still, interesting that he spoke Spanish.

"Bien. Bueno. Adios." He hung up. I walked back to him and looked up into his dark eyes.

"Where did you learn to speak Spanish?"

"Here." I rolled my eyes, feigning patience, willing him to go on, and surprisingly, he did. "Grew up with these guys and you gotta talk with them." That was weird and not what I was expecting. If he was conservative, wasn't he against anyone who didn't speak English? I must have had a weird look on my face, because he asked, defensively, "What?"

"You're a Republican."

"You know it."

"And you speak Spanish."

"Yeah."

I kicked a rock to the side. "Then how can you support those candidates who want to round up everyone who is not like them and deport them?"

He rolled his eyes and asked, "Do you really want to get into that darlin'?"

All I could think at first was how sexy his voice sounded when he called me darlin'. God, I was so fucking shallow sometimes. He brought out the worst in me.

But no, I wasn't going to be distracted by the slab of caramel man candy in front of me. I remembered my ethics.

I let out an annoyed breath. One minute he's fun and flirty and the next he was . . .

Not like me.

Not my type.

And he was an ass.

"You bring up politics all the time," I said, "and you haven't even asked me what mine are."

He smirked. "Because I know you're a fucking liberal."

Oh that's enough. We were getting nowhere. And I didn't need to be insulted like that. I mean, not that being liberal was bad, I was proud of it. But he didn't need to swear at me. I turned to back to the truck, done with the conversation. "You're a judgmental asshole. You don't even know me."

He just shook his head and started, "You come here from the city and you have no idea what goes on in a farm—" but I interrupted him, turning around and raising my finger.

"Oh no? I grew up as a kid of migrant farmworkers," I countered. "I never had a home, going up and down California and Mexico looking for work. My parents worked hard and saved their money and then went to school and got jobs so that my brother and sister and I would have a good life. So don't give me that 'you have no idea' shit. I'm no princess. I work hard and I play hard and I go about my business and try not to hurt anyone."

He looked exasperated, huffing out in a breath, "Then what's with the hippie-mobile and the crazy shit you eat?"

"I care about the earth and I don't want to wreck it," I yelled. And I made sure everyone knew it by my actions. My life was a political statement.

"Neither do I," he argued back. "That's why I work a ranch."

Hmm. He had a point.

At this point we had moved closer to each other, unconsciously, our steps closing the gap between us until I stood in front of him, my belly going in and out, and I noticed the sheen of sweat from the hot day on his forehead, the way his hair flopped over and how shiny, dark, and thick it looked ...

No.

I couldn't do this. I couldn't have a summer fling with this good-looking jerk. I wasn't going to be the hypocrite, telling everyone my politics, living it out loud, but secretly perving on a bigot.

"I just wish you'd stop calling me names," I said, looking up at him, my light brown eyes to his dark.

He looked down at me, his hand reaching forward and then

stopping. An emotion washed over his face that looked like desire.

"If I do, can I kiss you?"

Holy shit.

It *was* desire.

6

ARGUING PLUS BENEFITS

"NO."

The word was out of my mouth before I could articulate the reason why I didn't want Will to kiss me. The truth was, I wanted to kiss him, I wanted to explore that sensual mouth, get up close and personal, again, with the body I had slammed into when I first met him. I wanted to do more than kiss him. I wanted to feel every inch of his huge, hard body and I wanted him to satisfy the parts of me that tingled when I thought about him. I was suffering from withdrawal from not touching him, even though I'd just met him. Guess this is what happened when you met a man while he was naked.

But still, *no* on the kiss. Or, as I thought more about it, perhaps *hell no*.

His eye twitched. "What do you mean, no?" He paused, and then he smiled a sexy half smile. "So you'll kiss me anyway, even if I still call you names?" Now I was seeing a new side to him: Playful Will. I liked Playful Will as much, or more, as Naughty Sense of Humor Will and Mischievous Will. It balanced out Asshole Will and Conservative Will, and was intriguing. But no.

"No. You're my boss." There, a concrete reason percolated to the surface of my brain and came out of my mouth.

And threw cold water on everything, because I might be a party girl but I wasn't stupid and I was not going to throw away a job that I really wanted for a guy no matter how handsome he was.

"I'm not your boss," he said immediately and resolutely.

Now it was my turn to twitch. "How's that?"

"Your checks are signed by the Headlands Program, not the Ranch. I run the Ranch. Janine is your boss. Not me. You're just living on my land for the summer. The nonprofit has a separate board of directors from my family trust, provides its own staffing, and I donate the space, animals, and supplies."

Well, that cleared one hurdle.

I wondered why I threw so many hurdles up if there was no way in hell I'd ever be with a Republican.

But still, the answer was no kissing, and I thought of more reasons why. "You chew."

"So?"

"It's disgusting."

He stared at me and gave me a sort of chin lift. "What else you got?"

The big one. The sin. The crime—at least in my way of thinking.

"You're a Republican. I have never, to my knowledge, ever kissed a Republican."

His grin was now a full smile, not a half smile, and honestly, it was dazzling, like before. "Let's try this. I'll give you a choice. We can continue arguing politics all summer—and I think we're a match for each other and I'm looking forward to the arguments, darlin'—and I don't lay a hand on you. Or, we can continue arguing politics all summer, but I can fuck your hot body whenever you want. Which do you pick?"

I spasmed. His phone rang.

"'lo?" He strolled off to the side to take his call, his hand in his pocket, and I patted Trixie, who had come up around my legs.

I wouldn't have guessed that this was the way that my summer adventure was going to happen. Still, I was wildly amused and turned on, but simultaneously repelled. Decisions, decisions.

I'd just met the guy yesterday, but it wasn't like I'd never had a one-night stand before. I could be a bit wild. Well, *total party girl* might be a better description of me. But this was potentially more than a one-night stand. It could be for the summer, and frankly, that sounded like fun. Although I didn't need all the bickering that was destined to occur.

As I thought about it, however, I knew that if things didn't go well with him, I'd have to avoid him for months and that could be awkward, especially if I knew how he was in bed.

Yum, Will in bed.

But things were already awkward. I'd already had a preview of his body and it was spectacular. I wasn't avoiding him because I had seen him naked. Quite the opposite, actually.

So, what to do? I was definitely attracted to him and he was definitely my opposite. I felt pulled to him and pushed away at the same time.

He was nothing like the guys I'd dated before, who'd been mostly crunchy bohemian types, and a little feminine, honestly. Will was red meat man and I was a vegan. I really didn't think that this would work.

And a small voice inside me said that I was scared that if it did work, I'd just have to leave him at the end of summer.

As I thought about it, though, we were already sniping at each other at every chance, so it was hard to see how things would get any worse. Maybe they'd get better.

I needed to know more before I made a decision.

He finished his call and walked back to me and Trixie, stepping just a little closer to me than societal conventions allowed. I felt him even though I didn't touch him.

"How *Republican*, Republican are you?"

He leaned into me, his eyes amused, his voice low and certain. "Very."

This meant, as I suspected, that we disagreed on all the things.

Desperately wishing for a way to make this work, a flash of hope ran through me. Maybe we were just arguing semantics.

And I chided myself. How easily I considered setting aside my deeply-held beliefs just because of one hot man. What kind of feminist was I where my brain turned off because my body was turned on? Still, I needed to find out more.

"What do you think of women's rights? Are you a feminist?"

All the other guys I'd dated said they were. They might have said it to get me naked, but at least they'd said it.

He shook his head. Uh-oh. My stomach dropped and I felt disheartened. This was not acceptable. "Not really. Guys and girls are different. Treat 'em different. You gonna argue with me 'bout that?"

"Obviously."

He raised an eyebrow and gave me that devastating smile.

"Bring it on."

Ohmigod, I wanted him for real now, and I was pissed that he turned my brain to mush. I'm smarter than this. I stepped back, needing space from him and then I realized something. "Since you're not my boss, I can tell you, you're an ignorant dick for saying something like that. Women are still fighting for equal rights. The pay gap and the glass ceiling exist and we have to do something about them."

He smiled again and my fucking panties got wet. "And you're a commie pinko. What else you got?"

Seriously? "Commie pinko? What is this, 1969?"

A wicked look came over his face and he dropped his voice so low I felt it in my groin. "What's that about sixty-nine?"

Walked into that one. And then the idea of my mouth on Will with his mouth on me made me wetter.

No.

I couldn't.

Or I could.

Gah.

"How old are you?" I finally asked, changing the subject.

"Thirty-four. You?"

"I'm thirty-two."

None of this was helping me to make a decision of whether to go after him. I needed to press him about his backwards thinking. But I also wanted his body pressing into mine.

He let me off the hook by saying, "Tell you what. I'll show you some more of the ranch and you can decide whether you want arguing or arguing plus benefits."

I didn't know if I could stay focused on the tour of the ranch, and judging by the way he had his hands shoved in the pockets of his jeans, neither could he.

Still, I knew that I couldn't take him up on it yet. I wanted to, badly, but no.

Maybe.

7

HAY

SOMETHING FLIP-FLOPPED DURING THE ride in the gas-guzzling, mega truck back to the Headlands Ranch compound. Instead of me asking Will questions and receiving one-word answers from him in response, he started asking me questions: about my family (my older brother, responsible, my younger sister, not), my school, my work, and my friends. And me being me, of course I talked a lot. Aside from his obvious good looks, there was something so attractive about this strong, mostly silent guy, taking an active interest in me, seeming to really listen, and asking follow up questions. This was probably because we were talking about safe topics, not politics or country music, which would have put us both into our default positions of protecting our belief systems. It was much better when we were being ourselves, without the political designations.

As we drove, I became acutely aware of the distance between us in the truck cab. He was so close, but not, since he wasn't touching me. I kept watching him—the muscles on his powerful thighs flexing as he moved his leg from the gas to the brake and back; his meaty biceps and forearms clenching as he shifted the car into drive and back into park; his flat belly moving as he spoke or took a breath; his dark eyes looking at me during the times that he tore his gaze away from the dirt road; his hewn jaw jerking if he found something I said amusing.

He drove me to a few other places on the ranch, which, size-wise was ridiculously large. I had no idea how many acres we saw. It seemed like his family owned half of California. He told me his dad had retired and left the operations to him. He employed office staff and a lot of workers, both seasonal and full-time. I saw the rangeland for the cattle, more of the orchards, and some of the fields of row crops. He also drove me to a section that had vineyards, and then to the Headlands Ranch winery. Apparently nearer to the highway, there was a small tasting room for the winery and he told me that he'd take me there to try the wine.

Could I potentially go there on a date there with Will? I liked that idea. A lot.

When we arrived at the compound, he parked the truck and Trixie jumped out. I leaped out of the high truck cab, and Will came around and walked me up to the bunkhouse. So, appar-ently for every Asshole Will, there was a Gentleman Will, too. When we got to the bunkhouse, he looked down at me, ran his hand through his longish, wavy dark hair, gave me a half-smile, and took off.

I watched him saunter back to his house, Trixie prancing at his side.

I'd left my phone in the bunkhouse and when I got to my room, I picked it up.

> How was your second day of work?

This was Amelia. I texted her back.

I found out the hot guy who I thought is my boss is not actually my boss and he wants to do the nasty with me.

I thought this was summer camp, not a swinger's club.

We are complete political opposites and he is an asshole . . . sometimes.

How much of an asshole?

So far, less than fifty percent.

How hot?

Scale of 1 to 10?

Yes.

57.

Do the politics matter that much?

I don't know. I mean, yes, of course they do. This is me we're talking about. I live my beliefs. I'd be a moral failure if I slept with the enemy.

Girl . . .

I know. He's sexy as fuck, Amelia. I want to lick him. What do I do?

Lick him first. Ask questions later. If he's an asshole to you, dump him. It's not a moral failure to have sex with a handsome man you like.

That's the strangest advice I've ever been given.

But I just might take it.

I'm here to serve. Speaking of serving, Ryan's at the door. Gotta go.

Fuck it. I was jumping Will's bones as soon as I could. I needed to get laid and I felt so attracted to him, obsessively so. There was no privacy around here, but I'd find a way.

In the evening, after dinner, I drank beer with Janine, Stephanie, and Cookie, sitting on the porch of the bunkhouse, watching the sunset, but Will was nowhere to be seen.

The next morning, Sunday, was my last day of prep before the kids got there. Officially, I had the day to myself, but I wanted to ride the horses again. After the motherfucking metal triangle woke me up way too early, again, I got up. I put on jeans, a white tank top, and boots, and fortified myself with coffee and cereal made with soy milk. Then I went to the stables with Janine and Stephanie.

"Hello, gorgeous," I cooed to Happy, as I combed him, gave him an apple, and helped the wranglers put on his pad, saddle, and other gear. After the horses were ready, Janine, Stephanie, and I set off down the trail, headed on a new-to-me trail. Our horses walked around the perimeter of a citrus orchard, out into rangeland, where there were cattle, up a road by grapevines, and then back down another dirt road to the compound. I loved being out on the horse in the morning. It was such a natural way to travel, feeling the warm, early summer air on our faces and skin, my eyes squinting at the sun. I thought about getting a cowboy hat to shade my eyes and giggled to myself about going country, instead of edgy hippie. But boots and hats were utilitarian out here.

We returned to the stables well before lunch and I helped put away Happy's tack and groomed him. Janine chatted with Stephanie, and they left for the bunkhouse to clean up for lunch. As I headed out of the tack room, I saw Will go into one of the barns.

Opportunity.

Last night I'd made the decision. He was going to be my plaything for the summer and I was shoving the politics to the side. Either that or I was embracing the fact that he was a very enthralling boundary that I wanted to cross in the most sinful way.

I'd picked arguing plus benefits. Hopefully with only minimal arguing.

I walked into the barn through a small door on the side and stayed in the doorway, allowing my eyes to adjust to the dim light and the dust that had settled everywhere. This storage barn had bales of hay, farm implements, and lots of unidentifiable grimy mechanical parts.

Will stood by the hay bales, beginning to do something—no idea what—with some piece of equipment—couldn't tell you about that either. Because I was silhouetted in the doorway, I blocked the light and he noticed me. His face broke into a half-smile. "Need somethin'?"

"Yeah."

I strode slowly over to him, taking my time, making him wait, even though I didn't want to. I really wanted to run into his arms, to make him crash into the hay, taking my weight. I wanted to feel what his biceps felt like, gripping me, holding me.

The look on his face was a combination of wary and interested. When I got to him, he looked down at me, but didn't say anything. At first, he didn't move, just kept his hands where they were, one on the greasy farm equipment, one out. Then he carefully wiped them on a rag.

And then I decided to make the first move.

I reached over to him, put my index finger out, and trailed it up from his belly button to his chin, again slowly, taking my time. His expression got less wary and more interested. I looked him in his lovely eyes, put both hands behind his neck, and brought his face to mine to kiss.

Our lips touched, his soft lips on mine, and the kiss was sweet for all of about three seconds, and then, suddenly, Will Thrash was kissing me back like he meant it. Tongue engaged, devouring me. Hands in my hair, on my lower back pressing me to him, on my ass. My hands went crazy too, all over his strong back, his neck, his thick hair, his Wrangler-clad ass.

Now I've been kissed a lot, but never like this. It was like he had this frenzy inside him that he'd kept bottled up by being quiet all the time, and he just let it out, on me. His lips nibbled mine, his tongue chased mine, and after a really long time, he broke away and then was back, making his way down my neck, nuzzling me and sucking on my neck. I gasped, I couldn't help it, it felt so good.

I pushed on his shoulders, walking him back to the hay bales, and even though he had this rock solid body, he let me. In another instant, we were down on top of the hay bales, me straddling him, kissing him with all my might, an activity in which he fully cooperated. The poky hay stuck into the knees of my jeans, and poor Will probably had it pressing into his back, but he didn't act like he cared. In fact, I was pretty sure he didn't because he hardened under me, and I felt it between my legs. Having been given a preview attraction upon arrival, I couldn't wait to meet his cock in person. I reached down between my legs and felt his length under his jeans, and he groaned. With steady, gentle pressure, I stroked him over his jeans as I kissed him, and his eyes went wild.

Boy. Stepping over a boundary was a fucking turn-on.

And then we heard a loud male voice call, "Will?"

We both jumped up, startled and disheveled. It was Jimmy, the older wrangler, who appeared in the doorway. I brushed off my knees as fast as I could, and straightened my hair, while Will adjusted his pants. I reached behind him and dusted off his back, trying to get the hay off of his black t-shirt, but I wasn't fast enough because Jimmy walked in the barn, shielded his eyes to get used to the light, sized us up, and smiled.

"Hope I'm not interrupting anything."

Will didn't answer, but he was breathing hard and gave me a look I couldn't read.

"I'll just be going," I said. "See you later."

I resisted the urge to pick a straw out of his hair and left him to explain himself, if he wanted to, to Jimmy, who'd clearly figured everything out already.

8

SENSES

THE FIRST KIDS OF the summer are coming tomorrow!!!! I texted Amelia.

> That's not all that's going to come this summer, I imagine.

I laughed, called Amelia, and updated her on the new parts of Will that I had experienced, including the physical part, meaning, obviously, my kiss with him in the barn. I told her that I'd made the decision to get busy with him at the first opportunity as my summer fling. She heartily approved. I knew you didn't need a girlfriend to agree with you about a guy, but it sure felt soothing when one supported you like that.

I mean, this was the right decision, right?

Right?

Normally, when I kissed a man, if I liked him, I wanted to kiss him again, and perhaps go further. Since my fumbling high school days, I really hadn't had any bad kisses, although there had been some that had felt kinda *meh*. Still, though, I had a good and active sex life, even if no one had thrilled me in a long time.

But with Will? That kiss had me reenacting it in my head the whole day. I couldn't think of anything else. It was like kissing him was the key to opening him up. In the short period that I had known him, he had been quite reserved, and, well, an asshole. Now I knew that there was more to him. He had something passionate under that quiet surface that I wanted to experience again, and in full detail. He sure flared up immediately when I gave him the opportunity. Like a spark in the dry California chaparral. I'd never experienced anything like that, being with someone so ardent.

It was fucking hot and I wanted more. Now.

Instead of going back to find him in the barn, however, I spent the rest of the day attempting to work in the office, which in reality meant that I was daydreaming about Will's body and its various parts, until it was time for dinner, when I packed up and walked to the chow hall.

Part of me was apprehensive about seeing him at meal times. How do you act in public with a guy that you work with when you were almost in his pants a few hours earlier? But mostly, I was simply curious to see to how he would react. At least that's what I'd told myself.

He was already seated when I got there, so, like the other meals, I sat next to him. But this time, when I brushed up against him as I sat down, instead of flinching, he pressed his thigh into mine and kept it there for the entire meal. I liked this. I could feel his body and smell his clean smell. He kept sneaking glances at me and giving me half-smiles as I talked. Let's just say that I was distracted throughout the entire meal. Despite my lack of interest in my dinner, conversation surged, especially involving plans for the visually impaired students coming the next day.

"We're going to be focusing on tactile sensations for the participants," I told the table. Staff members before me had properly set up the Headlands Program for assisting with all sorts of disabilities. Besides various games, CDs, and training materials, the ranch even had a three-dimensional map of the horse arena so that the students could explore it with their hands before they got on the horses. That way they'd know what to expect. After I talked about the different things the students were going to do this week, I concluded, "This is going to be a week of waking up all of our senses."

Will stifled a smile and put his hand over his mouth, his nostrils flaring.

Dirty birdie.

Damn, if I didn't like it. A lot.

At the end of the meal, as everyone else picked up their dishes and went to bus them to the kitchen, I leaned over and whispered in his ear, "I'll wake up your senses this week if you wake up mine."

He looked me in the eyes, intently, raised an eyebrow, and said, "Deal."

Janine and Stephanie came back over to me and the three of us walked back to the bunkhouse, leaving Will to go to his. I felt like he watched me as we walked away, but I didn't spin around to look. Finally, as we headed up the steps, I turned and watched Will go up to his ranch house, alone, and suppressed the urge to chase him down and tackle him.

My dreams that night were spicy, to say the least, and starred him.

The following morning, I woke up before the triangle, because I was so excited to meet the kids. A surge of adrenaline propelled me out of bed and got me to breakfast early. I took my coffee to go and set up for the kids while I anxiously waited for their arrival. When the vans pulled up, followed by a pickup truck with their luggage, I ran out to meet them.

"Hello, and welcome to the Headlands Program," I said, as the six participants and their parents or adult leaders made their way out of the vehicles. "I'm Marie and I'm here to make sure you all have a wonderful time. I'm so glad you're here. Now, my first question when I got here was, is there somewhere to pee?"

There were a few laughs.

I walked up to each of the six participants individually, who ranged in ages from nine to eighteen, and shook their hands and talked with them, and let them touch me, if they wanted to. One participant in particular, a seventeen-year-old girl named Clarissa, had long, dark blonde hair plaited into dozens of braids, going down her head into rows with beads on the end, kind of like Bo Derek. When I met her, she turned towards me, held out her hand, and said, "Hair sings to me. Let me feel your hair and I will tell you what it sounds like." I bent and put my head in her hands and she trilled a clear, high, note. Then she told me, "Oh, your hair is fun. We are going to have a good time."

With these kids, the pace slowed down from my enthusiasm that morning. We made our way, with care, to the bunkhouse, and took our time setting everyone up. I was impressed once I realized that there was braille on all the signs in the compound. This place was set up for helping people.

After lunch, we headed over to the horses, and Stephanie took over.

None of them had ever ridden a horse before, and I was impressed by their bravery. Fear of horses is common. Horses are big animals, and they can feel overwhelming. Being around them, without being able to see them, had to be a disconcerting experience. After each participant had a chance to meet his or her horse, running their hands over their noses, feeling their manes, and touching the flicking muscles on their necks, we headed back to the bunkhouse for free time before dinner. As I walked with the group back to the bunkhouse, I saw Will off to the side, sweaty, take off his shirt and wipe off his face, his muscular torso on display, basically just for me. He saw me and grinned, and I knew the show was on purpose. He even flexed a bicep.

I'd have to think of a way to get him back.

9

COMPROMISE

THE EXPERIENCE OF ASSISTING visually impaired kids to ride horses would stay with me forever.

Once the kids were up on their horses using a special ramp, the looks on their faces seared into my memory. Sure, they were scared at first, to be that high up off of the ground on an unfamiliar and huge animal. Then, the looks turned to unadulterated terror once the horses started walking. A horse has a sway to its gait that you have to get used to. If you were blind, your body was often hunched over, since you relied on canes, guide animals, or caregivers to get around. But on a horse, sitting up engaged other muscles and other senses, which was so healthy. The wranglers held the ropes and guided each horse and rider slowly around the corral. And after a while, the faces of the children turned to delight.

They were riding horses, actually doing it. So powerful.

After, they described to me the sensations they felt—the scent of the barnyard, the sounds of the horses, the rough feel of the hide of their horse, the lumbering motion of the walk. They also talked about how they felt about riding, from fear to joy. We made a recording of their voices so that they could replay it and remember what they felt when they returned home.

Once we were done, every single one of them wanted to do it again and again.

So they went riding a lot.

Speaking of riding, Will was away from the compound this week, I guess taking care of things around the ranch. But he made a point to walk over to the corral on one afternoon and talk with the kids. He gave them individual attention. But he sure looked over at me often.

When he met Clarissa, of course she wanted to "sing" his hair, so he bent down, all six and a half feet of him and let the little seventeen-year-old touch his curly, brown hair.

I wanted to to do that.

She sang a sweet, middle note, and said that his hair sounded "True, passionate, and kind."

Interesting. It was sort of like an astrology reading by hair.

I really only saw Will this week at meal times, when we both had trouble keeping our hands under control. The flirting with him was now a combination of completely under wraps and blatantly obvious. At least I hoped it wasn't obvious. When I got up to refill the water pitcher, for instance, I made it a point to graze his crotch as I got up. He did the same, reaching across my boobs to grab the salt and pepper, and resting his arm just a second too long. And then looking at me, giving me an almost imperceptible eyebrow raise and smirk. And so it went on, in public, playing this game of who can touch the other one the most, without letting anyone else know it.

On Thursday, it happened.

"What's that noise?" asked Clarissa suddenly, her sunglasses on, blonde braids whipping around to turn her ear toward some scrubby bushes growing at the far end of the corral. I walked over to investigate and, holy shit, there was a full-sized rattlesnake right there. Not only could I see the snake, stretched out across the dirt, but also I could hear the rattle. About all that I knew about rattlesnakes came from cartoons, but I figured that just because it wasn't coiled up and ready to strike didn't mean that we should stick around and meet it.

"We're going to get out of here and go inside and I'll get someone to take care of it," I said, more calmly and confidently than I felt. "I think it's a rattlesnake." I also had no idea what I meant by "take care of it," not remembering the protocol I'd read previously, but I had no choice. I couldn't have anyone, let alone a blind child, get hurt.

Just then, Will's truck pulled into the compound.

"There's a rattlesnake in the bushes by the corral," I burst out, and I pointed to where I saw it.

He nodded, said, "I'll handle it," and ran to one of the barns. The caretakers gathered the kids and walked them to safety. Will came back, holding a shovel, with a ranch hand holding a bucket, and Janine holding a rake. My heart clenched. I didn't want them to kill the rattlesnake. It hadn't done anything wrong. But rattlesnake venom could be fatal. This was the part where wanting to save all of the animals in the world was really difficult. I didn't eat animal products, wear any leather, or do anything that would involve animal testing. But here, on the ranch, there was just no avoiding wildlife, and as much as I hated, absolutely fucking hated, what they were going to do—or at least what I thought they were going to do—I couldn't, and wouldn't, stop it. But I also couldn't let them do it either.

When I got near the corral, Will's head whipped around and he yelled, "Get away, Marie. Go in the tack house."

"No," I yelled back. "I want to know what you're doing to it."

He looked at me, anger flashing on his face, mixed with something else. Concern? "Stay away, it's dangerous. Right now we have it under control. I'll come talk to you in the tack house when we're done."

I felt so torn. "No."

I followed him. I knew that some people would say that it's just a snake, but to me, it was important. I didn't want to be responsible for killing any animal, even one that was not cuddly and cute. I didn't even buy tequila with worms in it.

Will turned, deadly serious, and spoke, looking me right in the eyes, and while it was authoritative, he also said it with kindness. "Get in the tack house, Marie. Don't distract us."

Okay, fine. I went in and sat on a sawhorse, pissed, scared, and hurt.

After about ten minutes, Will walked in the tack house, and came right over to me, standing over me, panting. He paused and looked down at me sitting. "You're upset."

"Yeah, Captain obvious."

"Can't have rattlers around here. Not with the Headlands Program. Had to kill it," he said firmly.

I knew he was right, but I didn't like it. "You couldn't have taken it to another part of the ranch?"

He looked at me, his tone kind even if his words weren't. "I'm not driving around with a rattlesnake in my truck. Can't take them somewhere else on the ranch 'cause they might come back. It's too far for animal control to come."

I sighed and kicked at the floor. "I know you think I'm crazy, all sad about the life of one snake, but that's just how I'm made."

He smiled and shuffled his feet. "I know. That's part of the reason why I think I like you."

That made my pulse run. Hearing it come out of his mouth was different than me guessing about it. "You think you like me?" I stuttered out.

He gave me his half smile. "The part that cares about everyone and everything? Yeah."

Oh great gobs of gooey goodness. Will Thrash likes me. I felt like I was in seventh grade and he had just asked me to a chaperoned dance. But I was still upset. "Will you tell me what you did to it?"

He looked at me, probing and serious, and reached a finger under my chin. "Do you really want to know?"

I nodded.

He spoke in his slow drawl, gently and clinically. "Janine pinned its head with the rake while I sliced it off with the shovel. We put it in the bucket and buried it out back."

To me, that sounded gruesome, but I suppose it could have been worse. I shuddered.

"That upset you more," he said, still standing over me.

"Yeah." I went to get up, but he put his hand on my shoulder, gently, pushing me down. He gave me a sexy chin lift and narrowed his eyes.

"Stay here for a minute." He left the tack house and after a moment, came back in, carrying something.

"Bought you a present." Really? I was surprised and touched. He'd been away all day. It was heartwarming to think that he'd thought of me.

"What is it?" I asked, eager to find out what he'd buy me, and feeling a greater thrill than I'd admit out loud.

He handed me the white paper sack and I opened it up. Candy?

"It's from Robitaille's in Carpinteria. It's candy, so I figured you could eat it—no animals in it. I asked and they said these had no milk or butter or anything."

My mouth opened at such a thoughtful gift and I tilted my head to the side. "That was nice of you."

He gave me a wicked look. "Not really. They were the official candy maker of Reagan's second inauguration."

I couldn't help but laugh. Of course he gave me Republican vegan candy.

I raised an eyebrow. "A compromise, Mr. Thrash? I didn't know you had it in you."

He looked for a moment like he was battling with himself to say something, but didn't. He blinked and he pressed his mouth together. Then he stood up, looked down at me, said, "See you later," and walked away. But I heard him mutter, "I know what I want in you."

Dirty motherfucker. I smiled.

The candy was delicious, though I still felt bad for the snake.

10

A HORSE AND A WHITE BIKINI

ON FRIDAY MORNING, THE kids left, I wrote a report of what we did, and then I packed up a daypack with a huge towel, sunscreen, water (in a reusable BPA-free bottle), organic berries from the ranch, my phone, and my e-reader. I put on my white bikini under my cut-off jean shorts and white t-shirt and set off to the beach, a hot twenty-minute walk.

This beach featured a small cove, with bluffs on all sides and rocks heading into the water, no one around on any side for miles. I lay out my towel, stripped off my shorts and t-shirt, and ran into the water to cool off and wash off my sweat from the walk. Oh, was it cold! Although it was a sunny June day, the Pacific Ocean felt arctic. I splashed around for just a minute, did a handstand on my way back to my towel, and flopped down on my back, sunglasses on, and my earbuds in with dance music on my phone. Goosebumps covered my skin from the frigid water and my nipples puckered. I wanted the sun to warm me up, and fast.

After a moment, I sensed a shadow over my face.

I opened my eyes and saw Will standing over me, wearing a

green Justin Workboots trucker hat, which barely controlled his hair, a tight, faded red t-shirt, and his usual jeans and boots. I tore out my earbuds and hoisted myself up on my elbows, looking up at him.

"What are you doing here?"

"Heard you went to the beach," he said, his expression unreadable. "Thought I'd give Thor some exercise."

"Your horse is named Thor?" I laughed, took my sunglasses off, and looked around. He'd tied the horse to a post at the edge of the small beach area.

He ignored my comment and looked my body up and down, his dark eyes now intense. "You can't do this to me," he said, and he crouched down next to me, rocking back on his heels.

"Do what?" I asked, only partially innocently, since I was sticking my chest out at him, determined to mess with him every chance I got. Guess this was also my way of getting him back for his naked torso display the other day.

He shook his head. "Display your sexy body like that and not expect me to touch you."

"Go right ahead, cowboy," I said, and the words were barely out of my mouth when he took off his hat, put it on backwards, kneeled, leaned over, and kissed me, pulling my wet body to his dry one and holding me to him.

This was a sweeter kiss than the one we shared almost a week ago, but no less energetic. As he kissed me, with plenty of tongue, I kissed him back, feeling his hot lips on my cold ones. I was getting his t-shirt wet, but, typical Will, he didn't seem to care. Instead, he ran his fingers from my ear down my neck to my shoulder, and he broke apart from me, looking to trace the dove tattoo on my collar bone. Without saying anything, he pushed me gently back down on the towel, threw his hat down beside us, and trailed his fingers down my side, lingering on the Noah's ark and all of the animals. Then he leaned over and traced this tattoo with his tongue and his lips, talking against my skin, "You taste like the ocean but it's so good."

Fuck. *This man.* So fucking sexy.

I let him touch me and felt the sensations of his rough hands going over my body. He moved his body over mine, between my legs, careful not to get any sand on the towel, holding himself over me, kissing me from my belly to my face. Then he brushed a hand over my left breast, holding himself up with the other one.

"Yes," I whispered, and then any self-control we had— minimal as it was—snapped.

He pushed my bikini top to the side, and cupped my breast, sucking my nipple hard, harder than it'd ever been sucked before, and fuck me, I loved it. It sent a sensation down my body straight between my legs. After lavishing attention on one side, he switched to the other, and the sucking made me wet, this time from me, not from the ocean.

"You taste so fucking good," he said against my breast. "Salty but not. It's so good." He nibbled his way up my chest and to my ear, which he bit lightly, and sucked.

Fuck, that felt good too.

His hand started to wander, as he felt my shoulder, grazed my arms, and held my hand, squeezing it gently.

He held my hand.

And then, he moved his hand over to my belly and kept going down.

I got wetter.

"I don't have a condom," I whispered.

"For what I'm thinking, we don't need one," he whispered back. "I wanna taste you."

Fine by me.

His hand went into my bikini bottom and aimed for the exact right place. I let out an involuntary breath. He rolled my clit with his thumb while he stuck two other fingers inside me, and that felt amazing. He rhythmically stroked me with his fingers, and then he stopped, kissed me again on the lips, and headed down my body. Leaving me turned on and bereft, he grasped the sides of my white bikini bottom in both hands and gently nudged it down, fully exposing my star tattoos on my hip bones. He let out a breath and reverently kissed one and then the other, and then pulled my bikini down all the way off of me, kneeled between my legs, and started licking me, clutching my ass with one hand.

He lapped me the entire way up my sex, tongue wide and wet, and I almost lost it just from that move alone. Then he did some sort of swirly, rolly thing with his mouth. I don't know what it was, but I didn't want him to stop and I told him so, loudly. He kept his fingers going for good measure. So, between the wide lapping of his tongue, the swirling and teasing, and his fingers in the exact right spots, it didn't take me long to come.

When I come, the world shuts down. I can't hear anything, I can't see anything. There is only my body, there is only tension, there is only the sensation of clenching all over, and then there is this sweet release, that lets it all out, flooding my entire body with pleasure.

God, that felt good.

But Will Thrash wasn't done with only one episode of Sex on the Beach. He kept going with his tongue and his fingers, and he brought me over the edge again, and again.

Oh my God.

Finally, I had to tell him to stop because I thought I was going to die from the pleasure.

He leaned back on his heels and looked at me closely, a satisfied look on his face, dark hair messy.

"I want nothing more than to bury myself in you. Go out to dinner with me tonight. Want you in my bed after."

I was in no state to argue with him.

"But what about you?" I asked. "Let me return the favor."

"Tonight."

He handed me my bikini bottom and I put it back on and adjusted my top. I can't believe I came in public. On the beach!

Exhibitionist.

Will carefully lay down next to me, staring at the sky, until my breathing regulated, and then he grabbed my hand and squeezed it. "Do you want to go back with me now or are you going to stay here?"

"I'll stay here for a while." I needed to think about what just happened.

"'Kay," he said, getting up. "Come get me at the ranch house when you want to go to dinner. Let's leave around six, 'cause it's a drive."

He kissed me, and I could taste my arousal on him. Then he put his hat back on, ambled over to his horse, got on, and took off up the bluff.

I lay on the towel, feeling sated and warm, and looking forward to a date with Will.

11

SOUP

I 'D NEVER PICKED UP a guy on a first date before, I realized, as I headed up the steps to Will's farmhouse, wearing a sleeveless, long, navy blue sundress that reached my ankles, and rope espadrilles. Sure, I'd picked up guys before, I'd asked out guys before, I'd initiated sex with guys before, but this felt different and more intimate—to walk up to his home from my room and get him for dinner. This wasn't a normal date.

Although I bet he asked me to come over because it was more convenient than him hanging around the bunkhouse, I thought that it reflected the strange balance of our relationship. I mean, I met him when he was naked and angry and then he immediately saw me almost-naked. He made the first move on me by making it clear what he wanted to do to me, but I made the actual first move by kissing him. There was a teeter-totter aspect to our new relationship, whatever it was—he didn't have all of the power and neither did I. I wasn't the type of woman who wanted him to be in charge of everything, make all the arrangements, and come to my door with flowers, sweeping me off of my feet.

He'd already given me candy, though.

And was taking me out to some unknown place where he'd made the arrangements.

Hmmm.

Not gonna think about the feminist thing right now.

Having learned my lesson to not barge in on the first day, I lifted up my fist to pound on the door, but it opened and Will stood there, looking down at me. Fuck me, handsome boy. He was wearing a dark blue, plaid, western-style shirt, jeans, and cowboy boots, but on him the clothes looked like they belonged, rather than a costume. His biceps and shoulders filled out the shirt, and he smelled fresh out of the shower.

Setting aside the politics, I was so amused to be dating a cowboy. I wondered where his hat was.

Before I could do anything, he grasped my wrist firmly, but gently, pulled me in the house, closed the door, pressed me to the wall, and kissed me, the whole length of his body pressing into mine. Naturally, I kissed him back and it was *yummy*.

"Hello to you, too," I laughed, when I could breathe again. He smiled and kissed my forehead and then took an evaluating look at my face.

"Did this hurt?" he asked, tracing my eyebrow piercing.

"A little," I said, "but it was also a total rush. I understand why people get all sorts of things pierced, because it feels like a high."

"I get the idea of pleasure mixed with pain, darlin'" he responded, looking at me closely.

I shivered at his words.

He traced his finger along the tattoo down the inside of my arm, and then continued, "Let's go get dinner before we don't make it out of here."

We walked over to his truck, which was now clean. I felt honored that he'd washed it for me. He opened my door and helped me up, Gentleman Will on display. Trixie came bounding up to go with us, and he let her up into the truck bed. To add to the list of new experiences that I was compiling this evening, I could now add that I'd never been on a first date with a guy *and his dog* before.

As we drove down the bumpy dirt road to the freeway, I filled him in on the parts that he'd missed with the kids from last week. He especially wanted to know how Clarissa liked everything and he seemed to really care that they all had a good time.

I didn't notice where we were going until we pulled up to a restaurant in Buellton, a small town near the ranch.

"Pea Soup Andersen's?" I asked, incredulously. A kitschy traveler's mecca, it had been here for decades, and advertised by signs with a couple of cartoon mascots who were splitting peas for split pea soup. Will gave Trixie water from a bottle and tied her to the side so she wouldn't go anywhere while we were eating.

"The soup's vegan." And he gave me a look, kind of triumphant for having already thought of it himself.

Ohmigod. He could really be sweet.

We walked through the tacky tourist shop and made our way to the old school diner in the back.

Consistent with the theme, the hostess was attired in a pseudo-traditional, Danish outfit. She seated us at a dark, naugahyde booth, old fashioned water glasses were placed on our fake wood table, and we ordered—me, soup and beer, him, pot roast and beer.

While Will was not a chatterbox by any stretch of the imagination, he was interactive, attentive, and polite, and I relaxed into a fun date. We ate, we talked, we laughed. Will paid, and we left the restaurant, giving Trixie attention before we headed back to the ranch in the truck.

Well, it *was* a fun date until he made an asinine comment, as we pulled in the compound, about the upcoming Presidential election, showing that he liked what a potential candidate—and coincidentally, a *complete idiot*—was saying.

And then he revealed that he voted for Bush. Twice.

Excuse me? How could he?

There was *no way* that anyone sane would agree with this candidate and no way that I could be with someone who voted for Bush.

It was a litmus test and Will failed.

What was I doing with this guy?

I was letting down the cause. I was an idiot for thinking that I could do this.

Had I been blinded by his body?

Clearly. We were such polar opposites. This wasn't going to work.

"I can't believe you would listen to anything that moron says," I snapped. "He's the worst thing ever for our country," and I stalked out of the truck. He let Trixie out and walked over to me and looked at me. "You believe in all the wrong things."

"I could say the same thing about you," he said sharply, with amusement under the edge in his voice.

I looked up at him, masculine and beautiful in the moonlight. And I was pissed. We had such a good date. But now I'd come back to reality and he was still the guy who called me names with whom I'd never see eye to eye. Finally, I spoke. "I don't know what we're doing. We shouldn't date. We don't have anything in common." Even though I knew it was true, saying it hurt for some reason.

"Oh no? I think we do—" he started to say, but I interrupted.

"Just don't talk to me," I snapped, and started to walk back to my room. "I don't want this to go any further. We're never going to get past it. I'm never going to agree with you on basic stuff that matters to me and that matters to you, so why should we bother?"

He hustled in front of me and stood there, blocking me, stopping my progress, holding up his hand, eyes on mine.

"We talked about this, Marie," he said in his low voice. "You're not gonna agree with me on a lot of things, and I'm not gonna agree with you. So what? Take it out on me," he invited, lifting his chin with his half-grin.

I paused, exasperated. "I'm not going to hit you, Will, even though you deserve it for voting for that imbecile and thinking the way you do. I'm a nonviolent tree hugger, remember?"

"That's not what I'm talking about," he rumbled, his eyes boring into me, his burly presence overshadowing me. He paused. Then he continued. "This is the part where we have angry sex."

12

REVERSE COWGIRL

"**I**SN'T IT WEIRD TO do this position the first time we fuck?" I moaned.

"Nope," he panted. "Just do it."

To back up.

At Will's words outside, I decided that, yes, I needed angry sex and I needed it right fucking now. I needed to get laid. I was going to take out my frustrations with him being an asshole Republican, and an asshole generally, directly on him. Now. Almost before he finished his sentence, I whirled around and ran to his house, him hot on my heels. He had his keys in his hand by the time we were at front door, unlocking it quickly, pushing me in, and slamming the door shut.

Immediately, I got to work, unbuttoning his shirt, fumbling with his belt buckle, reaching for the button fly of his jeans, trying to do this all at once and kiss him at the same time and getting nowhere.

"How the fuck does this work?" I yelled, during the time I was trying to unhook his I-am-a-cowboy-so-I-must-wear-a-dinner-plate belt buckle, not at all trying to keep my voice down. He was going to learn that I'm a very loud fuck. He took pity on me and whipped his partially-unbuttoned shirt over his head, somehow got his belt and belt buckle off, and started unbuttoning his pants. At this, I noticed something. No waistband of his underwear.

Holy shit, Will went commando.

Before he got his pants unbuttoned more than two or three buttons, however, he leaned over and pulled off his boots and threw them on the ground. I heard them hit the floor with a clump, and then another clump. Meanwhile, I reached for the hem of my dress, sailing it over my head so I was only wearing my navy blue satin thong, a matching bra, and my espadrilles, which had flat, dark blue ribbons criss-crossing up my ankles. He took a step back, stared at me, taking my long-legged body in, as I panted, staring at him, equally taking in his epic body, since by now he was only wearing halfway-unbuttoned jeans and clean white socks. Fuck, he was stunning. We both breathed in and out for a moment, just looking at each other, not touching.

Then.

"C'mon," he grunted, and pulled me to the stairs, holding my hand, letting go once we got there.

Not even taking the time to look at my surroundings any better than I had the first time, other than noticing that it was a very old house, I ran up the creaky wooden staircase after him, breathing hard—for a variety of reasons—by the time I got up to the top.

Apparently I'd taken too long getting up there because he hoisted me up over his shoulder in a fireman's carry, jogged down the hall with me shrieking, went into a room, and threw me down on a bed.

And then his big, warm body was on top of mine, his lips on mine, his cock hard through his jeans, and all of this feeling like it belonged there.

But still, I wanted to be on top.

Our kisses were like we were battling with each other for who was going to prevail, and there was quite a bit of wrestling for position going on. Given his muscles, I figured that he was holding back, because, finally, I wriggled and pushed until I was straddling him, him looking up at me, eyes wild, wavy hair mussed, breathing hard.

I'd no idea what I looked like and I didn't care.

Now on top, where I wanted to be, I took a second to glance around at what must be Will's room. I was in an old-fashioned bedroom with tall, whitewashed walls, several small old-fashioned black and white agricultural pictures on the walls, and a huge, dark wood, antique four-poster bed with a handmade, red and white quilt on top. There was a pile of clothes in the corner and loose change on a dresser top, but otherwise the room appeared neat.

Will immediately interrupted my inspection of his interior design by snaking his hand around my back and expertly unhooking my bra so that my breasts sprung free, pulling my bra off of my arms. And then he let out a breath. Knifing up, he did some sort of twist maneuver so that I was back under him again, and he was kissing my lips, then my neck, then my nipples.

"Goddammit Will, get my fucking shoes off and take off your fucking pants," I yelled.

He laughed, and reached back to untie the ribbons on my shoes, while I sat up and went to work on his pants, again fumbling in my anger and frustration. My shoes were off, one, then the other, and Will got up, looked at me, pulled off his socks, and undid the rest of his pants, letting them drop to the ground.

There he was.

So, remember how I said that Will was huge while unerect?

Now he was erect.

Oh boy.

My eyes widened.

"You're fucking huge, asshole, how is that thing going to fit inside me?"

Guess I was still yelling at him.

"It won't be a problem," he muttered. "I won't hurt you. Now get these things off," and he hooked his fingers in my panties and pulled them down, off of my body. He leaned over to a bedside table drawer and threw a condom on top.

Then he proceeded to attend to me.

As I ran my hands through his hair and down his back, he gave ample attention to my lips, feasted on my earlobes, kissed his way down my neck, all the while running his hands through my hair, tracing my tattoos, fondling my breasts. Then, he turned the direction of his mouth to my breasts and his hand went lower, finding my already soaking wet pussy, and exploring.

The man knew what he was doing.

"If you don't get inside me in one second, Will, I swear—" and he cut me off by kissing me, breaking apart, then ripping the condom wrapper open with his teeth and sliding it on fast.

"You ready?" he growled. "Think you are, you're so fucking wet—"

"—Right fucking now, Will. You need to—" I started to say, and he thrust into me.

Heaven.

"Oh, *fuck*," we both said together.

That was right where he needed to be. Right where I wanted him. Yes, he was huge, but my body accepted him like he was meant to be there. He stayed still for a moment, just pressing into me, and then started to move a little.

"Will, don't pussyfoot around, you asshole. Get moving."

He laughed, a strained sort of groaning laugh, and started moving.

Yes.

I might have said that out loud.

Because of the size of him, he hit every nerve ending in me. I had never felt sensations like that, stroking, teasing, rubbing every part of me that felt good. He leaned down and kissed me. "You. On top."

Fine by me.

We wrestled over to the other side of the bed, but he pulled out and grabbed my hips, helping me to turn around. "This way."

Now, I'd done this before but not while getting to know someone.

"Isn't it weird to do this position the first time we fuck?" I asked.

"Nope. Just do it."

Ah well, fuck it. I turned around so that I was straddling him, facing his feet, and lowered myself on his cock. "Touch yourself," he grunted.

Now he was talking.

I started slowly, then went to work, riding him up and down his magnificent cock, as I fingered my clit. Talk about pleasure. Between him filling me up and me heightening the sensation, I was completely in ecstasy. I moaned and panted. I could hear him grunting as I went faster and faster.

And then it hit me. I came, spasming on his cock, as I stroked myself into oblivion. He raised his hips, heightening the pleasure for me.

Fuck me.

When I came down, I panted, "Which way do you want it?"

In a second, he positioned me and I was on my hands and knees. He thrust into me from behind.

That felt incredible, too.

Then he pushed me down on the bed, me still on my stomach, him still on top, he leaned his body over top of me, and reached his hand in front of me, between my legs, and started fingering my clit again. "Go again," he said.

Again, fine by me.

As he thrust into me, and fingered me, I lay, somewhat helpless to the overwhelming sensations of pleasure. As Will fucked me completely, the exquisite and familiar focusing and clenching meant an orgasm was coming. When it burst, I screamed nonsensical words, and he sped up, thrusting until he, too, came with a loud groan and a shudder, and then he collapsed on my back.

After a second, he propped himself up so that he wasn't squishing me, then nuzzled my neck.

He kissed me down my spine and pulled out. And then he plopped himself next to me, and pulled me into him, cuddling with me.

And then I decided that I was a fan of angry sex. A life-long fan.

13

STARS

FTER A FEW MOMENTS, Will got up, padded down the hall, and came back cleaned up. He opened a drawer, put on a pair of boxer shorts, and crawled into bed next to me.

"I'm sorry I called you an asshole so much," I said quietly. "I got carried away."

"Don't need to be sorry 'bout that. I *am* an asshole. Not going to apologize for who I am. And you don't need to apologize for who you are." He paused for a second. "Plus, I'm a kinky sumbitch, so I like it that you get carried away. Want you to get carried away with me again."

Okay, then.

I snuggled into his chest and he played with my hair.

"It's still early," he said into the top of my head. "Wanna beer?"

"Yeah."

"It's a nice night. Let's go outside. I know the spot. You can borrow something to wear."

I thought about whether I wanted to wear something of his, or go get my own clothes, braving an inquisition at the bunkhouse. But there was little chance of an inquisition. Stephanie was gone for the weekend, visiting her parents. Janine knew that I had a date with Will, and approved, telling me that she thought he was great, and that he was like a little brother to her. Since no part of Will seemed "little" to me, this was a funny comment, but it was still heartening.

"I'll go get sweats and meet you outside," I whispered.

"'Kay. See you in a few," he whispered back, and then kissed me gently.

I gingerly got up off of the bed, found the small amount of clothes that I had lost in this room, and retraced my steps to the downstairs, adding clothes to my body as I went down the hall. Will followed me in his underwear, and once I reached the front door and had my dress and shoes back on, he put his finger below my chin, drew me to him, and kissed me again. Then he put his forehead against mine and whispered, "Hurry."

I walked to the bunkhouse from Will's house, across the courtyard. Although a few outside lights shone on the buildings, the stars were out in full force on this moonless night. I hopped into the bunkhouse, skipped down the hall, and divested myself of my date outfit, putting on a pair of comfy yoga pants, a tank top and hoodie sweatshirt, and a pair of Tom's shoes. Janine slept, so I tried to be as quiet as possible. I put my hair up into a rumpled bun on the top of my head, and headed out, where Will stood outside, wearing a dark t-shirt, black track pants with gray stripes down the side, and flip flops. He was carrying two open beers and a folded up blanket.

"What, no Wranglers, cowboy?" I asked, teasing him.

He smiled and handed me an open beer. "C'mon." He took my hand and led me toward a path that I hadn't been on before. I heard a jingling, and Trixie came running up beside us, tail wagging, eager to continue our date.

"Where does she sleep?"

"Doghouse or my room. Depends on what she wants."

With how devoted that dog was to Will, I bet she spent almost no time at all in the doghouse.

We walked along a flat path that headed northwest and then headed up a small hill to a bluff overlooking the ocean. The path glowed pale so we could see without flashlights, as our eyes adjusted to the lack of light.

We stopped. He spread out the blanket on the ground and gestured for me to sit. We could hear the crash of the waves, but no other sounds. He took my beer from me, set it beside his on the ground, and lay down on the blanket. "Make yourself comfortable."

I snuggled up next to him, but down his body, my head on his belly, my legs tangled with his. Trixie plopped down next to us. For a while, neither Will nor I said anything, we just looked at the infinite stars visible in this beautiful place. I felt the rise and fall of his belly and heard Trixie's panting.

"You know," he said to the top of my head, surprising me by opening up, "I've grown up a rancher, and my dad was a rancher, and my granddad was a rancher, and his dad before him. Don't know what I'd be doing if it wasn't for farming and ranching."

For once, I shut up and let him talk.

"I see my parents whenever I want 'cause they live here in a new house we built for them. I normally have Sunday dinner with them. They do their own thing, I do mine, but they're close.

"Dad's retired. I'm in charge now.

"Gotta offer to sell this place to some fancy developer. It would mean that I'd never have to work another day in my life. And I just can't get myself to say yes because I'd miss comin' out here and lookin' at the stars in the sky."

I propped myself up halfway and looked at him while he was continuing to share. "Farming and ranching is more than just a job. It's who I am. And if I gave it up, I dunno what I'd do. So I keep telling 'em no and they keep calling me back and offering me more money."

I looked at him, and traced his handsome face with my fingers. "I don't know what the right answer is. I just know that it's beautiful out here."

"Yeah," he said quietly.

He sat up and pulled me in front of him, so I could sit, leaning against him. He reached over, grabbed our beers, and we stayed there, under the stars, drinking beer in silence for quite a while.

After our beers were finished and the air chilled slightly, we walked back to his house hand in hand, with Trixie following behind.

14

FIRST IMPRESSIONS, REDUX

THE FIRST THING I heard the next morning was the clang, clang, clang of the triangle. That fucking triangle didn't let me sleep in. I'd have to steal it and hide it somewhere, or maybe melt it down into a horseshoe.

As I woke up, I also became aware that I wasn't in my bed in the bunkhouse with Janine, reenacting *The Waltons*. Instead, I was tucked into Will, his arms around my waist and his forehead in my hair, under his red and white quilt, in his antique bed, in his farmhouse. Bright sunlight bathed the whitewashed room and I felt sore, but also like I'd slept really well.

I moved away from him and he leaned back into his pillow, putting an arm up behind him, still sleeping, peaceful and pretty, hair tousled on his pillow. I was surprised that I'd woken up first. He seemed like an early-to-rise farmer, but I suppose we were active last night.

After we'd walked in the house from stargazing, he fed Trixie in the kitchen, closed her in there with a dog bed, and then got a look on his face that was a combination of mischievous and hopeful.

"I was thinking of redoing our first meeting."

"In the bathroom?" I asked, surprised.

"Yeah. But reenacting it a different way," he said, grinning.

Although I was mellow from him opening up to me outside and going for a walk under the stars, at his words, a thrill raced through my body. I hadn't had enough of Will for the evening.

I followed him down the hall, into the second door on the left, but this time, instead of pushing me out, he opened his arms to me and gave me a huge bear hug, then leaned back, tilted my chin up to him and kissed me.

The kiss started out sweet, but it didn't end that way. By the end of the kiss we were in each other's space. Chasing tongues, licking teeth, exploring the territory. We simply couldn't get close enough to each other.

I didn't look at the bathroom at all the last time. This time, I eventually got around to looking at it, and it was adorable— vintage white tile, an old fashioned tub built into one side, and spartan, but pleasant and country.

He'd been taking the lead this evening, but I decided it was my turn. I broke apart from our kiss, pulled up the hem of his tight t-shirt and lifted it over his head. I ran my flat hands down the smooth skin on his broad shoulders, lingering over his bulging biceps, feeling the veins in his forearms. Then I held his hands.

Letting go, I reached up and ran my palms up his torso, wanting to feel his washboard waist and his defined muscula- ture, wanting to make his nipples pucker. As I did this, he watched me, amused and intense. I ran my hands up and over his shoulders, and down his strong back, feeling the muscles, feeling his brawn.

Then I got to his ass. He had a very tight butt that fit into the Wranglers like they were made for him. As I've mentioned, I'm not a Wrangler girl, I go more for Levi's, but Will's ass swayed me to the other side. Still, right now he was in loose track pants and bare feet. I slid my hands inside the waistband and peeled his pants and boxers off of him, feeling his ass, and kneeling as I went down. His cock, splendid and full, popped out of his pants and stood at attention. I reached over to stroke him and I heard him hold his breath. Then.

"Take off your shirt," he whispered, letting out his air with his words. He reached over into the shower and turned it on to heat up the water.

"I'll do one better," I murmured and I peeled off my hoodie and top, slowly, looking at him straight into his dark brown eyes. Then I licked my lips, enjoying the tease, as I took off my shoes and my pants, and stood there in my underwear.

I decided that I just had to play with him some more. I loved messing with him, he was so reactive, even though he said so little. I loved his irregular breathing, the darkening of his eyes, the quiver of his cheek and jaw. Looking at him, I slowly unhooked my bra, then slipped it down my arms. Next, I shimmied out of my underwear. Then I kneeled again, before all six and a half feet of him, looking up at this mountain of a man.

And I smiled.

He widened his eyes and let out a breath like a quiet, "Whoooooooooo."

So I leaned over and I went for it.

As I've mentioned, Mr. Will was a very big boy, in height, strength, and junk. I didn't know if I could get all of him in my mouth, but I was going to have fun trying. So, I decided to go slowly and carefully, almost dividing it into sectors. First, the balls sector. I gently cupped them with my hands, rolling them, caressing them. Then I decided that he needed a big lick up his cock sector, so I started at the root and licked him all the way to the head.

He liked this.

I could tell because he started swearing and he really knew how to swear.

Then I sort of reached up and decided to take as much of him as I could in my mouth—which ended up being a surprisingly long amount. I swirled my tongue around and pulled out with a sucking pop, and then went back again. And again. Swirl, suck, pop, lick. Repeat.

Then I decided to lavish attention on the glans sector, and thereunder.

And then I made the rounds again back to the other sectors, trying to keep up a steady rhythm and gentle pressure.

I knew I was pleasing him because of the noises that came out of him—a moan, a groan, a quiet "*Yes.*"

But then he leaned his hips back, pulled out of my mouth and said, "Shower," and opened the curtain and helped me in. As the water surrounded us, he let me into the spray, warming me up, although I was already pretty warm, and comforting me. Then he pulled me to him by my lower back, pressed against me, and said against my neck, "You do that again and I'd consider voting for a Democrat."

"I see my plan is working," I said, joking.

He didn't look like he was joking. He sucked on my neck and asked, "You tested?"

"Yeah."

"You negative?" he continued.

"Yeah. You?"

"Yep. You on the pill?"

"Yeah."

"Then you good with bare?"

"Fuck yeah."

And with that, he picked me up by my ass and hoisted me against the flat part of the shower wall, above the faucets, under the spray, and slid into me. I quickly wrapped my legs and arms around him and held on.

I was already wet from the kiss at the beginning of all of this.

"Finger yourself, darlin'," he ordered, and I did, as he started to move.

It felt like all of my senses were engaged—touching the water, Will's righteous body, and the cool tile behind me; hearing the sound of our breathing, the slaps of our bodies and the splash of the water; tasting his marvelous mouth; seeing his hard body and dark eyes; smelling his skin and the musky scent of sex.

Even though I was wrapped around him, he held me up easily. I'd never thought this was a comfortable position, but with him, it felt easy. I liked this. A lot.

With the assistance of my own fingers and his cock stimulating me on the inside, it wasn't long before I exploded into a climax, Will following shortly behind.

After staying there for a moment, he slowly let my legs down, pressed his forehead next to mine, and said, "This is what I was thinking when I saw you the first time."

"Funny," I said, "I just thought, *yum.*"

"Same thing." He smiled, forehead still to mine, and then he kissed me.

We soaped up, the slippery suds sliding over our wet bodies, cleaned up, dried off, and went to his bed, clean and sated.

Will didn't object when I told him that I liked to sleep naked. Apparently so did he.

So now, first thing in the morning, his torso on display, arm behind his head, I got to watch him in the early sun. Even his armpit was fine. I nuzzled his Adam's apple and then he woke up too.

He blinked and looked around and then saw me and pulled

me into a tight squeeze. Who'd have thought that Will was a cuddler?

"We need to get up," I told him, "We'll miss breakfast."

"Fuck breakfast," he muttered against my hair. "We'll either make something later or I'll take you out."

"'Kay," I agreed.

He turned over in bed and pressed me to my back, so that I was looking up at him and he was on his side, looking at me. He traced the tattoo down my arm, gently, lightly.

"What does this mean?"

"Everything happens for a reason."

He raised a sleepy eyebrow. "The saving the animals and the peacenik dove and the earth on your ass I can figure out, I think. But what about the stars on your hipbones?"

I looked away from him for a moment, then decided to tell him. "Because someday I want to find my mate for life, who will have the stars on his hips too and we'll match."

"That's cool," he said, tracing my markings with his hands, fascinated. Then, a few moments later, he asked, "You hungry now?"

"I could wait."

"Good. Because we'll eat after I fuck you again."

I lifted up my arms and pulled him to me.

And if he hadn't announced that it was fucking, I would have called it something else, something with a name that meant that it was slow and gentle and patient. Something like making love.

15

MA

"I'M NOT EATING FUCKING quinoa for breakfast, however you say it. And I'm not going to ride in your hippie-mobile, whatever shit that is. Men drive. Men like me drive trucks. We don't eat kale and we don't ride shotgun in fucking sissy-ass cars while some woman drives us around—"

So Will's sweetness was good while it lasted. But apparently he had a breaking point, and that point was easy to get to. Actually, we got to it at breakfast, after I made him oatmeal with craisins, walnuts, and brown sugar, which he said was good but needed butter that he added. But then I mentioned that I liked quinoa for breakfast and I knew a vegan restaurant to take him to and he lost it. If we weren't in each other's pants, it seemed that we were destined for fighting about stupid shit, but the problem was that to both of us the stupid shit was a symbol for something greater. Something we couldn't reconcile. Something that mattered deep down underneath.

Quinoa was a symbol of my desire to help the earth. It was also a symbol of his distrust and dislike of anything politically correct.

He looked at me with disgust, and started that quinoa/kale/car/female driving diatribe, but I wasn't going to let him finish it.

"First, *some woman*? That's all I am? Then how can you stand to be around me?" I snapped. "You just want to fuck me. I'm an easy cunt. That's it."

"No, I don't 'just want to fuck' you—" he started, but I interrupted him.

"Why did you even start this, Will, if you can't stand me? I should just go. I'm fucking out of here."

I went to leave the kitchen and he got in front of me and stopped.

"I like you, Marie. I just don't like everything you like—" he said in a quiet and dangerous tone, but I interrupted him, again.

"Fuck you, you're a motherfucker," and I pushed him to the side. "If you don't agree with me, fine, don't, but you don't have to be an ass about it."

"I told you, I know I'm an asshole. That's just the way I'm made. But I think there's something here and if we can get past these arguments, I'd like to know—" but I interrupted him, again.

"We're not going to be able to get past these arguments because this shit? It's in our DNA. I believe what I believe and you believe what you believe and neither one of us is going to change. We both think we're right and we can't stand what the other one believes in. And you think differently than me in every possible way you can."

He looked annoyed. "Not true."

I waved a finger in his face. "And you're rude and sexist."

He sighed, exasperated. "Yes, I can be rude but I'm not sexist."

"Then what was that shit that just came out of your mouth?" I said, exasperated.

Looking at me straight in the eyes, he said firmly, "The truth."

Oh he was so difficult!

"Fuck no, that's not the truth."

We looked at each other, both seething, both breathing hard. He spoke first, closing a gap between us.

"I am fucking attracted to you, Marie, and it's not just your incredible body, although that's a big part of it. I like that you don't back down on me. I like that you push back. I like that you care about everything. I like knowing what you think. You don't hide it from me and I like that. I just think some of it is extreme bullshit and I'm not going to do it. But you, I want to be with you."

Yeah, right. I was an easy target. "No you don't. You just want to stick your cock in me."

He reached for me and I pulled back, wanting to withdraw. He kept going.

"Marie, you're not listening to me. I want to date you," he growled.

He wants to date me? Could I date Will for real? He made me pause for a moment, but then, I remembered who we were and I put my hand on my hip.

"Yeah, but can that go anywhere? What would it be like to be seen in public with me? When I have rainbow hair and my eyebrow ring and I'm wearing hemp clothes and I'm drinking green juice. You'd be the laughingstock of your friends and family for hanging out with me. You'd be ashamed."

"Don't tell me how I'd think—" he started, running a hand through his hair, but I interrupted, again.

"I've lived on your property for more than a week and I haven't met your parents, who I know live here too. That shows you're ashamed of me. You don't want them to know that a freak like me is living here, whether or not I'm dating you."

"You have that entirely wrong," he snarled.

"Oh no? Then why haven't I met them? I've met everyone else. I've even met the ranch foreman."

Will stared at me for a moment, eyes flaring, and said, "Come on then. You're meeting my ma and dad."

I looked down. I was in my yoga pants and hoodie from the night before. "Will, I'm not all dressed up—"

"You don't have to be. You look beautiful just the way you are. I'm not ashamed of hanging out with you. I'll prove it. Come. Now." And he fucking picked me up under my knees and shoulders, and carried me out of the house, Trixie nipping at his heels.

"Put me the fuck down, right now," I shrieked as I struggled.

"Only if you come with me," he said, not exerting himself at all as he walked.

"Fine," I said, with as much contempt as I could put into the one syllable, and he put me down.

He took my hand and physically pulled me across the courtyard, past several buildings, almost running, until we got to a newer ranch house off to the side. It had a grass front with a picket fence, and a few vintage farm implements and wooden wagon wheels as decorations. The one-story house had a slight ramp to the front door.

He opened the screen and knocked once, walking in. "Ma?" he called.

An elegant, low female voice with a Spanish accent called out musically, "William, come in. I'm in the living room."

We walked into the house, which was newish and clean. It was decorated in country, although not overdone, capital-letter, Country. The room had new, comfortable furniture, fresh flowers in chipped enamel vases, and impressionist paintings of California on the walls. We walked through the front room and the kitchen to another room where I could hear Fox News on the television.

Oh, God, Fox News. Here we go.

But then I walked into a room and saw a beautiful dark haired, dark eyed woman in a wheelchair. She was breathtaking, with clear caramel skin, high cheek bones, and lush lips. She was clearly Will's mom.

His mom spoke Spanish?

And was a double-amputee.

Fuck. Things were starting to come together. Janine had mentioned that his mom had been in a car accident and her recovery was the beginning of the Headlands Program. I was willing to bet that this accident was the reason, likely, why Will was an only child.

Fuck, shit, damn.

He was an asshole, but so was I.

"Ma, this is Marie Diaz-Austin. She's running the enrichment programs for Headlands, and she's also going to be my girlfriend."

Excuse me?

I'd have to talk to him about this, so I glared at him, then rearranged my face into a smile and shook her slim, cool hand. "It's nice to meet you."

"Marie, the pleasure is all mine. My name is Margarita, but you can call me Margaret. Are you enjoying the ranch?"

And with that, we launched into a discussion about the ranch and how much I loved it, studiously avoiding Will's presumptuous pronouncement about the future of our relationship, such that it was. After a little while, a tall, handsome older man, wearing a plaid shirt and Wranglers, sauntered in from the back of the house, shook my hand, and sat down by his wife, holding her hand. He had dark eyes and light brown hair and introduced himself as Bill Thrash.

I didn't know how I got myself into this. I went from pissing Will off, to being attracted to him, to yelling at him, to fucking him, to being sweet with him, to fighting with him, to meeting his parents. This was so confusing.

But damn, if Fox News wasn't on, it would've been perfect.

16

EATING DINOSAUR

I HAVEN'T HEARD FROM you in days because by now you're sleeping with Will, right?

Upon reading this text, I immediately picked up my phone and dialed Amelia. I needed girlfriend time and I needed it now. Between sex, politics, and my new job, let alone Will's statement that we were dating, I had a lot to cover with her and I wanted advice.

After talking with Will's parents, who were incredibly nice, his mom outgoing, his dad friendly, but less talkative, just like Will, we excused ourselves. He walked me to the bunkhouse, telling me that because his dad took care of his mom, he was rarely out of the house. His mom would go out to see the animals and loved the life on the ranch. And Will ate there on weekends and stopped in often. He told me he'd take me back if I wanted to go. I absolutely wanted to see them again.

He followed me inside the bunkhouse, all the way to my room, and when we got to it, he closed the door and kissed me hard. Then he said that he had to go check on things around the ranch and left. I heard him whistling for Trixie once he got outside.

I changed clothes into jeans and my vegan boots and went into the bunkhouse office to finalize my plans for the upcoming week, a group of thirty twelve- and thirteen-year-olds from Oakland.

Then I remembered that I hadn't checked my phone in a long time. Funny, now that I was enmeshed in life at Headlands, I didn't seem to check it very much, unlike how I spent every waking hour on it at home. There was just too much to do here —horses and fresh air and taking care of kids and spending time with Will, among my favorites.

Amelia answered immediately.

"How did you know we fucked?" I asked, without preamble.

"Ha! Lucky guess."

"That's not all that's lucky," I said, and she laughed. "Listen, though. It's an emergency. I need Amelia time. Can you come up?"

"Sure. When?"

"Uh, today?"

"I can leave in an hour and be there in two. Should I bring Ryan so that we can all go out to dinner?"

There was a reason why Amelia was my best friend and this was it. I told her to bring boots and jeans in case she wanted to ride a horse, and stuff to stay overnight and go out to dinner.

Two hours later, she and Ryan pulled up in Ryan's SUV, a surfboard tied to the top.

"I totally have to pee!" exclaimed Amelia, as she burst from the car and gave me a rushed hug.

I laughed. "I know the feeling. Go into that ranch house, down the hallway, two doors down on the left, and don't forget to knock first."

As she ran off, Ryan stepped out of the car.

I mentioned it before, but Ryan was so hot. Tall and lanky, but muscular, dressed in jeans—Levi's, thank you very much, that hung down nicely on his hips—and a plaid shirt over a white t-shirt. He had wild, curly blond hair and tanned skin, and when he smiled he had dimples.

He was Amelia's, but I had eyes.

"Hey, Marie," he said, in his low, sexy surfer voice, and pulled me into a tight hug.

Just then, Will walked around the barn, wearing a fitted, but faded black t-shirt that showed off his chest, a trucker hat squashing his waves, and his usual Wranglers and boots. Even from this distance, he affected me in the worst way. He saw us, and a strange look came over his face as he strolled over.

I called out to him, waving, excited, "Will, this is Ryan Fielding, my best friend Amelia's fiancé. She's using your bathroom." Will looked at me, and I could read a bunch of emotions that passed over his face—apparent relief that Ryan was not with me, surprise that my friends were visiting, and humor at Amelia being just like me.

The guys shook hands, gripping firmly. "Will Thrash."

"Ryan. Nice to meet you. This ranch is great. I work with coffee growers in Kona," and with that Ryan was off chatting with Will as if they'd known each other forever. Ryan was the type of guy who would be equally comfortable talking with drunkards at a demolition derby or at a formal dinner with the Queen of England, just a cool guy. So perfect for my girl, and he'd really helped her through her personal issues. I also knew from Amelia that he was dynamite in bed, so I was happy that she'd finally found her partner for life. They really were meant to be together.

The ranch house door opened and Amelia walked down, got a glimpse of Will, her violet eyes wide, and mouthed "Holy shit" to me.

"I know," I mouthed. Then I turned to Will. "I invited my best friend up to visit and I thought we could all go out to dinner. Would you like to come?"

"Sure, darlin'," he drawled, and Amelia got a look on her face that wasn't hard to figure out. She liked him.

"I'd like to take them horseback riding too, if I can find Jimmy or one of the wranglers."

"Sounds good."

Amelia walked up and I introduced her to Will and she shook his hand. She seemed to tremble in his presence, and I didn't blame her.

We agreed on a time to meet up for dinner. Ryan unstrapped his surfboard, saying that he was going to explore a secret surf break that was supposed to be around here. Amelia, who was already dressed for riding, and I headed over to the horses. Jimmy got us saddled up, me on Happy, Amelia on Astrix, and we headed out on one of the well-worn trails.

Once we were out of earshot of everyone at the ranch, Amelia started. "Marie, he's mesmerizing. No wonder you wanted to tap that. I'd want to, too."

"I know. He's stunning. I feel this overwhelming attraction to him, but also this repulsion because of his backwards politics. It's like we're both magnets, and if we get the sides right, there's no separating us, but if we turn the magnet around, there's no getting us together."

Our horses walked past sagebrush on the hills, which scented the air. The sun overhead warmed us.

"So is the issue that you may want to be with him for more than just the summer?"

"That's part of it. Part of it is that I feel like I'm a hypocrite. Like on the outside I'm all green and on the inside I'm not."

"But does he respect you?"

"I don't know. His politics tell me he doesn't, but his actions tell me he does." I paused. "Isn't it crazy? He's not my type. I mean, remember Jeremy?"

We rode on, through a lemon orchard and out to the rangeland where cattle gathered under the oak trees.

She laughed. "Man Bun. He wasn't enough of a challenge for you. What does your heart say?"

"My heart says that if I don't protect it, I could fall in love with him," I said, admitting and articulating thoughts that were buried really deep. "And then what would I do? I'm only supposed to be here for the summer. I can't be with him, I have to finish my school. I'm the girl who always moves on. I don't stay still."

"I think you're getting ahead of yourself and you have to trust what you feel," said Amelia gently, "and not worry about the consequences yet. There are ways of still going to school and seeing him, if that's what you want to do. This isn't all that far away from home."

"No. But what about this feeling that I'm turning into a cavewoman if I hang out with him. Is he going to start ordering me around and making me eat dinosaur?"

Amelia laughed. "Well, a certain amount of being bossed around is hot. There's a balance. If he respects you, and despite what you think, I think he does, then you'll work it out. You wouldn't be attracted to him if he treated you shitty. I think you guys just argue because you like each other. And cavewomen didn't eat dinosaur."

"I still feel the need to remind him that I am a modern woman. He's only two years older than us, but some of his attitudes are from a different generation."

She smiled.

"But he's fucking hot in bed."

Amelia laughed, a full-on laugh, and said, "Girl, now you must spill."

So I told her. I went into detail about Will's immensely huge junk, which made her eyes flash. I continued with a discussion about the way he went down on me at the beach, how he had me riding reverse cowgirl in his bed the first time we did it, how I then sucked him off in the bathroom, then he nailed me in his shower, and then he made gentle love to me first thing that morning.

"All of this since yesterday?"

"Yes."

"Ohmigod."

She needed time to recover.

Once she had been fully briefed on the situation, she said, "I have an idea."

"Yeah?"

"I think we need to throw these guys off their game. Ryan can be very take-charge too. After dinner, we need to do something that they wouldn't expect. Make *them* be along for the ride instead of us, for a change."

"Will likes to drive."

"So does Ryan. Okay, here's what I'm thinking," she said in a rush. "I'm thinking we take them to a strip club and see how they act with modern females getting lap dances from strippers."

I snorted. "Amelia! You're starting to think dirty, all the time, like me. And, um, that's random. How does going to a strip club with them serve any purpose?"

She looked a little embarrassed. "I've been talking about them with Ryan. I've never been to one and I think I should."

"Part of your rule-breaking is it?" I asked.

She looked at me, exasperated. "It was never a Rule but yeah, kind of." Then she said in a rush, "Okay, I have a list of reasons, wanna hear them?"

That's my girl, with her lists. I nodded.

"One, they're used to telling us what to do and so, for once, we can tell *them* what to do. Two, it's hot. Three, I want to see their faces. Four, strip clubs aren't just for men. Women can enjoy them too. Five, I think they won't be able to stand it and I totally want to torture them, especially if Will is anywhere near the horny bastard Ryan is. What do you think? Surprise them?"

"Totally. I can't wait to see the looks on their faces."

"Or what'll happen afterward."

_____

17

BLUE CLEAR SKY

S O, WILL TOOK US all to a steakhouse.

After Amelia and I returned, helped Jimmy put the horses away, and cleaned up, and Ryan finished surfing and showered, we all dressed to go out. Amelia and I both put on little dresses, mine electric blue, and shorter and tighter than her longer, strappy, black one, but her red platform heels were higher than my silver stilettos. Will wore a black western shirt and his usual jeans and boots and looked yummy. When I saw him, I couldn't help but whisper in his ear, "I dare you to wear a cowboy hat."

He looked me up and down in my dress, planted a wet kiss on my lips, grinned, and went into the house. He returned with a black cowboy hat, the first time I'd ever seen him wear one, which made him look dangerous, in addition to his usual sexy. Ryan wore his surfer jeans and button down plaid shirt and looked lickable too.

Then we piled into Will's big truck, boys in front, girls in back, because we were with cavemen, and drove up north to Santa Maria to a restaurant that Will liked.

We walked into the steakhouse and I could tell immediately

why he liked it. It was the epitome of "Beef, it's what's for dinner." It felt Western, with low ceilings, dark wood paneling on the walls, and branding irons as decoration. The home of some famous Santa Maria steaks, both Amelia and Ryan seemed excited to check it out.

But Will told me, with undisguised disgust, that he had gone online beforehand to make sure that they had a vegan meal, which, I found out, consisted of all of the side dishes that the restaurant had on one plate—baked potato, mashed potatoes, sweet potato fries, broccoli, mixed vegetables with broccoli, and corn. Like Will, the restaurant didn't know what to do with me. Good thing I thought this was funny and I didn't really care what I ate this evening.

It was also thoughtful of him to find out beforehand.

We were seated in a booth, all squished together, and ordered drinks, Amelia and I going immediately for cosmos because that's the kind of girls we were, the guys ordering beers.

After dinner, this restaurant became a saloon with a dance floor, which started immediately adjacent to us and ended up at a full bar. Country music played, ghastly twangy stuff, but a few people were dancing, which was fun to watch. Those country boys can move, swirling their partners around, unafraid to be seen dancing. Will had only had one beer, Ryan, two, while Amelia and I had three cosmos each. There was no way around it, it was going to be a sloppy evening.

After we ate our meal, and were relaxing, talking, and drinking, a new song came on. Will grabbed my hand and pulled. "C'mon. We're dancing."

I'd never danced to country music before, but I loved to dance, so I didn't argue. I was curious about what made him want to move.

"Why are we dancing?" I asked.

"Because I like this song," he said. "George Strait."

There was that George Strait again, he must be his favorite singer. The song said something about how you were giving up on love, when it fell out of the blue clear sky.

This was how I learned that Will could dance. Even in my heels, he towered over me, and spun me around easily, moving me where he wanted me to go, gently leading and guiding me with one hand on my waist and the other holding my hand. For such a bulky guy, he moved really well, which I should have guessed given how good he was in the bedroom.

I'd never had this much fun dancing with a guy before. Most guys I knew just sort of jerked around spasmodically or moved like they were in a trance. They danced *next to you*, not *with you*. But Will knew what he was doing and moved me around the floor, like he'd spent all of his life on a dance floor. It was simply fun to dance together, as a couple, as partners. Yeah it was country music. I got over it. He smelled good, he looked wonderful, and he moved so gracefully, in charge and having fun.

At the end of the song, he smiled, dipped me, then pulled me up and kissed me deeply.

I wondered if my internal swoon was audible.

The bill came and everyone argued about who would pay for it. Will won because he said that he'd invited everyone out, which earned him a kiss on the cheek from me and an "I got the next one" from Ryan.

And then Amelia said, "Marie and I have an idea. We know where we want to go next. It's a surprise. Are you guys up for it?"

Will and Ryan looked at each other and at us and Ryan shrugged and Will muttered, "Oh shit," and put his cowboy hat low down on his face.

I clapped my hands. "Excellent."

Once we got back to the truck, I pulled out my phone, found the link to the strip club that Amelia and I had scoped out earlier online, and gave the guys directions, street by street, without telling them our destination.

When we pulled in the parking lot, both of them turned around to look at us, and the looks on their faces were hilarious. Ryan looked turned on, Will looked both amused and aggravated.

We walked into the Peppermint Panda, a large club, with a bizarre-looking, randy panda bear as a mascot. Amelia and I, three drinks in, both thought that the name and mascot were *awesome. Hilarious.* We talked with the bouncer, and found out that there was no cover charge, but a two drink minimum—and each drink was twenty dollars. A hostess escorted us into the club, music throbbing, Will holding my hand, Ryan holding Amelia's.

Oxblood leather half-booths lined all the walls of the club. In the center, to one side, a dozen mostly naked girls occupied bar stools, waiting their turn. In the center, on the other side, perched a raised catwalk with multiple poles, lined with bar stools on all sides, presently being used by a lithe, athletic blonde who could really hold herself up on the pole. What was clearly a bachelor party on one side of us watched her carefully; a bachelorette party on the other side seemed more interested in their drinks. Looking around, it was a comfortable crowd, not intimidating or scary, with groups of guys, single guys, and couples.

The hostess stopped us at four bar stools right in front of Ms. Athletic Blonde, and a scantily-clad waitress immediately came up and took our drink order, two more cosmos each for me and Amelia, beers for Ryan and Will, two each. The waitress brought back eight drinks for the four of us and I looked at all of the alcohol and giggled uncontrollably. After an argument between Will and Ryan, Ryan paid.

Then Will leaned over to me and whispered in my ear, "I don't know whether to spank you or fuck you for this."

"Both, I think," I whispered back and he let out a groan.

I noticed that almost immediately, Amelia and Ryan got stuck together at the lips and stopped paying attention to anyone or anything around them, but I was having a blast checking out the scene. A younger guy in the corner received a very invasive lap dance by a busty brunette with long, curly hair. When she was done, he didn't move for three songs.

While we drank our drinks and watched, a number of girls approached, asking if we wanted to have lap dances. I waited for a cue from Will as to the right one. One girl was Gothic looking, with spiderweb leggings and black hair with harsh bangs. Not his type. Another was maybe Russian, with an elegant accent. Again, not his type. Another a slim Thai, another a curvy, freckled redhead, another an athletic African-American. Still, watching Will's reaction, I politely turned them all down, even though they were all beautiful.

But then, a seriously busty raven-haired girl came up, and kissed me on the boobs and said enthusiastically, "Are these real? Oh my God, they're huge!" and Will's eyes popped out of his head.

Her.

I looked over at Amelia, who was negotiating with a slim, leggy blonde, and we all moved to two adjacent booths, taking our drinks with us.

I smiled a wicked smile at Will and told her, "One dance for me, and another for him."

Again, he leaned over, and said, "You're getting it when this is done."

"That's what I'm hoping, cowboy," I replied saucily, and the music started.

In a flash, the girl took off her bra and shoved her breasts in my face. I couldn't help but giggle. She gyrated on my lap and kissed me on my boobs, completely feeling me up as I stayed still. I could smell her sweet perfume and feel her soft skin brush against me. She left bright red lipstick marks all over my chest.

I glanced over at Will, who seemed paralyzed. She gyrated, all in my business, her g-string inches away, her lips almost to my neck, high heels kicking out. I couldn't help myself, but five cosmos in, it was smutty, but also funny, and I giggled throughout. The song ended pretty quickly, she gave me a hug at the end, and told me that my giggles were cute.

Now it was Will's turn. She turned to him, took off his cowboy hat, and put it on, then straddled him. He looked over at me, a very heated look, and stayed still, as she moved over and around him, feeling up his chest, rubbing her breasts in his face, showing him her ass. Then she put his hat back on him and flipped her hair around and I lost him in a mane of her hair.

I was so going to get it.

Looking over at Amelia and Ryan, Ryan was faring no better than Will, hot green eyes on Amelia and then back to the blonde grinding in his lap.

We were both going to get it.

18

JUST GETTIN' STARTED

"OUTSIDE, NOW," WILL GROWLED in my ear and pulled me by my hand. I tripped after him in my silver stilettos, waving merrily at Amelia, who glanced at me, sized up what we were doing, smiled, and then was immediately yanked by Ryan in the opposite direction.

The expressionless bouncer stamped our hands and we went out to the dimly lit parking lot. He'd seen this routine before. Will didn't say anything outside until we got to the truck, when he pressed me up against the side, one arm on one side of me, the other arm on the other, his entire body melded to mine, and said, "All I could think about in there was how I wished it was you doing the lap dance."

"That could be arranged," I said coyly, and wiggled under him.

His dark chocolate eyes turned molten under the orange, sodium-vapor light. Opening the back door of his truck's cab, he ordered, "In. Now."

I clambered in the back seat of his enormous truck. He climbed in after me, sat down on the bench seat, and shut the door.

Before he could open his mouth again, I purred, drunkenly, "You want a lap dance, cowboy? I'll give you one." And I lifted up the skirt of my dress, way over my hips, and shimmied out of my black lace thong, keeping my shoes on. Then I unzipped my dress a little in the back and pulled the shoulders down, showing him my matching bra.

He didn't say a word, just looked fixedly at me, his breathing shallow.

Naked under my hips, with my dress scrunched up around my waist, I straddled him, and he let out a sigh. I grabbed his black cowboy hat and put it on my head, smiling at him. Then, avoiding his face, I kissed his ear, nibbling his earlobe, listening to his groan, then licked and sucked my way down his neck, as I rotated my hips in his lap, then grinded on him, likely getting all of my wetness on his cock, because of course he was hard, and probably had been so for a long time.

Then I got moving, just like the stripper, shoving my bra-clad breasts in his face, running my nails up his torso, gyrating in his lap.

Will could only take this for so long. "We're doing this here," he said, and I nodded, reaching behind, unhooking, and taking off my bra.

Then he unbuckled his dinner plate belt buckle, unbuttoned his pants, and shoved them down so that his straining, now purple cock, leapt free. Once he was situated, I immediately hovered over him and sank down, his cock filling me up all the way.

"Oh, *fuck*," we both said.

From this angle, he was so big and I was so wet, that every movement felt pleasurable. Every up, every down, every clench of a muscle, every twinge of his cock, every movement to the side or back and forth was an individual sensation.

Phenomenal.

I reached behind him, holding on to the back of the seat, and moved, slow and exploratory at first, then faster and faster, until I was riding him so hard and so fast, my ample breasts bouncing in his face. Then I exploded in pleasure, my body vibrating, screaming, "Yes, yes, yes!"

He grabbed my shoulders and held me down onto him as he came, pumping his release into me, grunting into my ear.

I collapsed in his arms and sucked on his neck as he played with my hair.

After a moment, we both came down off of our high, and I leaned back and looked at him, finally kissing him, and it was a deep, wet, tongue-driven kiss, in which he fully accepted, and which he eventually took over.

And then we broke apart, and I laughed, I wasn't sure why. Perhaps because I just had sex in the parking lot of a strip club, without caring if anyone saw. Perhaps because Will coming undone was one of the hottest things I'd ever seen. Perhaps because it was fun. Perhaps because I was starting to care about this guy and I loved turning him on.

Perhaps because I was thinking more about our similarities than our differences.

I lifted myself off of him, and got dressed again, straightening myself out as best as I could. Will pulled up his pants and got himself decent. Then he pulled me into a big hug and said, "Let's go find the others."

We left the truck, holding hands, not frenzied anymore, to see Amelia and Ryan leaving the club. I raised my hand and waved, even though they were right there, then ran over to Amelia.

"Where did you guys go?" I asked in a low voice in her ear. "I thought the guards wouldn't let you do anything inside."

"Ryan paid the guard five hundred dollars for a private room and told him to lock the door and look the other way," she answered, in my ear.

He was good.

I high-fived her. "Our plan worked," I whispered.

"Yeah," she whispered back, "but these guys don't need much encouragement."

We headed back to the truck. I was worried about it smelling like sex. But it ended up being no big deal because, *meh*, we all smelled like sex. Everyone rode quietly to the ranch and Will played country music on the radio.

He turned into Headlands Ranch, but instead of heading to the compound, he drove down a bouncy dirt road that I'd never been on.

"Where are we going?" I asked.

"Wanna show them a bluff," he answered.

We got to a large dirt area, overlooking the water, with nothing around us except the ocean and the ranch. In the dark, we could hear the crash and return of the waves. Ryan and Amelia held hands, looking out, and Will draped his arms around my waist, standing behind me, his chin on my shoulder, hat left in the car.

I shivered in the nighttime air.

"C'mon," he said, and walked me back to the truck, leaving me at the truck bed. He went to the cab, opened the back door, rummaged around behind the back seat, and came up with a blanket. Then he spread it out on the back of the truck, helped me and Amelia up, and climbed up, followed by Ryan. We all lay in the back of Will's truck, packed like sardines, Will and I spooning, and facing the opposite direction of Amelia and Ryan, who were spooning, and looked at the infinite stars.

Amelia let out a sigh and breathed, "It is so beautiful here."

After a while, quietly, we piled back in the truck, and Will drove us back to the compound. We said goodnight to Amelia and Ryan, who were in a downstairs guest room, and I trudged up the stairs after Will, my sandals in my hand.

When we got to his room, I paused at the doorway and, taking a step forward, asked, "Are we going to sleep now?"

Will answered from inside the bedroom, "Oh no, darlin'. We're just gettin' started."

19

QUIT

I FLOPPED DOWN ON Will's bed on my back, mostly sober, still wearing my dress and shoes, my feet dangling over the side. He walked around the bed to the side my head was on, and gave me the slowest and sexiest upside down kiss that I'd ever received in my entire life. The top of his tongue explored the top of mine, teasing and feathering in my mouth, and I reached up to his luscious ass and held him closer.

As I felt his back pocket, I realized something.

"I haven't seen you chew since the first day I was here, right? At least it's been a while," I said between kisses.

"Quit," he said, sucking on my lower lip, still upside down.

I pulled back and looked at him straight in his dark eyes, as he leaned over me. "What do you mean you quit? Just like that? Isn't it addictive?"

He shrugged.

"Will Thrash changed something for me," I said wonderingly.

His response was quiet, but immediate. "I like you in my mouth more than dip."

Fuck me. I didn't know what to say about this. For someone

who was stubborn, he also . . . wasn't. I reached up and ran my fingers through the stubble on his jaw, and then up through his thick, dark waves. But it had been a long twenty-four hours and there were a few other things that we needed to discuss.

"Will, you told your mom I was your girlfriend this morning. I'm not your girlfriend."

He pulled back. "Went too fast," he said. "Now I gotta convince you to be my girlfriend, don't I?"

"You went too fast," I agreed. "I barely know you."

He smiled. "'Kay. I like you, Marie. I like how fun you are. Think you want more than a fuck or two, so I'm just gonna convince you to go out with me on a regular basis."

"You can try."

His words made me happy but then I reminded myself that I was the public liberal privately sleeping with the enemy.

Right now, though, with him hovering over me? I shoved my thoughts to the side.

"'Kay. I'll take that for now." He kissed me again lightly, full lips on mine, still upside down. "I won't scare you off by saying what I think."

I froze for a second and tried to play it off like it was nothing. "What's that?"

His chocolate eyes met mine. "That this is gonna go somewhere."

"You did just scare me," I whispered, only half-joking.

"I know," he half-grinned back at me. "So now I think the only objection to being with me is that I'm a Republican, right?" he said, as he unbuttoned his black Western shirt and pulled it off, exposing a torso hewn by a farm but belonging to the gods.

I ran my fingers along his ribs and his warm skin, and racked my brain for another objection, but that was a pretty big one. "Oh, and you're an asshole," I said matter-of-factly.

"'Kay," he agreed easily.

"Only sometimes, though . . ." I trailed off, because now he was really distracting me.

He unbuckled his belt buckle and unbuttoned the top button of his jeans, and then started to kiss his way from my lips, over my neck, his torso in my face, smelling like fuck-yeah Will mixed with beer and strippers, a very amusing and strangely arousing scent. He got to the dove tattoo on my collarbone, and said, "You still have lipstick here."

"I do?" I asked, surprised. I got up. "I'm kind of a mess."

"I like it."

"You really are kinky, aren't you?"

"Yep," he stated, completely unapologetic.

I stiffened for a moment. "I feel gross, Will, I need to take a shower or clean up. I still have your cum on me."

"Like that too."

My eyes bugged out and I pointed at him. "You are a deviant!"

He grinned at me.

"Let me get a washcloth, at least, and clean up," I continued.

"I'll get it," he said, and walked out, returning soon with a handful of wet washcloths. I sat up and he unzipped my dress and ran a pleasantly warm washcloth over the tops of my breasts, cleaning off the cheap stripper perfume and indelible red lipstick. Then he helped me out of the dress and walked around and took off my shoes. He pulled off my underwear as I undid my bra. "Spread, baby." He gently took the washcloth and cleaned between my legs, stroking while he did it, which made me aroused. I felt better and taken care of.

"You know," he said quietly, "maybe you only get mad at me because you care what I think."

I had heard that expression before. Then it dawned on me. "You read *Fifty Shades of Grey*!"

"The fuck?" he asked.

"It said something like that in *Fifty Shades*. Something along the lines of 'you only get upset with people you care about.' You're a closet smut fan, aren't you?"

Will took a look at me and burst out laughing. This was the first time I'd heard him laugh—a full, male laugh, not a chuckle —and it was beautiful. White teeth showing, full lips smiling, waist shaking. I watched him in amazement as he let it out. It took him a moment before he could talk, and then he managed, "No, don't read that shit. No objection to bondage, though. I like it, truth be told."

So there was something else to think about.

But now, I noticed the other washcloth, and said, "Let me clean you." I unbuttoned the rest of his fly and eased him out of his jeans, and he fell on the bed next to me, head at my waist. I took the washcloth and cleaned him, caressing each part of his cock, which belonged in an art gallery.

"Now that you're here, and clean—" I started to say, but he interrupted me.

"Sixty-nine, darlin'," he whispered.

"'Kay," I whispered back, totally turned on.

"But first, you need a few more orgasms," he said, in a businesslike tone, and reached between my legs, fingering me. Then he suddenly got up, left the room, naked and erect, carrying the washcloths, and came back with a bottle of Nivea lotion.

"What's that for?"

"Don't have any lube. This'll do."

"*Will*," I said, warningly.

"Marie, you don't wanna do something, you tell me and I stop. Simple. But I've got a big sexual appetite, and I'm wanting to see how big an appetite you have, and whether we can satisfy it."

Well then.

Hell, I was up for anything. He wouldn't hurt me, at least not physically.

"Alright," I agreed.

And he lay back down, head by my pussy, and started exploring with his big, calloused hands, a nudge and a caress here, a press there, and slowly, very slowly, rubbing and circling my clit with his thumb. Then a finger, then two, inside me. And then he put some lotion on, and a finger ended up pressed into my ass. So now he was stimulating me in three places and it felt really fucking good. And after a little bit of this, he built up the sensations in my body and made me climb up until I exploded in a raging, fiery climax that put the other ones I'd had to shame, wringing out the tension from my body and letting it out with a yell.

I hoped Amelia and Ryan didn't hear that scream.

But he kept going.

And he built me up again.

And I blew up.

And then he did it again.

Fuck me, I'd just lost it, quaking, my body shattering so many times.

So, when finally I came back to the present, my awareness going beyond the sensations in my own body, I realized that right next to me was Will and his huge cock, and he needed attention. So, tentatively at first, and then bolder, I leaned over on my side and licked and sucked him, until I could get him almost entirely in my mouth, if I relaxed a bit. And he leaned over and licked at me, lapping and sucking my swollen pussy, while he kept his fingers where they were.

It'd been my experience with this position that it was distracting. Do I pay attention to my partner or do I pay attention to what is being done to me? It's normally so confusing.

But with Will, I wasn't confused at all. We just took turns, slowly, languidly, building each other up, then pausing for the other's turn, then back again.

"How close are you?" he asked, when I was pretty fucking close.

"Pretty fucking close."

"Me too. Think we can do this together?" he said against my pussy.

"Let's try."

I could feel him get close, the vein enlarging and throbbing in his cock, his balls pushing up, and I could feel me clenching, dying for yet another release, and between his tongue and his hands, he set off a chain reaction, that had me bouncing on the bed, sucking on him for dear life, which then released him, warm spurts in my mouth.

After a moment, we extricated ourselves from each other, and he crawled around to face me, trailing a finger up my torso, past my Noah's ark tattoo, over my breasts, and up to my chin. Then he turned me on my side so that he was spooning me and he kissed my naked shoulder, murmuring, "I like that, Marie."

I nodded. Me too.

20

MUCKING

"WE NEED TO HAVE a talk."

After breakfasting, showering, and packing up Ryan and Amelia to go back to Santa Barbara, Amelia pulled me aside. Then she pushed me outside the ranch house and started walking with me, leaving Ryan and Will talking in the house.

"I know what you're going to say—" I started, but she interrupted me.

"And that is?"

"That I'm crazy for what I'm doing with Will."

She rolled her eyes. "Girl, I knew you were crazy a long time ago. This new crazy, though, is for what you are *not* doing with Will."

We walked past the corrals and headed to the path that wended its way to the bluff and the beach. "There's not much that I am not doing with Will," I said, joking.

But she was serious. "Marie. You are my best friend. You saved my life. Multiple times. I feel like I need to do the same for you."

"What are you talking about?"

"You're not opening your heart up to him." I spluttered, thinking that she was sounding like that old Madonna song, but she kept going, giving me The Hand. "You're the most caring person I know. You teach preschool and you help kids and you want to be a counselor and you give me your time and you care about the environment and baby polar bears and all sorts of causes. But you don't take yourself on as a cause."

"Yes I do," I started, "I totally defend myself."

"You do," she agreed easily, "but you don't let yourself get in deep. When was the last time you were in a real relationship?"

I couldn't remember. I shook my head at her, but she continued.

"You have this big, tall, hunk of a cowboy, who looks at you as if he sees you, only you, and no one else but you on the entire goddamn planet, and as far as I can tell, he respects you, he pays attention to you, he makes sure that you are taken care of, and he buys you candy and fucking dances with you the way you've never been danced with. And you're questioning it because it's new and that's normal.

"You're the life of the party, always having fun, always making sure that others have fun. But as a friend, I want you to think about whether you are willing to go deeper than you ever have before. You're the caring party girl that I know and love, but you don't let anyone in. When are you going to do something for yourself? And I don't just mean get laid. Though, the fact that he is phenomenal in bed says something . . ." She gave me a knowing smile. "But I digress. I want you to think about really letting him care for you, not just with sex, but with everything. Sure, he's the silent type, but there's something burning under that Marlboro Man exterior, and based on what you tell me, he shows it with his actions, not with his mouth."

"His mouth is pretty good," I muttered, kicking at the dust in the trail. We were almost to the bluff where you could see the ocean.

"But that's it, see? You're not letting it be beyond sex. You care about everyone else and your heart is huge. But your heart needs to open up for you and see what it's like to let him in. Because it's obvious, to me, at least, that he's wonderful for you. There's no bullshit with him. He just wants you and he shows it."

I didn't have a response to this. I wasn't sure that she was right, but since she normally was, I wanted to listen to her.

Then I whispered, "He quit chewing tobacco for me." We stopped walking. We had reached the bluff and watched the waves crash on the shore.

I continued, "But he's not going to change his politics."

She shook her head and sighed. "You both care so much about the fucking labels and what ideology you're adopting that you aren't paying enough attention to the stuff that matters. The stuff beyond the label bullshit. Outside last night, looking up at the stars? In the grand scheme of things, we are all the same."

"You borrowed my Deepak Chopra?"

"And I'm not returning it."

I turned to her and gave her a hug and kissed the top of her head. "I'll think about it."

She nodded and we looked at the ocean for a while. And then we hiked back to the compound.

Once we got there, she got in the car to go. Will came over and gave her a kiss on the cheek, which I thought was sweet. Then Ryan gave me a big hug and shook hands with Will and invited us to visit his beach house.

After their car disappeared down the dirt road, Will gave me a quick but very public kiss and then left in his truck, Trixie in the back, to survey his land or wrestle a cow or something. I went back to the bunkhouse, where I'd spent very little time in the past few days.

Stephanie and Janine were both in there, so as usual there was no privacy. Janine asked me how my date went with Will, which meant that now Stephanie knew about it as well.

I'd barely thought about the repercussions of Will and me hooking up on the relationships with the rest of the staff.

I told her, vaguely, that we had a good time and he wanted to date me. It seemed like she wanted to ask more but she didn't. We chatted about their weekends and then I left, needing some time to think. Since I usually fed off of the interactions with others, this was unusual, but I needed to think about what I was doing with Will.

It was just sex, right? We were so sexually compatible. He turned me on and I apparently turned him on. He was hot and seemingly constantly aroused. It was fun to be with him. It was fun to have sex with him. But we'd never be together, together, because we were too different.

And that was it.

Maybe.

Fuck.

What Amelia had said made me think. Having more than just sex with Will? I didn't know about that. I didn't know if I could show him all of me. I mean, while I was the type to organize a party, cheer up a friend, or start a Kickstarter project to get rid of the garbage patch in the middle of the Pacific Ocean, I didn't usually open up to people, especially guys. I think it had to do with how I grew up, moving around all the time, always moving onto the next person. If you got too close to someone, it hurt, because you had to say goodbye and maybe you'd never see them again. So it was safe to be friendly and have fun, but not fall very deep.

I'd dated all kinds of guys, but had been in very few relationships and the ones that I'd been in didn't last long. I never really let them know what I felt, but rather hid it under my party exterior.

Will seemed to dodge my image as a party girl and go right for the *me* underneath. He just decided that he liked me and that was it. His actions, after yelling at me when I bumped into him naked that first day, were all caring—taking me to Andersen's for vegan split pea soup, cleaning me up before sex, immediately introducing me to his mother when I complained about not having met her.

Why did I complain about not having met his parents if it was just sex?

So it boiled down to the fact that he was so vehemently anti-politically correct, while I, essentially, was politically correct in every possible way. And while this may seem like a stupid thing to worry about, because these beliefs were so central to both of us, it mattered at a basic level. I wanted to be tolerant of others, but I thought of his politics as that of the intolerant. How can you be tolerant of the intolerant?

I mean, you want people to agree with you. At least about the important stuff.

Right?

Fuck.

I didn't know what to think anymore. It was a lot simpler when I'd just decided to jump Will's bones and be done with it. Now that there was this possibility of more, I was scared.

Wanting to escape my thoughts, I wandered over to the barn and the corral to see what the wranglers were doing. Although I officially had the weekend off and could do whatever I wanted, I loved hanging around the horses.

Jimmy, the old wrangler, and Hector, the young wrangler were mucking out the corral, a daily activity. I grabbed a rake and helped them and they looked at me gratefully.

"Enjoying Headlands?" asked Jimmy, a guru with a drawl.

"I love it here. It's so beautiful and I love the work that the Program does for kids. I met Will's mom and dad and I am so glad that they opened the facility for others."

Jimmy paused for a moment in his mucking and turned and looked at me.

"Will likes you," he said.

"I don't know about that," I said, trying to be modest.

"I've known him since he was born. Never seen him take a woman to meet his parents."

Really?

"His parents are so nice."

Jimmy nodded.

"I just wish they wouldn't watch Fox News all the time," I said.

"They are the last of the old-fashioned California Republicans. Not this new stuff. Old style. Don't raise their taxes or tell 'em what to do on their land."

I raised an eyebrow. That was interesting. I'd assumed that his parents were the Fox News ultra-conservative.

Maybe I needed to just talk to them.

Was *I* being intolerant of *them*?

Hector came by with fresh hay after we had mucked out the corral and the stalls, and we fed the horses and made sure they had fresh water.

A fresh start.

And then it was time to get cleaned up for dinner.

In the chow hall, I sat next to Will, his leg pressed up against me again. He smelled clean and had just taken a shower. After dinner, he asked me to spend the night but I told him no because I wanted to stay in my bunk. I needed the space.

But in the middle of the night, after tossing and turning in my bottom bunk, I snuck out of the bunkhouse and knocked on Will's door in my jammies. He let me in and I tumbled into his arms. He kissed me deeply, took me upstairs to his room, and kept me awake for a while. I eventually fell asleep in his strong arms, tucked into him, under his quilt, in his whitewashed room, in his old-fashioned farmhouse that was starting to feel like home, and I slept very well.

21

CAMPFIRE

"IT SMELLS FUNNY."

"I have to pee."

I stifled a laugh as I watched the noisy kids from Oakland spill out of the old, yellow school bus, their voices an indistinct chorus, becoming distinct as they stepped outside into the fresh midmorning air. Standing with the wranglers, we welcomed fifteen boys, fifteen girls, plus a few adults.

This was a seriously racially diverse group, probably reflecting the melting pot demographics of the East Bay. The kids looked shiny and new, with cell phones, wearing fresh jeans and clean tennis shoes, compared to the five of us program staff, who all had trail dust on us from riding horses early that morning.

I could see their young faces taking in the ranch buildings, the animals in their corrals and pens, and the landscape of brown hills, orchards, vineyards, and fields. None of them had ever been on a farm before.

"Hello!" I yelled cheerfully. "Welcome to Headlands Ranch! I'm Marie!"

"What the fuck is this shit?" I heard from one of the boys, a tall African-American with a very precise haircut, dark smooth skin, and a grouchy look on his face.

"I have to use the bathroom," whined a ponytailed Asian girl, the only one of the group wearing cowboy boots over her pale jeans.

"Ohmigod it smells," said a redhead with freckles, wearing clothes that were a little too big. She held her nose. "It smells bad."

"What, there's no WiFi here?" complained a Hispanic boy, very sharply dressed, in a button down shirt and skinny jeans.

I ignored them all and kept talking.

"I am so glad all of you are here. Let's get you set up and then you'll meet your horses."

"Cool," said a small African-American girl with a shy smile, her hair in three thick braids.

A few other kids smiled at me and I was instantly charmed by the combination of their enthusiasm for the farm with their inexperience due to their urban background.

A tall, attractive, bald man with mocha-colored skin and dark eyes, wearing well-fitting jeans and a plaid button down shirt, came up to me and said, "Nice to meet you, Marie. I'm Maurice Jenkins, and I run the Bay Area program for these guys."

"Nice to meet you," I said, shaking his hand.

"I'm the boys' group leader," he continued, "and Tricia Pham," pointing to a petite woman with amazingly cool dark jeans and a fluttery top, "is the girls' group leader." I shook her hand.

After settling the kids in the bunkhouse, we headed over to the barns, the stables, and the corrals, to see the horses. As we were walking over, Will pulled up from his rounds around the ranch in his now again mud-covered truck, and hopped out, moseying over to meet the kids with Trixie at his heels.

He looked mouthwatering in a faded, tight blue t-shirt that

showed every ridge of his torso and his usual jeans, belt buckle, and boots. His hair curled underneath a trucker hat, sticking out at the bottom. He looked at me and smiled.

I heard Tricia Pham breathe out "Oh. My. God."

I called out, "Everyone, this is Will Thrash, a genuine rancher, whose family has owned Headlands Ranch for four generations."

Will looked at all the kids and gave them his grin, speaking in his deep drawl. "Welcome. Glad you're here. Hope you like ridin'." Then he looked at me. "I know Marie does."

I hoped that no one else would pick up on his innuendo.

It still made me hot.

We spent the rest of the morning organizing the kids into their groups, assigning them to the wranglers, and having them meet and pet their horses. Then it was time for lunch. Will sat with me, leaning against me as much as he could without being obvious—or at least I hoped we weren't being obvious. Then he left to go meet with some visitors who looked like they were from the city. I wondered if they were the developers that he was so worried about earlier.

After lunch, the kids learned how to care for the chickens, goats, and other animals, and I planned a campfire for that night.

THE CAMPFIRE WAS A FAILURE.

The fire wouldn't light. Between me, Jimmy, and Hector, we couldn't get it to start. So Hector came back with a bottle of lighter fluid, which made the boys perk up and Will grumble about his insurance premiums and the cost of Worker's Comp insurance. He'd been pretty sullen since his meeting with the suits, but had come by the campfire and stood in the back, leaning against a tree, watching me but not participating.

Then it took too long for the tall flames to die down into coals so that we could roast marshmallows, so we didn't do that.

I made an attempt to get the group to sing "Row, Row, Row Your Boat" in a three-part round, but I had to do it all by myself, because all of the adults said, "I don't sing." Will looked at me with a "No way in hell am I singing" look on his face.

This seriously pissed me off. He really was an asshole sometimes.

But these were kids. Everyone knew the song, right? My singing voice wasn't great, but what good was a campfire if you didn't sing around it?

It didn't work. They just stared at me.

Will put his hand over his mouth, chuckling.

That wasn't nice.

No one laughed at my jokes, except Cookie, who always looked like he wanted to laugh at me. God. These kids just didn't want to look uncool.

Will silently left in the middle of all this, clearly amused by my enthusiasm and the lack of response of the kids, and not helping in the slightest.

As he walked away, I saw him stifle a laugh as I tried, yet again, to get the kids to sing, saying "Come on, everyone! Let's do this!"

I needed help. I didn't need to be left struggling alone by the guy who wanted to get in my pants. Jerk.

After a few more attempts at group activities, I gave up, letting the kids just hang out around the campfire. Some took out their cell phones, while others chatted with each other. They seemed to like this better than an organized activity.

I implemented a no cell phone rule beginning immediately.

What a depressing end to the day. I wanted to make connections with the kids and have some fun. I did not want to be a freak show.

When the kids were finally in bed that night, I went to my bunk and crashed, tired, and for once not thinking about joining Will in his bed.

But I couldn't sleep. I was pissed.

I got more pissed the more that I thought about it.

Will should have set aside any embarrassment and supported me. I'd needed help getting these kids to open up and, instead, he'd left me.

I texted Amelia.

> Will just treated me like shit.

Will should have set aside any embarrassment and

What?! Honey. What did he do?

> I had a bad first day with this group of city kids from Oakland and he just laughed at me and watched me crash and burn instead of helping to make it better.

You know what the right answer is, right? You need to talk with him. Guys can't read your mind and sometimes they don't know when they hurt you.

I sighed. She was right. She had such a healthy relationship with Ryan, she knew what to do. I got out of bed, put on flip flops, put my hair up in a messy bun on the top of my head, grabbed a hoodie, and headed over to Will's house.

When he opened the door, barechested, in sweats, he started to say, "Wondered if you were gonna come over—" but I pushed him inside, and started immediately talking to him in the hallway.

"I'm pissed at you. You treated me like shit tonight.

Remember last week, when Clarissa said your hair sang that you were true and passionate and kind? Well it didn't feel like that. It felt like you were a jerk and an asshole. I needed some help and you didn't stick up for me. You treated me like I was the monkey exhibit at the zoo. And you want me to go out with you? Well this is why I won't. I'm just an amusing cunt to you, not girlfriend material. You don't say much, Silent Sam, so I watch your actions. And your actions tonight were shitty, Will."

He stared at me, his brown eyes big, and then he reached over to brush my cheek. I flinched and brushed his hand aside and continued, "I was being laughed at enough by the kids and they were completely disrespectful. These are tough kids, Will. They don't know about camp life. I bet a lot of them are raised by a single parent or a grandparent or have family members on drugs or aren't doing well in school because they have no support and no role models. I need to do silly things with them. Wholesome things. They don't need everything to be cynical."

Will let out a deep breath and put his head down. Then he raised his head and looked at me.

"I'm sorry," he said, his eyes softening.

"What?"

"I'm sorry," he repeated sincerely. "You're right, that was a dick move. Fucked up. Didn't mean to hurt you. I didn't realize—"

And then the house started shaking, the pictures started violently moving on the walls, the lamps started skidding toward the end of the table, and I heard the crash of glass breaking.

Earthquake!

22

CAMPOUT

EVERYTHING AROUND US THAT was supposed to be still, was moving. We stood in the front room of Will's old farmhouse, the antique ceiling light swinging, a spindly wooden chair falling over, and papers and photographs falling off of a side table.

Crash!

That sounded like the dishes fell off of a shelf in the kitchen.

Breaking glass.

Oh no!

The pictures swung off-kilter on the walls.

We'd been placed in a life-sized cardboard box, and now a malevolent giant was shaking that box with us in it.

I wanted to get out of that cardboard box.

We needed to get out of the house, *now*.

Will grabbed my hand and pulled me outside the house, down the porch, and to the middle of the Headlands compound. As we ran, I stumbled and he caught me. It was hard to run during an earthquake.

The moonlight illuminated the dark ground. We could hear the leaves on the trees rustling, and we could actually see the earth undulate, starting from the hills and working its way down to the fields. Watching the earth move in waves like it was the ocean was one of the eeriest things I'd ever experienced. While quiet outside, as the earth moved, it made a low groan. The buildings creaked.

I realized that my arms and legs shook and that I was suddenly close to tears. I didn't want to panic. I didn't know if I was the type to panic.

All I knew was that I had to keep it together because we had a lot of people and animals to take care of. I could collapse later.

I took a deep breath.

As suddenly as it had come on, the earth quieted down. After an earthquake, your body had the memory of the movement stored and it always felt like, "*What was that? An aftershock?*" Your body and mind played tricks on you and afterward you often felt the ground moving for a long time.

He spoke first, quickly, still holding my hand, which he squeezed. "Here's the plan. You okay?" I nodded. "I'm gonna run, help my dad with my ma, make sure she's okay, then meet you at the bunkhouse. You get the kids out. Don't want them to be in there in case there are aftershocks. Think we'll just set up camp in a field. Safest place in an earthquake is out in the open. We'll keep 'em away from structures until we can check for damage. We'll clean up in the morning when we can see better. I'll get tarps, you have 'em get blankets. I'll tell the ranch hands to help." He looked me up and down, hard, and seemed to be satisfied. He squeezed my hand again.

And then he took off, barefoot, sprinting to his parents' house, wearing just his black track pants, his back muscles rippling. I ran to the bunkhouse in my flip flops. I could see several wranglers headed toward the barn.

As I ran up to the bunkhouse, I heard voices and knew that this was a vigorous enough earthquake to wake everyone up; I would guess that it was at least a five on the Richter scale, if not higher.

Once I got inside, kids were screaming and Maurice was on the stairs, talking with Tricia and the adult chaperones. I ran up to them.

"Will wants us to evacuate the buildings, and we're going to have a campout under the stars until we can check for damage in the morning. Get the kids to grab a pillow and sleeping bag and any cushions and head outside. Count heads. We'll regroup in the field."

I ran down the stairs and into Janiqua, the girl with the three braids, in pink pajamas, bleary eyed, and close to tears. I wrapped her in my arms and snuggled her close, hugging her hard. She half-sobbed into my chest. "Are the horses going to be okay?"

Gently patting her head, stroking it soothingly, I said as quickly as I could without making it seem rushed, "Yes, sweetie, we're going to take care of all of the animals. They have safe places to be. We'll make sure of it." I pulled back and looked her in the eyes, giving her a small smile. "Now put on shoes and get a sweater, your pillow, and sleeping bag, and meet me out front."

I hustled into each room, repeating the instructions. The kids obeyed quickly. They sensed that this was important because inside there was damage. A few of the empty bunk beds had tipped over and the office was a mess.

Enrique, the sharp-dressed Hispanic kid, came up to me, wearing pajamas with Stewie from the Family Guy on the pants and a gray t-shirt, an anxious look on his face making him look much, much younger. "I want to call my mom."

I relented, giving him a tight smile. "Bring your phone, it's okay, but wait until we get outside to use it." I felt the relief appear on his face.

Once we all got outside, the girls huddled around Tricia, the boys around Maurice, and we counted noses, made sure everyone was there, laden with pillows and sleeping bags, and we headed over to where the ranch hands were setting up a camp site.

I wasn't sure that I wanted to sleep on the ground, but I faked enthusiasm.

"C'mon guys, it's a warm night and the stars are beautiful. It will be fun."

Some of the kids looked at me like they believed me. James, the sweary kid, looked like he was finally interested in something. I guess it took a natural disaster to have him come around.

Will came running up, still barefoot, still without a shirt on, his hair wild, and asked me, "Everyone okay?"

I nodded and he started talking with the kids. Claudio, one of the ranch hands, had set up a few old-fashioned Coleman lanterns and the adults had flashlights.

"All of you are gonna get taken care of by Marie. I'm gonna check on the horses and the other animals and then I'm gonna come back and check on you. Power's still on and we have a backup generator, so we should be fine. This is just a precaution. Don't want nothing to fall on you in the bunkhouse and it's a nice night to see the sky. I'm gonna go see how the wranglers are doin' and I'll come back and stay with y'all."

Will headed over to join the wranglers at the corrals to check on the horses and make sure that all of the animals were secure. I could hear neighing and the horses did not sound happy.

I hoped that Happy, my horse, wasn't scared.

Cookie came up to me. "You want I should make some hot water for cocoa?"

"Good idea," I said.

He lumbered up to the kitchen and I went over to help the chaperones and the leaders set up the kids, arranging sleeping bags and pillows, and getting everyone tucked in. The kids seemed to like huddling together in their sleeping bags outside on a farm, and talked quietly among themselves.

Despite things calming down, I felt anxious and jumpy not knowing the news. I stayed put with the kids, walking around, making sure that they were all okay.

Cookie came out with an urn of hot water and paper cups and made instant hot chocolate with marshmallows for those who wanted it. This quieted the kids down as they sipped their treat.

Will and the wranglers came back from checking on the horses and he came right over to me, resting a finger on my wrist and leaning over. "You're working hard, Marie," he said in my ear. "Good job. Like your level head."

"Thanks," I whispered.

He looked at me like he wanted to say something more, but didn't. He paused and went on. "Don't think it's safe to go back yet. There's debris everywhere. We'll get it in the daylight. No sense making a racket that will keep up the kids."

I nodded.

"No structural damage that I can tell right now. Everything's wooden and has survived a lot of earthquakes. My ma is fine, their house is new and earthquake-safe. They're going to stay put." The look on his face was reassuring and made me feel better. I just wanted to stay by him at all times. "Hang on," he said, and ran his hand down my arm to my hand and gave me a squeeze. Then he let go.

He left me for a moment to go into the house. He came back, still shirtless, but with a stack of quilts, blankets, and pillows. In front of everyone, he knelt and made up a bed for us, out in the open, under the dark night sky.

A cool breeze touched our cheeks, but it was otherwise a silent and warm night. There were a few eyes on us, curious, but, well, fuck it. We walked around, turned the lanterns off, and wished the kids goodnight. He handed me a pillow, and whispered, "C'mere darlin'."

I fell into his arms, standing up, getting a hug that I desperately needed from him. It was like that old fashioned saying, his strength gave me comfort. It really did, feeling his massive arms around me, embracing me, my cheek nestled into his powerful chest. He kissed the top of my head and whispered, "Time for bed."

I figured that it'd be uncomfortable on the ground, but since it was a group sleepover, I wanted to participate rather than throw a fit. The earth actually wasn't that hard with the folded blankets that Will had used as cushions. We both got down on the ground and he curled up behind me, putting his arms around my body, his chin on my shoulder. He gave me a big squeeze with his bare arms and his warmth seeped through my clothes. I felt completely enveloped by him, and snuggled into him. I lay there for a while, listening to the quiet night sounds and the sounds of the kids sleeping, but then fell asleep tucked into Will, under his red and white quilt.

While I didn't want to overthink my summer adventure, I think that without saying a word, Will-style, something had changed.

I think we were together now.

AFTERSHOCKS

"SO MY LITTLE NOAH got her animals safely on the ark last night," a male voice murmured in my ear, full lips brushing against my skin, a finger trailing up my side, under my shirt, to where I was tattooed.

That was an electrifying way to wake up.

We had felt aftershocks last night, and while I'd slept lightly, I'd nevertheless rested. Now at dawn, my body creaked, stiff and sore from sleeping on the ground. The tarps and blankets felt damp from morning dew. Even though the sun had started to come up, Will was still holding me.

Still holding me.

I didn't understand why Will was being so affectionate, but I didn't want him to stop. Sleepily, I turned over and snuggled into him even more, burrowing into the silky skin of his hard chest.

"We gotta get up and check the damage," he said quietly.

"Okay," I whispered back, and darted my eyes around to see if anyone was looking, but no, they seemed asleep. So I gave him a good morning kiss, in which he fully participated, and at length. It was hot. Then he hugged me, extricated himself, and stood up and stretched.

My eyes popped out at the sight of his tan torso flexing in the morning, and his flat waist leading to his waistband where his track pants hung low, showing a bulge.

Right. We need to check the damage. No distractions.

I headed to the bunkhouse.

A disheveled interior greeted me and I went to my room to dress.

The triangle rang.

Seriously, Cookie? After last night? A triangle?

Once clothed, I went back out to the makeshift camp. Will, now dressed, walked around inspecting all of the buildings.

We roused the bleary-eyed kids and went to breakfast. I noticed a sense of camaraderie that was missing yesterday—kids helped each other out, talked with each other more, and were friendlier and more outgoing. They'd just shared a scary experience and it had brought them closer.

And they helped clean up. Before they got started, Will gave them a lecture that consisted of one sentence: "Part of livin' on a ranch is workin'." And then he strolled back over to his house to set it to rights while I supervised the bunkhouse cleanup.

Will didn't show up at lunch so I had Cookie make him a sandwich and I took it over to the ranch house. I knocked and walked in and found him sweeping up glass in his kitchen, listening to some God-awful country music.

"Sorry about the breakage," I said, leaning against the doorway.

"Not your fault. Just old stuff anyway," he said matter-of-factly, tipping the dustpan into the trash.

I wandered through his house while he took a break to eat his lunch, and I noticed how sparsely furnished it was. All of the furniture was antique, except for a back room that had a big television and a comfortable couch that screamed straight man.

It gave the appearance that he'd inherited it with all of its contents and hadn't changed a thing.

Going back into the kitchen, I heard the song change to yet another sappy country song. I had no idea how he could listen to this shit.

"Who sings this?" I demanded.

"George Strait."

I snorted. "Do you only listen to George Strait?"

"Internet radio," he answered. "George Strait channel."

That explained it.

"Listen to it," he ordered.

I leaned up against the kitchen counter and listened to the song. It was horribly schmaltzy, but it swayed me once I paid attention to the lyrics. George sang about a boy and his father and how the best day of the boy's life was when the father spent time with him camping as a kid, and then when he brought a classic car home that they could work on when he was a teenager, and how he wanted to be like his dad when he grew up.

It was super cheesy.

I had no idea why I had tears in my eyes at the end of it.

He looked at me and gave me a half smile. "You can figure out why I like this song. My dad was like that. Spent a lot of time with me. These kids don't have it like that. But we can give them our time, at least for a week."

I nodded.

Will had a generous heart, no question about it. We continued working and cleaned the house up.

Later on that afternoon, I set up a tie-dye station for the kids.

The first group of kids came over, which included kids who were enthusiastic, and James, the sweary one, who most certainly was not.

"Would you like to do tie-dye?" I asked him.

James stared at me, scandalized. "No."

I smiled, enthusiastic. "Oh, try it. It's fun!" I said.

He scowled and looked up at the sky. "Only fun for hippies like you. It's not cool where I'm from."

Just then Will came by on his way from the corrals. He gave me a chin lift and walked over to the picnic tables where the kids were gathered. "Whatcha doin'?" he asked.

"Making a shirt," said one of the girls. "I'm going to give it to my sister."

Will looked over at James. "You're not gonna make one?"

"No." James wasn't as sullen with Will as he was with me.

"Why not?" Will seemed genuinely perplexed.

"Won't wear it."

"Neither would I, not my thing, but it looks like it might be good to make one for my girl here. Do you have someone you can give it to?" Without waiting for an answer, Will continued, "Here, I'll make one with you." Now he gave James a chin lift. And without any fuss, he went over to the pile of white t-shirts, pulled out two, handed one to James and called over to me, "Marie, how the hell do you do this?" Once I was next to him, he lowered his mouth to my ear and continued, under his breath, "You're making me into a fucking hippie."

"Never," I whispered back.

I showed Will and James how to bunch up the t-shirt and add the rubber bands and how to dye it. When they pulled off the rubber bands after dying the shirts to expose the design, James actually looked pleased with what he'd made. It looked professional. The bright red, green, and yellow dye made it look like it could be sold in a groovy shop and I told him so, getting a small smile in return.

Progress.

Will's shirt was cool, too, black and dark blue. "I dare you to wear that shirt, cowboy," I whispered in Will's ear.

"Rather see you wear it, with nothing underneath," he whispered back, then he hung up the shirt on the makeshift clothes line I'd set up, and took off.

Later that night, when everyone was asleep, I walked over to Will's. I knocked on the door and he let me in, saying, "You can just walk in, Marie."

I countered, "When I did that the first time, I interrupted you in the shower and you were scary pissed."

He gave me a full smile. "Wouldn't mind if you did it again," he said, raising an eyebrow.

Who was this guy and what had he done with Will? I took a step back, feeling uncertain and confused. "Why have you been so nice to me all day? It's like you changed personalities, Will."

He looked down at me. "Figure I don't need to be an asshole to you, even if I am one."

Okay. That sounded good. But I still wasn't sure.

"And I want those knockout legs wrapped around me again. Tonight."

24

MORE

A S I STOOD THERE in Will's front room, I realized where I was and how I felt and the thought hit me that this was going way too fast. Will wanted me for sex, plus more. In other words, a real, modern relationship. Not a summer fling.

And at some point, he'd decided that we were together. I had sort of agreed, burying my opinion about our differences. But after a day—just a day—of letting him in and of being out in the open with our relationship, I had qualms.

The sex, at least for me, was the easy part. We were extremely sexually compatible. It was the "more" that I was hung up on. Could I fall for Will Thrash? Someone who, down at his core, believed things that were the opposite of me?

Conservatives believed in national defense and—in my opinion—were driven by fear and caution. I was an idealistic tree hugger and wanted the world to hold hands and get rid of weapons. Conservatives chose the economy over the environment. I chose the opposite. The conservative leaders I saw in the news were focused on white America—Christian, xenophobic, traditional values. This clashed with my core belief of focusing on the plurality. I wanted tolerance, progressiveness, and welcoming of all people.

I shook my head. I didn't think this could go anywhere. We were too different.

And even if we could figure out our politics, could I be with him, even if it would go nowhere? Absolutely nowhere? He lived up here and I lived down in Santa Barbara and that would not work, long term. I was used to moving on. I could not get attached, could not do so for longer than the time I was here.

But even for the summer, he wanted a relationship and a relationship meant that we could talk about things. So, for starters, I pinpointed one thing that was wrong with him being sweet.

"I don't trust you being nice to me. I only trust you when you're an asshole. When you're nice, I think that something's wrong, that you're kidding, that you're going to turn around and hurt me. It's a lot easier for this just to be about sex."

He stared at me and shook his handsome head.

"Gotta fix that," he said, and he thought for a moment and continued slowly. "How can I say this? You made me realize that I don't have to be a dick to you, like I am to others. I can be, well, decent." He smiled self-deprecatingly. "You're the first woman I've ever met who doesn't back down on my shit and you're so beautiful, the hottest I've ever seen. Your smoking body, your beautiful face. Fuck. But it's not just that. We're mirror images of each other. We have the same values. Can't you see it? I know what you believe in. You don't hide it. I like that. You've got a heart, Marie, and you give it to everyone—to kids, to animals. I want you to give it to me. I'll take care of it. But I see I've gotta make you trust me. That's where we are isn't it?"

My eyes widened and I nodded.

And he kept going, spilling out the honesty, stepping forward. "I don't know what I'm doing, all I know is that I can't stay away from you. I haven't been in many relationships. And when I have, they haven't lasted long."

I stepped back. "Me neither. That's why I'm scared of what you're asking." He went to take a step forward and stopped, looking at me, his dark eyes big.

"But you feel it too, don't you?" he asked, suddenly looking tentative. I had never seen Will look this open. Vulnerable.

I closed my eyes and thought for a moment. "Will, if I let whatever this is go forward, then I feel like I'm setting myself up for hurt. I have to leave at the end of the summer. You're never going to leave the ranch."

"Don't be so sure about that," he muttered.

I paused. "What?"

"I told the developers no." He looked up at the ceiling.

"No?" I didn't understand what he was talking about.

"To millions. Again."

My stomach plummeted. "Shit." How long would he be able to resist that kind of pressure?

Reading my mind, he continued, a look of disgust washing over his face. "Yeah. They're gonna buy up the neighbors, though. I'm gonna get squeezed out."

This pissed me off. "What the fuck? We need farms. We don't need ranchettes! Shit." While I was talking, he headed toward me so that I had backed against the wall. He placed one hand on the wall next to my head and I felt his warmth. He leaned in toward me.

"I don't know how long I'm gonna be able to hold out. The money could buy my mom better treatment. I'm told that there are experimental things that could help her. Having some cash around . . ." He trailed off. "Not easy to say no. If I sell, I could go anywhere. And if I don't." He sighed. "Since I've already gone too fast, I might as well keep at it. I want you to stay here, with me, after the summer. You could live here and finish your degree. It's not that far to UCSB. Lots of professors live up here. You could set up whatever counseling practice you want, up here. Do whatever you want. I just want to be with you."

I took a deep breath.

I couldn't do it.

I liked him. I was attracted to him. But I couldn't do it.

"Will, this is just sex. We're dating for the summer. Don't make it something more."

The pained look on his face tore me apart.

"Fuck," he said, pulling his arm back and taking a step away from me. "Serves me right." Then he continued, louder, and getting angry, "So let me get this straight. I treat you like shit, you want to stay. I'm nice to you, you want to go. What the fuck do I have to do, Marie? I like you and I think you like me. I want you. I want you in my life and I want you in my bed. You, the hot woman who saves animals and kids. You, the one who fights for what you believe in. You, the one that I know what I see is what I get. You deserve to be treated right. I'm trying to do that and you say you have to go?"

I tried to melt into the wall. "That's crazy, isn't it?" I whispered.

"Yeah," he whispered back, angry and biting and in my face. "I don't want to go back to treating you like shit. I want to take care of you. I want to fucking worship the ground you walk on."

Worship the ground I walk on.

Shit.

We stared at each other.

"Look," he said, pissed. "Forget it. Take a break. Go back to the bunkhouse. If you want to be with me, come back. I'll wait. Go. Just fucking go."

I opened the door and went to leave, pausing in the door. I looked at my feet, willing them to move forward, to leave. Just like I always leave, like I move on.

Fuck.

I was pushing him away.

I was pushing away the guy who made my pulse run. Who made me more turned on than anyone. Who surprised me with his thoughtfulness. Who said more by his actions than by his words.

The guy who was raised by a double-amputee, Spanish-speaking mother, and opened up his home to disabled kids and kids who'd never have a chance to ride a horse otherwise.

The guy who turned down millions of dollars because it meant more to him to have a farm than to have a ton of cash.

Who swore to me every time he was with me that he wanted me more and more.

Who argued with me about my politics, but when it came down to it, he was right there with me, saving the world in his own way.

All of a sudden, the thought of spending the night alone came to me. A night not in Will's arms. No Will to ask me how I was doing. No Will to dance with. No Will to fuck. If I couldn't do it for one night, I couldn't do it ever again.

A breeze came in through the door and whipped around me.

No.

Fuck no.

I couldn't do it.

Stepping back into his house and slamming the door shut, I turned to him and burst into tears.

"I can't," I whispered. "I can't stay away from you."

I ran into his arms and he nuzzled his face into my hair. "I can't stay away from you either," he said gruffly, squeezing me tight. "What do you need, Marie? Go for a walk? Go for a drive? Something to eat?"

"I need you to make love to me. And mean it."

"That can be arranged," he said huskily.

25

MIRRORS

ONCE IN WILL'S BEDROOM, he slowly walked over to me and leaned down and kissed me. Just a kiss, very gentle and very sweet, no touching me anywhere else, his hands behind his back. Releasing his hands, he reached over to me and tucked my hair behind my ears and ran his fingers down my face, wiping away the last of my tears with his work-rough hands. He leaned over and kissed the trails where my tears had been. And then he held me for a very long time, fully dressed, my head in his chest.

Once I'd relaxed in his arms, he loosened his grip and reached to the hem of my shirt, pulling it up over my head, and trailed his fingers down my torso, pausing at my dove tattoo, lingering over my bra, exploring the Noah's ark tattoo.

He took off his shirt and I returned the favor, exploring the lines of his chest, enjoying the feel of him.

Our pants came off. Will yet again had gone commando. My underwear and bra disappeared. His erection pressed into my belly as he hugged and kissed me and the contact intensified as I hugged and kissed him back.

He guided me to his bed, walking me backward, pressing

into me, until my butt hit the bed. And then he helped me up and kept going, until I was lying on my back across his bed.

Holding both of my feet for a moment, he looked at me, his eyes hungrily examining my body. Then he moved his hands up the insides of my legs, lightly, just his fingertips, making me shudder. Once he got to my pussy, he touched it gently, and then climbed up on the bed.

"Spread more, darlin'," he said, and I obeyed as he pushed my legs out as far as they would go. He kissed and suckled his way up from one knee to the inside of my upper thigh, and then stopped and started with the other knee. This time, once he got to my pussy, he licked it, just once, but thoroughly up all of the available real estate.

Then he smiled, dropped his head, and attended to me, gently licking and sucking, manipulating my pussy with his fingers, over and over again, his dark curls bobbing between my legs. I felt him worship me, letting me enjoy the consuming pleasure of his tongue on my sex. Squirming on the bed, my nails raking across the sheets, I started moaning, and then I got louder and louder as the sensation grew and grew and I came, my body shuddering, the pleasure rippling through my body.

He stayed with me, riding out the orgasm on his face, until I had calmed down and I realized that he was hovering over me, looking at me, positioning his cock at my entrance. His eyes were so passionate, so fierce, it was hard for me to look at him. He put his head down as he entered me, one slow delicious inch at a time, until he was fully seated within me.

After a moment he started to move, very gently, very carefully, caressing me with his hands, his fingers running over my breasts and massaging them, then going down my side, then holding my hips on one side, and then repeating the process on the other. I ran my fingers across his cheek and down his broad back. His cock hit a divine place inside me and I bore down on him, trying to clench around him, and take as much as he could give. He kept going and going, gently thrusting as he made very sweet love to me.

Suddenly Will pulled out and I whined, wanting his cock in me, wanting the fullness, wanting the pleasure. "Come back," I complained. "I was close."

"C'mere." He got up, erection sticking out at an unholy angle, and pulled me up by my armpits. Then he took my soft hand in his large, coarse farmer one, and pulled me from his bedroom, down the hall, me padding after him, naked as could be.

"Where are we going?" I whined.

"Wanna try this."

He led me into a bedroom, smaller than his, which was furnished with only a double bed. It also had a closet with double mirrored doors. Stopping in front of one of the mirrors, he gently turned me to face it and came around behind me, putting his chin on my shoulder, pressing his cock into my lower back and holding me around my waist.

"What do you see?" he asked quietly.

"You and me."

"Put your hands on the mirror. Brace yourself," he ordered.

I did as he said and he spread apart my legs, positioned himself behind me, and thrust into me. *Oh, yes.*

My eyes looked down at the ground. "Lift your head. Look at my eyes," he commanded.

I did. I saw his eyes, dark and demanding, and totally focused. On me. Totally into me. He pulled my hips back so that I was sticking my butt out against him and he began to thrust behind me, my arms still braced on the mirror. He held me tightly, one arm on my hip, the other hand snaked down between my legs, and he started to rub my clit, to the same rhythm of his thrusts, a sensuous pressure, not too light, and not too hard. Every time he thrust into me, my full breasts jogged up and down.

"What do you see, Marie?" he asked as he did this, but his voice this time was more urgent.

"You fucking me," I exhaled, beginning to pant again.

"Look closer."

I did. I looked at his beauty—his dark brown hair and eyes, his high cheekbones and narrow nose, his square jaw, his full lips. I saw his strong arms holding me, veins popping out down the side, his chest flexing. I saw his height, his stature, his presence.

But then I looked at myself in the mirror, being fucked by this incredibly hot guy. And I liked what I saw. I saw a pretty bleached blonde, edgy, but with some softness in her brown eyes, and the height to match him. I saw how sexy it was for me to be receiving what he was giving out. I saw that we fit together. We looked right together. Sure, I had tattoos and an eyebrow piercing, but that stuff didn't matter. We looked right together. It looked like I was meant to be with him, like no one would question why Will was with me. All that shit about our politics and beliefs didn't matter.

We looked like we belonged together.

"We are mirror images of each other," I whispered.

"Damn right," he said. "Now, tell me this is going somewhere," he ordered, as he increased the pace of his thrusts, his cock making my pussy spasm every time it received him, and the speed with which he was massaging my clit.

I moaned in response, the orgasm on its way.

"Tell me this means something. That this is going somewhere," he said again.

"Stop manipulating me through sex," I gasped.

"Tell me this is going somewhere," he repeated, vehemently.

"No!" I yelled.

He kept going, increasing the thrusts, fucking me hard against the mirror, watching my eyes the entire time, not letting go of my clit, bringing the tension, the pleasurable tension in our bodies up more and more, until we had to have a release. We had to. We'd die if we didn't.

"Tell me this is going somewhere," he yelled.

"Yes! Goddamn you, Will!" I screamed, "This is going somewhere. I could fucking fall in love with you if I let myself."

And with that, he said in my ear, "So let yourself," and thrust in hard and stayed there, so that it set off my reaction, and I shook, my legs collapsing, Will holding me up. My body flooded with the pleasure of the release of that sweet orgasmic tension and this set him off. He thrusted into me hard and high up in my body, hitting my fucking womb or something, and came.

I don't know how he held me up, but he did, his muscles shaking, and then he gently pulled me backward and onto the bed with him.

"This is going somewhere," he whispered as he held me, and I nodded my head to agree.

26

TORTURE

"**W**ILL?"

"Yeah, darlin'," he said in my ear, as he tucked in behind me in his vintage bed. We'd both showered after he'd fucked the confession out of me, and now dry but clean, we lay naked in his bed.

I wiggled into his warm body and let out a deep breath. This idea had come to me while we were showering and the more I thought about it, the more I had to do it, even if I didn't really want to. "I need something."

"Anything," he replied immediately, nibbling on my ear and making his way down to my neck, biting it gently, his hands tracing the curves of my side. I could feel him start to stiffen again behind me, even though he'd held me up in the shower not thirty minutes ago and fucked me against the wall until I had cried out, again and again.

"You're not going to like it."

He stiffened. "Tell me."

"Here's the thing. You're stunning. You distract me with sex. But I need to know that we can get along without it. As a couple,

I mean. Because if it's only sex, then it needs to stay that way. If it's not, though, well, I need to know."

He looked at me curiously. "So what do you want?"

I took a deep breath and let it out. "I want you to date me."

He smiled in relief and hugged me close. "'Course, baby. I want to do that."

"No. I want you to date me and just date me." I rolled over on my other side, body to body, facing him, and looked at him.

"What does that mean?"

I got embarrassed for a moment and looked down to his chest. "No sex."

He chuckled and wrapped his arms around me. "What do you mean, no sex?"

"I'm serious, Will. I want to go out on dates. I want to get to know you. Go to restaurants. Do couple things. Not just fuck."

He put a finger under my chin and lifted my head up to look at him; he looked confused. "Let me get this straight. We have the best fuckin' sex I've ever had in my life and you want to quit? What kind of fuckin' game is that?"

"It's not a game," I said, quietly and sincerely. "If it were a game, I wouldn't tell you what I wanted. I would just be playing you for no reason."

He shrugged. "Fair enough. Don't like it though."

"This is more like an experiment. To see if there is more to us than just physical compatibility. If we can get past the Will-is-a-Republican and Marie-is-a-Democrat shit. And if it works, then cool, we'll know. If not, well, then we'll know too."

He looked at me and winced. "I don't know if I can do that. After having a taste of you, fuck, I don't want to let you go."

That was sweet. "You're not letting me go. Not permanently. Just for a little bit. I want to see, you know, what it's like just to date you. I want to spend time with you. I want to find out how far apart we are on our issues. I want to sleep with you in this bed, just sleeping, not fucking."

"You want to torture me."

"It will be torture for me too," I whispered. "But I have to know. I have to know if there is something more here than just physical attraction."

He blew out a breath. "Okay. For how long?"

I thought about it. "Two weeks? That's as long as I've known you, practically. Next week we have the kids from the ASD program and after that we have the kids from East Los Angeles. Then we have a week break. So after the L.A. kids go home?"

"I'm going to have the biggest fuckin' blue balls on the planet if we do that. I can't keep my hands off of you. You know that George Strait song? No of course you don't. Well, he has a song, 'I Get Carried Away.' That's how I feel about you."

I was going to have to listen to that song and think about what that meant, but I knew that I liked it. As I lay there, I had an inspiration. "What if I make you a deal?"

"Yeah?" He nuzzled my neck.

I said it all in a rush. "You make it just over two weeks with me spending the night here, and no sex, and you take me out and I take you out and we spend time together, and come Friday after the L.A. kids leave, if we still like each other and want to continue this, I'll let you do anything sexually to me that you want."

He drew back and stared at me. "*Fuck.*"

Suddenly nervous, I felt like I needed to clarify. "Just don't hurt me."

"I'd never do that." He looked disappointed that I'd even suggest that.

I wiggled into him, my breasts pushing up against his chest, his dick in my belly. "Then, anything," I repeated.

He looked away. "Fuck. You probably want to start abstinence now, don't you."

Smiling shyly, I said quietly, "Not really, but I think we should."

He held me close, moving his lips to my ear, "Then there's no fuckin' way you are sleeping naked with me because that's just wrong."

I thought about torturing him a little bit more, but decided against it. "Okay," I agreed.

"What am I getting myself into?" he muttered.

"Me," I said, and he squeezed me tight.

"Okay, baby, you got yourself a deal. Two weeks from Friday, anything I want, and be prepared. Until then, we do it your way."

He released me and I got up and put on a t-shirt of his and my underwear, and he put on his boxers and we crawled into bed together. Because it was late, we both fell asleep quickly, but it was an uneasy sleep for me.

When I checked my phone the following morning, there was nothing from Amelia, so I texted her.

> What is it about bossy guys? Why are they so hot?

> Because they care. They are IN. TO. IT.

Yeah, I thought. Will cares. But I needed to know how *I* felt.

After breakfast, Will and I walked with a group of kids over to the corrals for their morning riding sessions. The kids were talking about the blockbuster movie of the summer.

When we were almost there, I heard one of the snobby girls, Emma, talking to Truc in a sneering voice. "Listen, *Fob*, have you ever seen a movie that wasn't a bootleg?" Truc immediately burst into tears.

Stunned, Tricia, the group leader, and a few other kids drew in their breath.

Tricia opened her mouth to start talking, but Will beat her to it, stopping Emma and asking, "What did you say?"

"Nothing," she said sullenly.

"What's that mean?" he asked Tricia.

"Fob means fresh off the boat. It's a nasty thing to say to another person."

Will's brows knit together and he looked at Emma. "That's not cool," he said in a low and dangerous voice. "You and me, we're gonna have a talk about prejudice. With everyone. Now."

He stopped the group and made them gather around.

"My mom's from Spain. She speaks Spanish. Marie's dad is Mexican. He was a migrant farmworker. That's how she grew up. We have people here from different countries, or their parents were from different countries, and we treat them all with respect.

"Prejudice is when you judge someone based on what they look like, not on who they are. We all do it. I do it myself. Do it all the time. I did it to my girl here, Marie, because I thought she was a lazy liberal." He smiled. "Turns out she's a caring, hard-working person who doesn't deserve to be judged like that. But words can hurt. Would you want to be called what you called Truc?" he asked Emma.

"No," she said quietly, but still petulant.

"Where you did you learn that word?" Will made a very good authority figure.

"At school," she said in the same voice.

"Do you think Truc likes to be called that?"

"No."

"Yeah," he said, looking at me. "People can prejudge each other. Words can hurt. I've done it myself. Let's make a pact, you and me, that we aren't going to call anyone names on my property. I'm not going to do it and you're not going to do it and everyone else here is not going to do it."

"Okay," whispered Emma.

"Okay," whispered Will back to her. Then in a louder voice, he asked everyone, "Are any of you going to call anyone names on my property?"

"No," the chorus came back.

"Good," said Will. And he came over to me, held my hand, and led everyone over the corrals.

27

MARIE GOT AN IDEA

FOR THE REST OF the week, the kids from Oakland rode horses, made crafts, took care of all of the different farm animals, and generally had a blast. After a rough start with the terrible campfire, the earthquake, and the overt racial slur, the group responded by bonding. I saw Emma talking with Truc several times at meals, James smiled at me once, and Enrique put his phone away in his duffle bag.

Both Maurice and Tricia came up to me and told me that they were going to do the program again next year. Success. Having no phones, no television, no distractions—except for friends to talk to and animals to take care of—really made it a place to put aside differences and make connections. I loved it. It felt like a perfect world. A utopia.

At the closing campfire Thursday night, the fire lit quickly, we roasted marshmallows, and everyone participated in singing my silly songs. And I even thought I saw Will join in from the back.

During the week, I noticed that while Will was a tough cowboy, he was also a kid-magnet. These children really looked up to him. Every time they saw him, they'd call out, "Will, Will!"

and he'd walk over, all burly, and talk with them, his face smiling and animated. He had no guard up around the kids. He'd ruffle the hair of the guys and tease the girls and the kids all seemed to adore him and want to be like him. After his lecture about prejudice, even though it was just a sentence or two, it seemed to do the trick. I heard not a word of teasing about race among these children. At least for now. At least with this group. And sometimes that's all you could hope for.

I realized that his lecture, in part, was an apology to me for what he said when we met. We still needed to talk about a lot of things, however, like our beliefs, our politics, ourselves. But knowing that he had the ability to instruct kids to set aside their beliefs was a start to me opening up to him.

I wondered if he could set aside his own beliefs. I wondered if I could. I wanted to talk with him, and while he wasn't hard to talk to, he was never chatty. I needed to come up with a way to fix that.

But I was scared. What if it really was just about sex? What if we really did get on each other's nerves and had nothing in common underneath the mutual physical attraction?

It would hurt to discover that there was nowhere to go.

And realizing that it would hurt meant that I really did like him.

While Will had not tried to get into my pants this week, he gave zero fucks about public displays of affection. Whenever I was near him, he touched me, either with his arm around my shoulders, holding my hand, or tracing a finger down my back or arms. It felt comforting and I really liked it.

But he hadn't kissed me since I asked him to knock off the sex.

I missed his mouth on mine.

I missed other parts of him too.

Then it was Friday, and the kids went home to Northern

California, dusty, wearing tie-dyed shirts, and boisterously singing "Row, Row, Row Your Boat" in a round on the bus ride home.

After they left, I went into the kitchen and made myself a snack of hummus and pita chips. Looking at my vegan food supplies, I realized that I needed to make a trip to a health food store to restock some of my favorites. I also noted that the bottle of tequila I'd brought with me had remained unopened.

That gave me an idea for tonight.

After I ate, I walked over to the barn to check in with Happy the horse. One of the farm hands, Claudio, was mucking out the stalls.

"When did you come here?" I asked.

He talked slowly, in a thick, Austrian accent. "I come here for school and then I start to work for Mister Will. And then I don't want to leave. At first I come to California. I rent red convertible Mustang. I try the surfing. But no, I am not surfer. Here, with the horses, I belong."

"I understand," I said. "I feel like I belong here too."

Will walked in the barn, hung up a bridle and reins in the tack room, and then came over to me. Claudio excused himself. Will put a foot up on a hay bale next to me, boxing me in by Happy's stall, and asked, "What do you wanna do tonight?"

"Get you drunk and see if I can get you to answer questions," I immediately responded.

He chuckled. "So you're gonna hide your true agenda."

I pushed his broad chest in protest, as a joke. He didn't move, just looked down at me, his brown eyes mellow. I responded, "Nope. But I got a bottle of tequila and it has our names on it."

He groaned. "Shit. Tequila. You sure that's a good idea?"

"Yes!" I clapped my hands. "I know! We'll go on a picnic. There has to be a good spot for a picnic, right? We can watch the sunset and drink and talk."

"Sounds terrific," Will muttered, not sounding like he believed it at all.

"It's all settled," I said. "I'll talk to Cookie and pack up something."

Will shook his head like he couldn't believe me, but he also looked amused.

Good. Hopefully I could get him talking. But I wasn't sure that I wanted to find out what he was going to say.

28

TEQUILA

WILL AND I WALKED away from the compound to his favorite bluff, which had quickly become my favorite bluff. A clear, cloudless sky meant that it was an absolutely beautiful summer evening that would surely turn into a superb night for stargazing.

I carried a blanket to sit on. He carried a small picnic basket with sandwiches made by Cookie—ham for Will, peanut butter for me—potato chips, watermelon, vegan chocolate cookies, water, and a huge bottle of tequila with a couple of plastic cups. So it was going to be a party. Woo-hoo!

But I had an agenda. I probably didn't really want to know the answers to any of it, but what could I say? I couldn't help myself. I *had* to know.

Still, as we walked, I was suddenly shy. This felt weird. I was never shy. But I guess I didn't want to spend the evening fighting with him about politics, or getting jealous of past girlfriends. And truthfully, I also really liked him and I didn't want to find out anything I wouldn't like.

I still felt an overwhelming urge to ask these things.

I couldn't bring myself to say a word until we got to the

picnic site and spread out the blanket over the low vegetation. Since it was one of the longest days of the year, the sun was still high in the sky. The ocean crashed below us, no one else around. We settled on the blanket, sitting cross-legged, facing each other.

"Guess I shouldn't be worried about you takin' me out here and takin' advantage of me, given our agreement," Will joked.

"Nope. I do want to talk," I said sincerely.

"'Kay."

"See, that's it. You always have one word answers. Maybe for every one word answer you have to take a shot of tequila—"

"No," he interrupted. "We can each take a shot to get started. And if the other says somethin' that deserves a shot, that'll be it."

This could get interesting rather quickly. I nodded. At least he was playing along.

He got out the bottle and the plastic cups, poured me a healthy shot and himself a healthier shot, saying, "I'm bigger than you," and downed it.

I drank my shot. It warmed me up immediately. With the kids around this summer, I hadn't been drinking as much as I usually did. We'd see if my tolerance had changed any over the past few weeks.

Will handed me my sandwich, unwrapped his own, took a bite, and said, "Shoot, darlin'."

Now that it was my chance to grill him, I couldn't do it.

That is, I chickened out about asking him about politics. That was the deepest issue and I couldn't start with it. Better to start with basic information that I didn't know.

"Where did you go to school?" I asked, taking a bite of my sandwich.

"College? Cal Poly, up the road. I've gotta degree in Agriculture. Went to high school in Santa Ynez with all the farm kids." Local boy stays local.

"Where have you worked?"

He chewed a bite of his sandwich and swallowed. "I've only ever worked here. Even in college, I came back here on weekends."

"How come?"

"Don't want to be anything other than a rancher. That's what I am."

I looked at him as I chewed my sandwich. "Take a shot."

He burst out laughing. "I just took one. You've only asked two questions."

"You said whenever the other one says something that deserves a shot, you take a shot. Your work history deserves a shot. You must have the shortest resume on the planet."

"Yep." He sighed. "Fine, but fuck. You're gonna get me fucked up."

"That's the point. You already asked me about me days ago, and I answered. But when I asked you questions, you barely answered me. So now it's my turn. How many girlfriends have you had?"

He stared at me and his cheek twitched. "That's dangerous territory darlin'. You don't wanna do that."

I let out a breath. "Will, it's a girl thing. I want to simultaneously think you've only ever been with me, but I also want you to have the experience of a professional escort."

"It's juvenile. You don't need to know that shit. It'll just make you mad. If you told me who you'd been with before me, it'd piss me off."

I'd admit that I liked him jealous. But still, I couldn't let it go. "What are you hiding?" I asked, more forcefully, lifting up my chin and challenging him.

"Nothing." He glared at me and took another bite of his sandwich. An idea came to me.

"Were you ever married?"

"No."

"Engaged?"

He let out a breath. "Yeah."

That surprised me. But it was what I wanted to know. "Really?"

"Yeah," he repeated.

"What happened?"

"She told me that I was an asshole and then she went back to Texas. I was with her for all of college. I was young. Think I knew deep down she wasn't the one. She hid all sorts of shit from me that I found out later. Don't like it when I don't know what a woman is really thinkin', I'd rather hear it. I didn't fight it when she left."

I was simultaneously sorry for him and not sorry for him because now I could be the one sitting with him on a bluff by the ocean, drinking tequila. It also explained why he liked my openness. "I think that deserves a shot," I teased him.

"Only if you take one too," he replied instantly.

"Fair enough."

He poured us both another shot of tequila, smaller than the first one, and we both downed it. I was starting to feel very warm now. Another thought came to my mind. "You don't have any kids or anything do you?"

"Fuck no."

"Have you ever been with a man?"

He stared at me.

"What?" I said defensively. "It's just a question. It deserves an answer."

"No," he said emphatically. "Just because I have a gay uncle doesn't mean I'm into that."

"You have a gay uncle?" I'd like to meet him, the real black sheep of the conservative family.

"Yeah."

I nudged a little closer to him, knees to knees, the tequila starting to talk. "What is the kinkiest thing you've ever done with someone."

He looked me straight in the eyes and put his finger under my chin. "Darlin' you don't want to know the answer to that."

"Yes I do." I totally did.

"Don't want to argue with you."

"Yes you do." We stayed that way for a little bit, like children, staring at each other, willing for the other one to give. "Another shot of tequila, Will."

"Fuck, Marie."

"Do it and answer the question."

He poured another shot and downed it, and answered. "Fine. Fucked a woman up the ass while her friend fucked her with a dildo and licked her pussy."

I burst out laughing. "You are a deviant," I whispered admiringly. "A real live threesome."

"Needed lotsa of lube," he continued.

"Holy fuck." I whispered again.

"It was a little awkward," he said, "you know, getting the position right—" Then he stopped. "You don't want to know this shit. Told you I was kinky."

"Agreed. It's hot, though. How did you get to be so kinky?"

"Internet."

"That's not an answer."

"Just how I'm made?" he said, as a question, grinning.

"That's not much better."

"College?" He was starting to chuckle now.

"Still not an answer."

He paused for a moment and looked thoughtful. "Dunno. Never thought about it. I guess I like a little pain mixed with the pleasure. If something is too easy, it doesn't feel right. I feel like you gotta work for what you want."

That sounded familiar. If he was being nice to me it didn't feel right. I inched closer to him, although if I got any closer, I'd be sitting in his lap. "So what do you do now that's so kinky?"

He pursed his lips for a moment and then said, "Orgasm denial. Bondage. Not into fringe shit."

I considered that. It actually sounded okay to me.

"Why anal?"

"I'm a guy."

"What is it with guys being fascinated by it?"

"Dunno."

"Just another hole to stick it in, I guess."

He burst out laughing. "Wouldn't put it that way. Your turn to take a shot. I'm two up on you. We gotta even this out."

"Ever been in a threesome with a guy?"

"Nope."

"Just two women?"

"Yep. Well, once three."

"What?"

He smiled.

"How many times."

"Couple."

"These one word answers are gonna get you in trouble," I warned him.

He laughed, a barking, unusual laugh for him. "I'm tryin' to avoid ripping off your clothes, vixen. Never told anyone this shit. Anyone. Not one soul knows this shit. Give a guy a break."

"How many times have you had threesomes?"

He sighed and hiccuped. "With the same women? Or different women?"

"I don't want to know the answer to that do I?"

"Nope. Multiple." He took a bite of his sandwich and so did I. Then I gestured to the bottle.

"Take a fucking shot."

"Fine." He poured the shot, took the drink, then continued. "My turn. Kinkiest thing?"

"You have already asked me questions days ago," I giggled. "This is not let's ask Marie. There is no grilling Marie session. I'm an open book. I chatter away—"

"What is the kinkiest thing you have ever done, Marie?" he asked again, louder and slower.

Now it was my turn to blush. "Well, once I gave a guy a blow job while he was driving."

Will looked at me in admiration. "How the fuck did he manage to keep driving?"

"No idea. It was down Highway 101 at seventy miles per hour. It was stupid."

"Yeah, road head's just dangerous, not kinky. Tell me something kinky."

"I was arrested for walking topless around campus protesting Instagram's ban of showing boobies."

He immediately looked interested. And aroused. "Seriously?"

"Yeah. I do protests. I'm the fuckin' liberal, remember?"

He stared at me.

I couldn't resist teasing him, and said, faux innocently, "I wore nothing but jeans and a smile, big guy. I'm pretty sure my picture is on the internet."

He glared at me. "We're both taking another shot for that one," he muttered. He gave us each a shot. I was getting very, very drunk. I didn't know how Will was handling it. Since he'd drunk more than me, he had to feel it by now.

"Another time, a guy went down my pants and finger-fucked me while I was sitting next to my parents. We were at a concert and under a blanket so they never knew how many orgasms he gave me while the concert played."

He looked at me. I kept talking.

"I've acted out porn while it was playing on the screen."

His gaze burned.

"There was this one night in college. With a woman."

"That's it," he interrupted. "We should stop talking about this."

"Yeah."

We stared at each other.

"Are we allowed to kiss or is this no touching for two weeks?" I asked.

"This was your idea," he said. "But I thought of a way around it."

29

OGRE

"WE'RE GONNA DO THIS right, Will. No 'way around it.' No sex means no sex. The point of this is to get to know you and peel the layers off of you."

"Like-an-ogre," he said, his words starting to slur a little. "I mean-an-onion." He blinked.

Then I blinked and cocked my head to the side. "Did you just make a *Shrek* reference?"

He shook his head, very slowly, looking at me with wide eyes.

"Liar," I laughed, pointing at him and waggling my finger in his face.

"My favorite movie," he muttered, shrugging, looking away from me and towards the ocean. The sun was starting to go down and the colors of the sky were changing from blue to a grayish purple.

"*Shrek* is your favorite movie? Of all of the movies out there, you pick a cartoon?"

"Yeah. Always felt like him. Get the fuck off my land and stay away from me, I'm just a big ugly ogre. And then I gotta deal with the donkeys."

"Donkeys meaning Democrats or donkeys meaning asses or donkeys meaning donkeys?"

"Yes," he answered, decisively and unhelpfully, his unruly hair waving as he nodded his head.

Oh, politics. I didn't want to go there with him. That'd just lead to us yelling at each other, I was sure of it.

By coming up with the get-Will-drunk idea, I'd just wanted to loosen him up, to see if he'd answer my questions with more than one word answers. Mission accomplished. As he'd been talking, I'd had been thinking about what he was saying, and most of what he said, I liked. I wasn't really happy to find out about his ex-fiancé or all of the girls, but who would be? And to be fair, it wasn't like I was a saint. I had a history too.

But I couldn't believe that he'd done threesomes and four-somes. Sheesh. Even I wasn't that much of a sex fiend. I had read a book or two where people had had orgies and threesomes but I couldn't believe he had actually had sex with two or three women at once. Only Will. I guess he was a big enough man that it was hard for one woman to satisfy him.

That wasn't a good thought.

I mean, he had consistently told me that he was kinky, but there was a difference between this guy, in real life, having crazy sex with a bunch of women, and some made up tortured billion-aire with a dungeon of pain. He was way more experienced than I was, even though I was no prude.

I'd never been particularly sexually shy, or indeed shy about anything, although apparently there was a long way along the sex adventure spectrum I could go. I was nowhere near the virginal side of the spectrum, but kinky? Nah.

My sex life had been fun and plenty spontaneous. I believed that our bodies were meant to be lived in, and I enjoyed mine.

But Will took sexual pleasure to another level, and I think it was because he was so in to it, like what Amelia had said when I texted her earlier. In. To. It. It was different being with someone who was intensely generous, devoted to making sure you had as good a time as he had, and completely focused on you, not on him. But it wasn't like he was always in charge, either, which was fun. We were equals in bed.

Beyond learning that he really was kinky, it was heartening to learn that he was also the straightforward country boy he seemed to be. He'd finished college and had been incredibly responsible on his farm, which made me appreciate him more.

But where did we go from here?

After drinking however many shots of tequila that I'd ingested, I felt like I was on that edge—the one teetering between just drunk enough, and far too drunk. I wasn't far too drunk but I was sure as fuck was not sober. But with a half dozen shots, one right after another, Will was surely feeling it more than me. Six shots of tequila for anyone would make them feel loose. And now his lack of sobriety was starting to show, with his words running together. It was cute, mostly because he was trying to hide it. He kept reaching out and putting the back of his hand on my cheek and carefully caressing my face, which felt ultra-soothing.

So with finally getting him to tell me something about himself, and him being so sweet, I didn't want to spoil it by getting into a drunken argument with him about politics.

Somewhere deep down, though, I knew that I was avoiding the deepest issue we had between us. I needed to bring it up before I did something stupid like fall in love with him. Because if that happened, then I'd have to deal with the fallout of that shit and I really didn't want to do that.

One thing he said dawned on me.

"You're not an ugly ogre."

He raised an eyebrow.

"You're the most handsome man I have ever seen," I said quietly.

"Shucks," he said, and I burst out laughing again.

"Most people start swearing more when they get drunk. You start swearing less?"

"Guess so. I'm drunk, though. I mean, I'm not drunk, though." Then he got the sweetest look on his face, almost imploring. "Is kissing off the, uh, I mean, off the table?"

"No," I answered, smiling and getting a little closer.

"Then c'mere, baby," he said, pulling me up from my cross-legged position and into his lap, then leaning back and lying down so that I was straddling him.

There was no other way of describing our kiss than a stupid, drunk, sloppy, wet kiss. It was epically bad. By the end, he was on top and we were both giggling, nose to nose.

Will giggling was a thing to behold.

"We're better at kissing without the tequila," I said against his tan neck.

"Shucks," he said again. "I'm sorry. Told ya you were gonna get me fucked up. I'll kiss you better when it wears off."

"Okay, you got a deal."

He smiled, still on top of me, now between my legs, and leaned down to kiss my cheek, I think, but missed and kissed my ear. "Wanna hear my loophole?"

"Yeah."

"So, no sex, right? For-like-two-weeks?" he slurred, as he nibbled my ear.

"Right," I said, laughing. He was a pretty obvious drunk.

"So no," he paused for a second, "fucking, meaning no," pause, nibble, "sexual intercourse."

"You got that one right, cowboy." I wiggled under him and he came up and looked at me in the eyes.

"But kissing doesn't count."

"You already know that." I ran my hands through his hair and enjoyed the feel of his body on mine. Even if we weren't having sex, and even if he was not himself right now, he still felt good pressed to me. He still felt like he belonged there.

"Does oral sex count?" He was serious, but I burst out laughing.

"It has sex in the name, Will," I scolded him.

"Okay, so what about sex with yourself? That's not sex with me." And he reached over and pushed my hair behind my ear and kissed me behind my ear, sloppily. Drunk, Playful Will was around.

"What are you saying?" I asked, distracted by his attentions.

"If you went in the shower tonight, after this," pause, kiss, "fascinating discussion—"

He paused and brought his head up to look at me again.

"What?"

"Nothin'," he said.

"No one word answers, dude," I said, and I shook my finger at him.

"Just thinking about you in the shower and that is not helping the stiffy you gave me by the image of you walking around in public topless."

"You just said stiffy," I giggled.

He looked at me, confused, eyebrows furrowed. "What would you call it?"

"Boner."

"That . . . that too," he slurred. "So, if you get yourself off, and I don't touch you and you don't touch me, then we're not breaking your rules," he concluded, proud of himself.

I hated to burst his bubble.

"No."

"No?" he asked, taken aback.

"No sex."

"If I went and stroked off by myself, though, would that count?"

I thought about it. "I guess not."

"So what's the difference if you do it while I watch?"

"It's still sex if you're watching me."

"Darling, you keep talking the way you did earlier and if there was no tequila in me, I'd come. Now . . ." he trailed off.

"Yeah?"

He didn't say anything.

"You're going to need help getting back to the house aren't you?"

"Maybe," he said, sheepishly.

"Whose idea was it to go two weeks?"

"Yours," he said, and kissed me on my lips, enthusiastically, and better this time. He awkwardly got off of me and helped me up.

Then we packed up the picnic and went back to his house, where he immediately fell asleep with his clothes on.

30

ICE CREAM

"**D**ON'T YOU MISS BACON and eggs?"

It was Saturday morning. We had both woken up feeling the night before, but Gatorade and Advil had fixed it. We'd shuffled into the chow hall in our sweats. Cookie had given Will a spinach and egg casserole for breakfast, while I'd retrieved my cereal and soy milk from my stash and poured myself a bowl. We had sat together in the middle of the room and eaten with the wranglers and ranch hands. After they took off to check on the horses, Will started asking me questions.

"Not really," I answered. "I have more of a sweet tooth. The one food I really miss is ice cream, but there are some good vegan ice cream brands out there, so I make do."

He rolled his eyes and then gestured at my bowl with the fork in his hand. "How long have you been a vegan?"

"Three years. Before that, I was vegetarian. I haven't had meat since I was sixteen."

He just stared at me and shook his head. "You're missing out."

"I'm not going to kill any animals, Will."

"You don't kill a cow to eat ice cream." He bit a piece of bacon.

"True. But I think that we raise animals in inhumane conditions and I'm not going to support the mistreatment of any animals. I don't support all of the growth hormones and antibiotics that are force fed to them. And then there are all of the resources that are required to produce the cattle—all of the land and processing and fossil fuels that are—"

"Inhumane conditions," he repeated, interrupting me.

"Yes. I saw this PETA video—"

"Fucking PETA. PETA's never been to my ranch. Have you seen our cattle?"

Here we go again with the arguing. Round one million.

"Well, clearly *you* don't have inhumane conditions—" I started, but he interrupted.

"I don't use growth hormones either."

"It's just something I believe in," I said, defensively. "It matters to me. I'm not going to change it."

Will looked over at my rice milk box, disgusted. "What you eat—it's not even food. It's—I don't know what that is that you eat. Why don't you just eat a normal meal like everyone else?"

"Because I don't want to."

An expression came over his face, impish and adorable. "Would you do it on a dare? What if I took you to a fancy, organic, no-growth-hormone ice cream place. The good shit. Would you eat it?"

I took a deep breath. Ice cream really was the thing that I missed the most about being a vegan. The other stuff, no. I didn't need it. "Are you asking me if I'd compromise a belief for you? I mean, that's what you're asking me, right? Would I change something about me if you dared me?"

"Suppose so, yeah."

Raising an eyebrow, I scolded him. "That sounds an awful lot like a game, Will Thrash. You accused me of playing games, but now you're the one doing it."

He set down his fork. "I need more coffee before I can argue with you," he muttered.

"No you don't." I let out a sigh. "Okay."

He did a double-take. "Okay, what?"

"Okay, I'll do it if you do it too."

"Meaning?"

"I'll go eat ice cream—"

"—compromising your beliefs," he said, now teasing me.

"—if you wear the tie-dye all day and go with me wherever I want. We drive in my car. And we're going to go to every hippie store I can think of, Will, and you're going to try a lot of new things."

He laughed. "Can't picture me wearing that tie-dye."

"Neither can I, so I want to see it, big guy. And that's just the beginning. I'm thinking yoga and drum circles and spiritual enlightenment book stores. You're going to learn about the Law of Attraction and we're going to go to the Democratic headquarters in Santa Barbara."

"Oh, now that's just mean," he drawled. "I offer to take you to have an ice cream cone. That's a date. You're punishing me."

"Take it or leave it. I'll eat ice cream and in exchange you do whatever it is I want you to do."

"No."

"No?" I couldn't believe he said no—I was really going to break my vegan-ness for him. I started to get mad but he spoke.

"I'll wear the shirt and you can drive your car and we'll go wherever you want except nothing political."

Guess he didn't want to go there either. That sounded like he was giving in. I reached over and shook his hand. "Mr. Thrash, I think you have yourself a deal."

After breakfast, we wandered over to the stables to check on the horses. Happy didn't really eat his breakfast, but I suppose he wasn't hungry. His stall looked clean. The wranglers must have already mucked it out.

Since I had this strange living arrangement where I slept with Will in his house—just sleeping for now—but my stuff wasn't there, I went to the bunkhouse and showered and changed, putting on white short shorts, flip flops, and a blue and white striped sailor shirt. Then I walked over to Will's house.

When I walked in, he was nowhere to be seen. "Will!" I called out. I heard him yell from upstairs, "Come on up."

When I got up to his room, he was standing in his bedroom, dark hair wet and wavy, barefoot, shirtless, wearing Levi's.

My boy actually owned jeans other than Wranglers.

And he looked gorgeous in them—dark wash, low slung, hugging his ass just right. They hung below his boxers, so I guess he only went commando in Wranglers.

He smiled, a rueful smirk. "I can't believe you're actually making me do this." And he reached over, picked up the black and blue tie-dyed shirt he made, and put it on.

Hoo-boy. Mr. Will always wore his shirts a little tight, and this was no exception. It hugged his chest, and his arm muscles bulged in the sleeves.

"Don't feel like myself," he said, running his hand down his abdominal muscles.

"You don't look like yourself," I said, and looked him up and down. He looked like a hunky guy that you'd see at Whole Foods, but he didn't look like my Will. It neutralized him. Truly, it was astonishing how much his clothes and his cowboy persona defined him. He looked beautiful, but it was different.

Almost too different.

I had half a mind to let him take it off.

But *nah*. This was too much fun.

"Can't wear boots with this," he said. "It feels wrong." And he pulled on flip flops and sunglasses.

I hadn't realized how much I was attracted to him as a rancher. Making him look like someone he wasn't felt off. I needed to throw him a bone.

"Tell you what. I'll buy me some Wranglers today and wear them for you, okay?" He shrugged. "Just Wranglers, no shirt."

"Deal," he said immediately.

We walked out to my car and he shuddered. "Can't believe I'm letting you talk me into this," he said under his breath.

"I heard that." I unlocked the doors and we got in.

"I don't know which is worse. Driving this hippie-mobile or being driven."

"I'll drive," I said. "I know where I want to go."

"And I'll take you to McConnell's for ice cream."

Ooh. Local, old fashioned, the good stuff.

Yum.

I almost forgot I was vegan.

31

KEYS

"**O**PEN YOUR MOUTH, DARLIN'."

I obeyed and licked the sweet, slightly salty white cream that Will held out for me.

And then I let out a loud moan of pleasure.

Oh yummmmmmm.

Sea Salt Cream & Cookies flavor ice cream.

Three years of no ice cream, that is, no real ice cream, made McConnell's taste even more exceptional. If I went non-vegan, Will was right, this was an excellent way to do it. It was tasty and it met my ecopolitical objectives—a family-owned business since the 1940s that used local, high-quality ingredients, and didn't have the bad shit in it.

And it was a date, with my boyfriend, buying me an ice cream cone on a hot summer day. Thinking about the word boyfriend made me feel all squishy in my belly. I wasn't used to calling him that, but if we were together, wasn't he my boyfriend?

My boyfriend, Will Thrash.

I needed to think about that sometime. I needed to talk to

Amelia about that too. Now wasn't the time, though. Now was the time to enjoy my treat.

"What do you think?" he asked, pulling the cone away from my lips.

"Itsogood," I groaned and I grabbed the cone from him. He had bought his own chocolate cone to eat.

As I licked my ice cream, Will watched me, paying attention. I played it up, giving my ice cream cone lots of tongue action, moaning and dribbling cream on my face. What can I say, as usual, it was fun to goad him. A patron or two noticed. But all he did in response was to narrow his eyes and ask me quietly, leaning over, cool lips brushing against my ear, "How much more of our two weeks do we have until I can get you naked and fuck you?"

My response was to lean back in my chair, grin at him, lick my ice cream all the way around the tip, and then slurp it up loudly, never losing eye contact with him.

He groaned and went back to his own ice cream cone.

I'd driven Will to Santa Barbara in my biodiesel Mercedes Benz, windows down, hair blowing, sunglasses on both of us. He dutifully sat in the passenger seat, but he didn't belong there. As a feminist, I didn't want to admit that, but he was not used to being driven; he was used to driving and he was used to driving in his big ol' truck. It was funny how much that little thing pushed his boundaries. He made no comment, but I could tell that he was uncomfortable. I did, however, let him befoul my radio with country music.

As we drove, we talked about the ranch and about the Headlands Program and the fact that there had been no major aftershocks from the earthquake. While Will was still Will, meaning not a chatterbox, he answered my questions, most of the time with more than one word, and asked me plenty of questions about where I lived in Santa Barbara and where we were going.

The clock hit lunchtime once we got there and I drove him to a vegan cafe. He looked especially pained when he reviewed the menu, but he ordered pasta with vegetables and ate it.

Then we went to the ice cream shop.

Once I finished my cone, I needed to go run a few errands.

The first place we went was my apartment. I had a tiny studio downtown, with not much in it. Even though it ate into my paycheck to pay the rent all summer, I didn't want to let it go because it was in such a great location. I packed a bag of more clothes, checked my mail, and grabbed a few other things that I had forgotten.

As I did this, Will looked around my apartment. I decorated in early stereotypical hippie, with tie-dyes, tapestries, paisley prints, candles, scarves, and incense everywhere. I had photographs of my friends, especially Amelia, crammed on every surface, and my refrigerator covered with art from the preschool where I had worked. Will walked around slowly, looking at all of it and not saying a word. Once I packed up, he carried down the heavy case and I carried a box and a bag of stuff. We put them in my trunk, and headed to Tri-County Produce, my favorite grocery store, which was supplied by local farms.

As we walked in, I immediately saw an ex-boyfriend, Jeremy, who Amelia called Man Bun, working there.

Oh shit.

Awkward.

Well, he was one of the many guys before Will. There were lots and lots of them, and they just didn't do it for me. Not like Will. Man Bun, while cute, was boring. Not an ounce of originality or enthusiasm about anything. He'd probably smoked out all of his brain cells anyway.

Still, I couldn't ignore him.

"Hi, Jeremy, how are you?" I asked, as we walked down the bulk aisle.

"Marie. Hi," he said, enthusiastically, and then he did a doubletake when he saw Will, who looked like a Burning Man god in that shirt. Man Bun recovered and asked, "So where have you been? I haven't seen you around in a while."

"I'm working up near Buellton," I said, "at Will's ranch. This is my boyfriend, Will Thrash."

Will's eyes shifted to me for a second at the word "boyfriend," but then he leaned forward to shake poor Man Bun's hand with what I was sure was a burly man death grip. Oh dear. Man Bun didn't wrestle bears in his spare time the way Will did.

"Will Thrash of Headlands Ranch?" asked Jeremy. "I think we're stocking some of your berries right now. Want me to show you?"

I nodded and we walked over to the fresh produce, which took up half of the floor space of the place and, sure enough, there were Headlands Ranch berries there. "I don't think we need to buy them, do we Will?" I asked.

"We've got plenty at home."

I thanked Jeremy, stocked up my vegan supplies, and got the hell out of there.

We filled up my gas at the lone biodiesel fuel station, Will looking at first repulsed and then slightly interested, and then we drove back to the ranch.

Home.

I let Will drive.

When we got back to the ranch, he parked, got out, went into his house without saying a word, and as I was taking things out of the trunk, he came back with something small, and put it in my hand.

"A car key?"

"Key to my truck. I'm not fucking riding in that again."

"Thanks," I said and kissed him. He helped me carry the bags to the bunkhouse bedroom and then left, whistling for Trixie, so that he could go and check on the fields. I dropped my groceries in the kitchen, and then went into the bunk room, where both Janine and Stephanie were sitting on their bunks, chatting.

I threw my keys and Will's key on the bed and my purse down, and then turned to unpack my new things.

Janine, noticing the extra truck key, asked, "Did you get another car?"

"No. Will gave me the key to his truck."

She looked shocked. "Did he really? Wow."

I looked at her questioningly.

She continued, with a knowing glance at Stephanie. "Well, it's kind of a joke saying, but if a cowboy gives you the keys to his truck, you know he's serious. It's almost more than an engagement ring."

Ohmigod.

32

WINE

I DRESSED WILL UP *like a Ken doll today*, I texted Amelia.

Why the fuck would you do that? He's already
Woody from Toy Story.

He is not. He's cooler, more like Johnny Cash,
the man in black.

True. And?

I wanted to see if he would do it. I made him
dress like me. Tie-dye. No Wranglers. He wore
Levi's and flip flops and Ray Bans.

And?

He looked hot. But he didn't look like Will.

And?

I'm not going to do that again. He can stay the
way he is.

And?

It was fun to try it.

And?

He's my boyfriend now.

Amelia?

<Sobbing into my coffee, so happy for my best
friend since third grade>

That evening I leaned against a shirtless, boxer-clad Will in
his bed, spooning, wearing a tank top and pajama bottoms. He
hugged me close but did not let his hands roam. He didn't kiss me.

"Forgot to buy you Wranglers today," he murmured in
my ear.

"That's because when we went to my apartment, I found a
pair from high school and packed them up. I think they still fit."

"You used to wear them?" he asked, with some admiration in
his voice.

"I rode horses when I was little," I said, "and I've always been
a horsey girl." Then I admitted, "I think they'll fit. They might be
a little tight."

"Lookin' forward to seeing that," he said. He ran his fingers
down my bare arm and kissed me behind the ear, which made
me sigh. His lips pressed against my skin as he asked, "What do
you want to do tomorrow?"

"I haven't been to your winery yet."

"Take you after I do the morning rounds." Just then I heard Trixie whimpering from the kitchen. "Mind if I bring her up? Sometimes she gets lonely."

I loved having Trixie around. I wondered why he didn't do it more often. "Not at all."

He got out of bed, all golden muscle and sexy. I heard him go downstairs, open the kitchen door, and the next thing I knew, Trixie had bounded up and was on the bed next to me, wagging her tail.

"Settle in, girl," he said to her, and rubbed behind her ears. Then he leaned over me and kissed me, deeply, lots of tongue, my breasts against his chest, and just when it was getting good, he pulled away, with a pained noise.

I looked at him, breathless. He looked back at me, breathless.

How many more days? Why did I insist on this?

He let out a sigh. Then he rearranged us, with me tucked into him and Trixie curled at the foot of the bed, reached over to turn off the light, kissed my neck, said "Goodnight," and went to sleep.

It took me a while to fall asleep. Not because I felt uncomfortable, but because quite the opposite.

Sitting in the bunkhouse office, the next morning, I finalized the plans for the activities for the upcoming week. I started thinking about what the "anything" that Will was going to do to me at the end of it.

Then I got an idea.

I found the website and ordered, assured of discreet brown packaging.

And then I joined Will and Trixie in his truck.

We drove past the rows of crops in the fields, trees in the orchards, and grapes in the vineyards, ultimately pulling into the gravel drive of the winery, with olive trees, rosemary, and lavender landscaping.

We walked hand in hand up to the corrugated metal building, decorated in industrial chic inside.

A young woman with a nose ring, dyed black hair, and a lot of tattoos stood behind the bar.

So Will employed someone else who looked like me. Maybe he wasn't as pure cowboy as he seemed.

"Hi, Mr. Thrash," she said, smiling.

"Genevieve, this is Marie, my girlfriend." He wasn't shy about using that word. "Let her have a flight."

"Sure thing, Mr. Thrash. You too?"

"Nope, I'm driving and gotta do some more work later."

She set out six wine glasses and poured a healthy amount in the first glass, a dry white Central Coast blend, telling me about it. "All of our wines are certified organic." A group of people walked in and she excused herself to go serve them. I sipped the wine, which tasted lovely.

"So you can handle two edgy female employees?"

"Yeah?" he said, wary.

"I guess I expected you to hire all country girls, but you have a thing for tattooed ones too?"

He sighed, exasperated. "She's an employee and she's twenty-two. You're my girlfriend, not my employee." I tipped back the last of the glass in a rush.

Genevieve came over and gave me another glass of white wine, describing it to me.

A strange mood, a funk, came over me. I needed to push him now. Stop pussyfooting around. I *had to know* if it was going to work between us. He seemed to think it would, but I wasn't convinced, and if I just tiptoed around our issues—his politics, my politics, my feminism, his anti-feminism—then we'd never get them resolved. Even though part of me just wanted to let these things go and let us off the hook, I knew that I had insisted on this period of time for a reason. And if it wasn't going to work out, I needed to know before I really got hurt. Before I really opened up my heart to him.

And I wanted to know more about his kink.

I looked at him, then I looked over at Genevieve, then I looked back at him. "Tell me more about the threesomes."

"This isn't the place, Marie."

"No one's listening."

I was right. We stood to the side of the bar as Genevieve helped the other patrons. They were noisy and there was no way that they were paying attention to us.

He looked really uncomfortable, but he started talking and I think it was because he knew that I'd bug him until he talked. "What do you want to know? There was a bar in college that I went to, a country bar, and a lot of times it was easy to pick up a woman and her friend." He paused. "You don't want to know this."

"I don't want to be in a threesome with you. I just want you. But it's hot and I want details."

"You don't want to know. That shit will only make you jealous and that's not a good idea. It's ancient history anyway."

I swallowed the last of the second glass of wine and Genevieve noticed, came over, and poured me the third glass. These were huge tastes, not the two fingers one normally got at a winery. I guess it helped if you were there with the boss.

"I don't talk about it. To anyone."

I looked at him.

"Christ, do you really want to know about the pussy that was before you?" he hissed.

Oh, no. He didn't say that.

He referred to other women as pussy. He just referred to me as pussy.

I got mad.

I knew I had some wine, although not that much, and I knew that I was being unreasonable. I knew I pushed him on it and probably for no reason other than I wanted to get this shit out of him.

I knew it wasn't fair.

But I didn't like being thought of as just a pussy.

That meant that deep down, he didn't think of me in the way that I was starting to think of him. I was a convenient piece of ass to fuck.

I mean, really, I didn't like him. We were too different. We'd never agree on the stuff that matters, even if we tried.

Right?

Fuck.

I'd brought this on myself.

"Is that what you think of me?" I hissed back, "Some pussy to stick your dick into? Is that what you think of all women?"

"Of course not."

"But you just said it."

He sighed. "You asked me before why I'm not a feminist. This is one of the reasons. Can't talk to you the way I would talk with a man. Men and women are different. We do different things, we see the world differently. Doesn't make one better than the other. You talk to me differently than you talk to Amelia."

Yeah, I've objectified men. I just looked at him, not answering, not caring that I was being unreasonable.

"We all do it darlin'. Doesn't mean that I don't respect you. Doesn't mean that I have something against women. I just don't support the political feminist agenda."

There.

This, this wasn't going to work.

It wasn't working.

I shouldn't have started it with him.

"This is the problem, Will. You are so closed mouth and sometimes what comes out of your mouth is totally wrong. Totally against my ideals."

"Fuck your ideals," he retorted, immediately.

"See, that's the thing," I said, wagging a finger in his face. "You can say fuck my ideals, but what about yours? What about yours big guy? What have you said fuck it to, for me?"

"Quit chewing for you," he said matter-of-factly.

Oh no. He did.

"Wore your damn shirt. Sang your songs. Drove in your car. Don't want to be listing this shit, just pay attention, Marie. It's not a one-way street here. We're both giving and taking. Wake up."

Wake up.

Fuck.

I glared at him.

"Take me back to Headlands," I demanded.

He nodded.

We got up, waved to Genevieve, and got the fuck out of there, driving back to the compound. Not saying a word the entire time.

When he stopped the truck, I opened the door, managed out, "Thanks for the ride," and ran into the bunkhouse, down the hall, into the bedroom, which was mercifully empty, shut the door, and called Amelia.

I briefed her about our fight and she started asking questions.

"He's just so yucky conservative."

"You knew that from the first," Amelia replied.

"He referred to women as just pussy," I complained. I started pacing the room.

"We've done that," she said reasonably.

"Ugh, but it was different with him."

"We do it too, Marie. We talk about men's bodies too. Does he walk all over you?"

"No."

"Does he listen to you?" Uh, oh. She was getting into lawyer interrogation mode.

"Yes." I kept pacing.

"Does he force you to do something you don't want to do?" Major badass lawyer interrogation mode.

I blew out a breath. "No."

"Does he want you to change?"

I felt defensive. "He dared me to eat ice cream."

"A dare is different. And did you?"

"McConnell's."

"Good choice. Yum. I may have to go there with Ryan soon. Sorry, I'm digressing. He doesn't make you not be *you*, though, does he?"

"No. He takes me as I am. He just argues with me when he doesn't agree with me. But he doesn't tell me to not be me," I said in a whisper.

"There's your answer," she said gently.

Fuck. Maybe.

"How do you feel about him?"

"I only want to be with him. When we went to Tri-County, I saw Jeremy—"

She snorted. "Man Bun? How is he?"

"Well he paled in comparison to Will."

"I could have told you that."

"Actually, the cowboy is all I'm thinking about these days. And we aren't even doing it."

"Huh?"

"I told him I wanted a sex moratorium until we worked out our shit."

She laughed. "And he agreed to that?"

"Yeah."

She paused for a moment. And then she continued, rocking my world. "He loves you. Straight up. No lying. He's fallen for you. No guy, especially no tough cowboy, would give you that unless he really cared about you."

"He gave me the keys to his truck," I said in a small voice.

"Shall we start working on table arrangements for the wedding? That's my favorite part—"

"Fuck off, Amelia. Speaking of weddings, how are plans for yours?"

Giggling, she started on her favorite topic. "It's going to be sooner, rather than later. And I can't wait, honestly. My mom wants it to be all big and Ryan doesn't care, but I want it to be small and informal." She stopped. "Wait. Don't change the subject. How is the heart opening, Marie?"

"I'm working on it."

"Really?"

"Maybe."

But I stayed in the bunkhouse the rest of the night.

33

DOGHOUSE

"YOU DIDN'T COME TO me so figured I'd come to you."

The mattress dipped as Will sat on my bunk next to me, dressed, wearing boots and his green trucker hat. He was so big, he totally dominated my sleeping space.

It was early morning. Cookie's triangle hadn't rung yet. I was sleepy, bleary-eyed, and completely out of it. Janine and Stephanie slept, one of them gently snoring.

"We gotta talk about this shit. Figured I'd give you time. But I don't like you in here and not in my bed with me."

I sat up in the bottom bunk and blinked at him. This early, it was hard not to stare at him. He really was gloriously handsome, with his deep brown eyes looking concerned. He handed me a cup of coffee, which I took, silently.

"Take the time you need, Marie, but don't shut me out. Don't stay here tonight, stay with me," he said roughly. He got up off the mattress and started to walk to the door.

"Wait," I blurted. He paused, his hand on the door jamb.

"Yeah?"

"I'll stay with you tonight."

He nodded and took off down the hall, the sound of the clomping of his boots getting quieter as he got farther away.

"And maybe every night for the rest of my life," I whispered.

I took a sip of the coffee and it tasted very good.

Maybe I needed to stop thinking of excuses to get mad at him and start thinking of reasons to be with him. I knew that I'd never been with anyone like him. He was so into me and he didn't care who knew or who saw. But identifying how I felt about him? That would require honesty with myself that I wasn't sure I was ready for. I knew that he attracted me on a lot of levels. And I knew that it grew stronger each day. And I knew that he was more complicated than I allowed him to be. I'd given in and called him my boyfriend. We were together now. But admitting to myself how I felt about him? I still couldn't do it.

Then the triangle rung. I got out of bed, showered, dressed, and walked to the chow hall for breakfast.

Will sat in there with Jimmy, eating pancakes and bacon. I made instant oatmeal, added dried fruit and agave, and joined them, sitting next to Will and brushing up against him on purpose. He responded by wrapping his arm around my shoulders and giving me a squeeze.

I don't know if all was forgiven on either side. All I knew was that I liked being next to him, and he made me feel cared for and comfortable when he wasn't pissing me off.

Will and Jimmy were discussing needed maintenance around the ranch.

"You know Al Gore gets a dollar for every compact fluorescent light bulb that's sold in the US," said Jimmy.

Will laughed. "As much as I'd like to believe that, I don't think it's true. That's probably some internet shit. Some bulbs cost less than a buck. And I think they'll save us cash down the line. We might want to get LEDs, though. The prices are coming down."

So Will could think independently from the party line. I knew he had a brain. I felt heartened to see that he used it.

After breakfast, two vans pulled up with the kids, six boys from ages nine to fourteen, from the ASD program, along with their parents and therapists. The upcoming week made me nervous and I hoped that the autistic kids would find a connection forged somehow, somewhere, with something or someone.

As the children got off the van, most of them milled around, but the oldest-looking boy, jean-clad, cute, gangly, with brown hair and brown eyes, came right up to me, looking at my shoulder, struggling to make eye contact. "Hello. My name is Charles. What is your name? I have high functioning Asperger's and my father tells me to introduce myself to every adult I meet." And he shook my hand firmly, looking at my ear. I could tell that he had been told to introduce himself and make eye contact and he just couldn't. I instantly fell for him. What a sweetie.

I smiled at him and said, "Nice to meet you, Charles. Thank you for introducing yourself. My name is Marie."

I noticed that one younger boy named Travis acted particularly rambunctious, running around the area in front. But then Travis saw Will walk over with Trixie and immediately ran to her, petting her head as she wagged her tail and licked him.

I thought of something. "Will, how come you didn't dock Trixie's tail. Don't most Australian Shepherds have a docked tail?"

"Some do, some don't. Couldn't cut her tail for vanity. Seemed pretty stupid."

My heart cracked open a little bit more. Will wouldn't hurt a dog.

Travis's mother came over to me, and said, "Can the dog stay around him? He opens up around animals and . . ." She trailed off, looking close to tears.

I reached over and squeezed her hand. "Of course. I think that Will can spare Trixie for a little bit."

"'Course," he said amiably. "She'll love the attention. He can spend as much time with her as he wants. She'll be happy to stay out of the doghouse."

"She doesn't sleep in the doghouse and you know it," I said, chiding him and giving him a gentle shove on his chest.

He leaned over and whispered in my ear, "She was in the doghouse with me last night and we're not gonna do it again."

For some reason, this made me warm all over. He put a hand on my bicep, squeezed it, and he took off, loping to the barn.

34

HAPPY

LATER THAT DAY, I wandered back over to the barn to visit Happy. When I got to his stall, I noticed him pawing at the ground, agitated, sweat running off of him. This wasn't my sweet, docile horse. Something bothered him. I walked outside and called over to Will, who stood next to the corral.

"Can you come here? Is there something wrong with Happy?"

Will came jogging inside, shot into the stall, and put his ear to the horse's belly while Happy moved, agitated, and pawed the ground. He took a step back and looked at Happy, then felt under his jaw.

"Fuck."

He ran outside and called to the wranglers, who were still in the corral with the other horses. "Jimmy! Call Sully now."

Jimmy nodded and started punching numbers into his cell phone, running toward the barn.

"What's going on, Will?"

"Think he's colicking. We're in for a long ride. We gotta act now, though."

"What does that mean?"

"There are no sounds in his gut. Means it's probably not working. His pulse rate is high. Has he been eating?" he asked Jimmy, who had come inside.

"I didn't really notice, but it hasn't been as much as usual."

"Fuck, shit, damn," growled Will.

"He didn't touch his hay the other day and his stall was clean," I said.

"Oh no," whispered Janine, coming over. "Why didn't we notice?"

Jimmy explained, to me, "With animals, it's like having a baby. They can't tell you what's wrong, they can only show you that they are in distress." He paused, talking into the phone, "Dr. Sullivan, please, it's an emergency." He continued, looking at me, "There are a couple of different types of colic. If it's the impaction type, well, that means something is stuck in his system and we can flush him out with oil or water. But if it's the twisted type." He paused. "Hope it's not." Then he started speaking into the cell phone. "Sully? It's Jimmy at Headlands. I think we have a colicking horse." He walked over to the side of the barn.

"What does that mean, the twisted type?" I asked Will.

"Well, sometimes a horse can't recover from the twisted type of colic. Or it's a really expensive surgery and we don't have the budget for it. And if we can't do the surgery, it means euthanizing the horse."

Oh no. Happy. No.

No animal could get hurt on my watch. Never.

"Should we give him Banamine?" asked Janine.

"What's that?" I asked.

"It's a muscle relaxer," said Will. "It's just a Bandaid, it doesn't fix the problem. It would mask the symptoms for a while but then they might come back. Still, it might make him feel better. What did Sully say?" he asked Jimmy.

"He's on his way."

"This is gonna be a long couple of days," said Will.

Stephanie came in the barn. "Will, there's some woman from Hamilton Development here to see you."

"Just what I need," he spat, and stalked out.

"What can I do?" I asked Janine.

"Sit and wait. It's like being in the waiting room at the ER. We need to see what the vet tells us to do."

I looked out the barn door and saw Will talking with an extremely beautiful woman in black wide-legged trousers, a cream silk blouse unbuttoned one button too many, and fancy stilettos. Her hair was that sort of layered, highlighted, expensive golden blonde, and she was tall, with curves and long legs. She was completely out of place on a ranch, but she looked like she belonged talking to Will.

She represented Hamilton Development? What happened to the guys in the suits? Not that a woman can't be a developer, but she didn't look like she was his regular contact, because he shook her hand, like it was an introduction.

Then he stood back from her, arms crossed, trucker hat back on, an expressionless look on his face. She smiled at him flirtatiously and touched his bicep.

Um, no. He was mine.

He took a step back. She looked like she was pleading with him, and he relented and led her to the ranch office.

I didn't like this one bit.

I went back in the barn and waited for the vet to get there, feeling helpless. The wranglers tried to get Happy to drink, but he wouldn't do it.

About a half hour later, Dr. Andrew Sullivan walked in, a young, red-haired Irishman with freckles. He shook hands with

Jimmy, Janine, and Stephanie, and introduced himself to me, with a thick Irish accent as Sully. Then he walked over to Happy and started to examine him.

I waited to the side with the rest of the wranglers, for as long as I could stand it, then I had to leave the barn. Too much tension. It really did feel like the waiting room of an ER and we were waiting for the pronouncement by the team of surgeons. I felt like everything was crashing around me. Happy was in distress. Developers tormented Will. And I needed to deal with my shit about him.

As I walked outside, I saw the development lady stalk back to her fancy car and drive off in a huff, and then I saw Will, off to the side, his face looking thunderous. I ran over to him and tackled him, grabbing him around his waist, hugging him tightly. He squeezed me back, burying his face in my hair.

He didn't say anything, he just held me.

After a little bit, he spoke. "Don't need this shit."

"Do you want to talk about it?" I asked, nuzzling his chest.

"No," he answered in my hair. But he kept going. "I got a colicky horse. Pushy developers who want my land, thinking that some fucking cunt is going to sway me. She fucking made a pass at me just now. It's total bullshit."

Oh no. "Seriously?"

"She started taking off her shirt. Like that would convince me to sell."

Now I got pissed too. "Fucking cunt," I hissed.

"I yelled at her to get her ass out of here and she hightailed it. But shit, it's tempting to sell because they're buying up the neighbors. I could sure use the cash to pay for things like horse surgery or my mom's treatment. Can't bring myself to do it and it's killing me."

"Will, you can't sell."

"I know, darlin'."

I felt a horrible trembling come over me. Like I was going to be sick to my stomach and collapse at the same time. But I had to say it because it was true. "If you have to euthanize Happy, and I hope you don't, but I'll support you." And then I burst into tears.

He looked at me, anger dissipating, finger under my chin. "Marie." He hugged me even tighter.

"Can't believe I'd say that. Can't believe I'd think that. But I can't believe you . . . I can't, it's too hard."

"Shh, darlin'. Maybe the horse will be okay."

I sobbed, but managed out, "Maybe you can make some money and buy up the neighbors. Is that a pipe dream?"

"No, it's not. The avocados are coming in now, we should be harvesting a good crop this year. Prices are up too. It's not impossible to be able to come up with a down payment on the neighboring parcel."

"We should go talk with them," I sniffled.

He nodded. "You okay?" he asked.

"No. I feel totally responsible for Happy being sick. I saw that he hadn't eaten the other day. I should have said something sooner."

"Not your fault," he said. "It happens." He wiped away a tear on my cheek with his hands.

"I'm really not happy that some woman made a pass at my man."

"Me neither," he said. Then he stopped. "So you're admitting I'm your man?"

"Yeah," I said. "I am."

"Don't worry, I'm not lookin' at her. It's only you," he said into my hair and then he leaned down and kissed me. Then he broke apart.

"Shouldn't ask this, but I gotta. How come you got so pissed at me yesterday for using the word pussy, when you used the word cunt pretty freely right now?"

"I think I was looking for a fight and looking for an excuse to be mad at you."

He smiled. "Don't need that, do we?"

I shook my head.

"Let's see what the diagnosis is."

35

MATURE AND RESPONSIBLE

A FEW TENSE DAYS passed as Happy was given medicine, pumped with water, and we waited.

And waited.

And waited some more.

At first, he seemed to get better with the medicine.

Then he got worse.

And then it passed.

He had the impaction type of colic, thank God, not the twist. But still, it made me realize that I lived in an ideal world and I needed to sometimes go out and visit the real world. I was still going to work for my ideal world, but things in real life were messy.

I couldn't save all of the animals. I'd try to. But I couldn't.

Still, if we'd been forced to euthanize Happy, I knew that I'd have been torn apart, but I would have supported Will. I would have cried for days, but there were some grown up decisions that had to be made and that was one of them. I hated it, but it was true.

Thankfully, it didn't get that far, but it was eye-opening for me to know that I would have made that decision. I never would have thought that I would.

But I never would have thought that I'd be dating a Republican, either. Sometimes things weren't always what you thought they would be.

The kids from the ASD program were adorable. They loved riding the horses. You could tell that they were affected by the sensations of the sway of the horse, the movement of riding. While there weren't any huge breakthroughs, there were no major problems, either, and I considered that a victory.

Travis and Trixie were inseparable. Travis's mom planned on getting him an Australian Shepherd when they got back home. Will gave her the number of where he got Trixie.

When the kids were packed up in the van, Will turned to me, "One week down."

So.

That.

Since the night that I had slept in the bunk, I never went back. I slept in Will's bed every night. Every night, he gently kissed me goodnight and hugged me, but that was it. Every morning I woke up with Will's cock poking me in the back. And we didn't do anything about it.

I was sick of it. It was worse because I knew that it was my idea. And my thoughts were getting more and more sexual, since a package had arrived for me that day. I couldn't wait to use it. Still, we weren't done with the moratorium. There were some things that I had put off talking about because I was scared of the answers. No time like the present, I guess.

I turned to him and said, "When you have a second, can we talk?"

"Sure. Now?"

I nodded. We went to his house, to the back man cave with

the television, and sat on the couch. He sat next to me, pulling my legs into his lap.

"Can we have a mature discussion about politics?"

He looked at me and held my calves firmly, comfortably. "Yeah."

I reached over and touched his cheek. "Tell me why you're a Republican."

"Don't want to pay taxes."

I looked at him. He let out a breath and continued. "I guess it's just a personal responsibility thing. I'm not opposed to helping people. I do it." I nodded. "Republicans give more to charity than Democrats. But it's just that I don't like being told what to do by the government and I don't like paying for it. The social stuff—gay marriage and all that, I don't care about. Not my issue."

"What do you mean not my issue?"

"People can do what they want in their bedrooms. Don't want to tell them what to do and I don't want them telling me what to do. Don't want someone regulating my land and I don't want someone taking my money through taxes and spending it on stupid shit. Roads? Sure. Schools? Sure. But some program to do I don't know what? No. People can figure that shit out on their own without the government. I don't want to be forced to do it."

I looked at him and listened. "How can you support candidates that I detest?"

"What kind of question is that?"

"I'll rephrase. How can you support candidates who want to build a wall between here and Mexico? Who want to deport all immigrants? Who let corporations get away without paying their fair share in taxes?"

He sighed. "Do you believe in everything that your candidates believe in?"

Okay, he had a point. "No."

"I'm not gonna change that. We can go issue by issue, but I'm not going to defend everything everyone else does. Growing up as a farmer, you can't be liberal around here. Farmers are about water. You ask a farmer what a problem around here is and they are going to say liberal entitlement."

"That doesn't make logical sense, though."

He smiled. "Maybe. I don't care what others do. I'm just me."

"Anything else Mr. Thrash?"

"Probably so, darlin'. I dunno. If you want to know, ask and I'll tell you. Why are you a Democrat?"

"I want to help people. I don't think that people do it on their own and I think that they need help to do it. And I want a clean environment and sustainable future for all the generations to come."

He nodded. "Me too."

"We're not all that much different are we?" I whispered.

"No baby, it's mostly just the name. And some other shit, too," he grinned, "but we can figure that out."

Then he did this maneuver where he moved my legs off of him, laid me down on my back on the couch, and pressed himself on top of me, whole torso to whole torso, his legs between my legs. And he kissed me like he was going to love me up, but he kept his hands to my hair.

It made me hot all over and my pussy throbbed.

And this made me mad at myself. I had needed the time to cool it with Will, and to think about it, but now my body was taking over and it was not good. Days of sexual thoughts were not helping, and now having his beautiful body pressed to mine, was just too much to take.

"Get off, we can't do this for another week."

"'Kay," he said, starting to move off of me, and I grabbed him back.

"Don't go."

He laughed. "Which is it, darlin'—"

I interrupted him. "I need your fucking cock in me and I need it right now. It's been days. You better do it."

"I need it there too but we have a deal, so no."

"No? You asshole."

He looked down at me, then pressed his forehead to mine. "This was your idea. I want my end of the bargain. No. I want the 'do anything' in a week."

I shivered with the anticipation of pleasure. "You can have it now."

"No."

I shoved him by the shoulders. Of course it didn't phase him. "Stubborn fucking man."

"I'm stubborn? Look in the mirror baby."

"Asshole," I hissed.

"It's been what, a week since you called me that? We just had a mature, responsible, adult conversation about politics and I thought we made progress. So now what is it? You're so focused on the names, on the shit. What is it?" His eyes were flaring, looking at me.

I looked away from him. This was it. This was the problem. After all the names, all of the excuses, all of the shit. I couldn't open my heart to him because I had to leave.

"If I decide to be with you, what will happen to me? To us? After this summer, I mean," I blurted.

"I'll take care of you of course, we can—"

"But how is that gonna work? With me in school, I mean."

"Darlin' I love you but half the time you don't let me get a word in edgewise—"

I froze.

"What did you say?"

"You don't let me talk," he said patiently.

"The other part."

He looked me straight in the eyes, intent. "I love you, Marie. Have since the day you slammed into me gettin' outta the shower."

"You love me?" I started to shake, trembling underneath him.

"Don't you feel it too?"

I just looked at him, eyes wide, unable to answer him. "I don't know," I said in a small voice and looked around in a panic. "I need to take a break for a minute."

And he got pissed. Fast. "Shit," he spat. He got off of me and stood up. "Figure out what you feel, and when you do, come find me." And he stalked out of the room and upstairs.

Now what should I do?

My body shook and I felt close to tears. I wanted to run upstairs and talk to him. I wanted to call Amelia. I wanted to figure this out. I didn't know what to do.

Instead of doing the mature thing, I got up off of the couch and bolted out of the house, running as fast as I could to the beach.

36

LOOPHOLE

THE WAVES CRASHED on the beach and withdrew as I dug my feet into the sand. The summer sun pounded on me. I felt like the water and the sun would wash away my emotions: this agonizing need to get away from him. To escape. To get out of there. I needed time to think.

I started walking up the beach, thoughts zooming in my head, buzzing around, and not letting me rest.

Or maybe I needed to stop thinking.

Could I imagine life without Will?

No.

Turning to the waves and watching the splash of the water, I realized that answer came immediately. Even though I'd just been compelled to leave him, the thought of leaving him for real horrified me. So was that what love was?

And then I thought about him.

Not just the overwhelming physical attraction I felt to his beauty and his masculine power. But the way he'd shown me his true nature through what he'd done all summer.

He brought me vegan Republican candy.

He stuck up for Truc.

He apologized immediately when he was an unsupportive dick to me at the disastrous campfire where the fire wouldn't light, and he never did it again.

He made a hippie black and blue tie-dye with James when he didn't want to.

He wore that tie-dye the whole day in Santa Barbara, in public, in front of my ex-boyfriend, when he didn't want to.

I turned and walked the other way down the beach, looking for shells, lost in my thoughts.

He stood out under the stars with me and lay under them spooning with my friends in the back of his truck.

He was the most generous lover I had ever been with. He went down on me first, expecting nothing in return. And the most jaw-dropping, with his dark eyes, tanned skin, and cut body.

He loved his double-amputee mom who'd inspired the program I worked for.

Reaching down, I picked up a sand dollar, small and perfect, fingering it.

He gave me the key to his ridiculously huge truck.

He bought me vegan Pea Soup Andersen soup. And sweet and salty local, responsible ice cream.

He quit chewing tobacco, immediately.

He donated his property to helping kids like Charles and Janiqua. He cared. He wanted to make the world better too. He didn't want development around him. He grew organic produce. He raised his animals humanely. He ran a legacy family business with grit and pride.

Then I thought about the way he looked at me when I called him my boyfriend. The way he looked at me always.

He was incredible.

I threw the sand dollar into the surf, watching it splash.

Fuck, I was in love with him and I didn't even know it. I

couldn't admit it to myself because I had tried all summer to keep a distance, to not analyze, to not let myself fall for him. But it had happened anyway.

And I had been in love with him for a very long time.

It didn't just happen right now. It happened a while ago.

But I just realized it now.

I'd been fighting it all summer long, throwing up excuses, walls, barriers, because of fear. But now, my heart felt like it had cracked open the whole way. Amelia was right. I'd needed to open it. I'd tried to keep it shut.

But this guy had gotten through to me.

For every bit that he was gruff, he was kind. For every bit that he fought with me, it was with a twinkle in his eye—at least most of the time. He didn't care that I had my tattoos or my eyebrow ring. He didn't care that I was the daughter of migrant farmworkers. He didn't care that I swore all the time or called him names.

Maybe I should tone that down.

But he took the time to do what I wanted. He thought about me.

And I, him. I wanted him to be happy. I didn't want him worried about sick horses or a disabled mom or stupid developers or taxes or his blueberry crop. I wanted him swearing in pleasure as I sucked him off. I wanted him sleeping peacefully. I wanted *him*, period, and all the things that came with him—dog, ranch, politics, all of it.

Because I loved his dog Trixie. I loved his four-generation ranch. I loved his surly Republican-ness. I loved his efficient way of talking, using just one word if he could get away with it. I loved the way he dressed in Wranglers and boots. I loved the way he danced in dark, dusty steakhouses.

I loved the way he slept next to me, cuddling me all night long. And I loved the way he explored my body sexually, waking me up. And I loved the way he gave me the space I needed to figure this all out.

And then I started crying for real. Ugly, loud tears. Because if I loved him, then I didn't want to leave him. This pain was what I'd been protecting myself against all summer. It wasn't just sex. It was more. And I didn't want to go back to my studio in Santa Barbara. I wanted to live with him forever and love him and fight him and drool over him and lick him and have his babies. I wanted to talk with him and dance with him and eat every vegan or non-vegan meal with him.

Hell, if I really thought about it, I wanted to marry him.

And I'd never felt this way about another person in my life. That magnet that symbolized our relationship? The one where we were either completely repelled or completely together? It was turned so that we were stuck and that was it. Once I allowed the feelings to open, they were all in. All of them. I had all of the feelings for Will.

Fuck.

I turned and ran up the path to the bluff.

When I got to the top of the bluff, sweating, panting, I kept running. I ran back the trail to the compound, past the horses, and into Will's house, without knocking, without stopping, yelling, "Will! Will?"

He appeared at the top of the stairs, the hard look on his face showing me that he was still pissed at me.

So I yelled from the bottom of the stairs, "I fucking love you, Will Thrash. I've never loved anyone in my life as much as I love you. Don't you ever leave me, you asshole."

He stared at me, not saying anything. His jaw ticked.

I continued. "I'm sorry I had my head up my ass all summer. I was scared and I didn't know what to do. You make me feel like home. You comfort me. You protect me. I don't hide anything from you."

He gripped the top of the stairs, not moving, not saying anything.

"I love you. Say something, goddamn it."

His eyes were the darkest I'd ever seen them, his hair wild and so sexy. "You gonna change your mind again, Marie?"

"Never," I said fiercely.

He let go of the bannister and took a step back, shaking his head. "You gonna keep looking for a fight?"

"Not intentionally."

He stared at me. "You gonna quit pushing me away?"

"Yes," I gasped.

"Then c'mere, baby," he said, and those were the sweetest words I'd ever heard.

And I ran up the stairs and into his open arms.

"I love you too," he said, "and I will never leave you." And he held me as I crashed into him, kissing him with whatever breath I had left after my run from the beach. He lifted me up and I wrapped my legs around him, holding him as close as I could, and he spun me around, then pressed me against the wall.

I broke our kiss, still crying, a total mess. "Don't make me go away at the end of summer," I sobbed into his shoulder. "Let me stay with you. I can't go. I can't be away from you." He held me against the wall and kissed me again. Then he let me down, but still kept his arms around me, his face the most beautiful thing I'd ever seen. And his next words made me feel a sweet relief, like all the burden of the summer had lifted.

"Then don't. Stay here. I'll take care of you. You can get your degree—it's not that long of a commute—and set up your therapy practice and do whatever you want. You can see your friends whenever they want."

I took a deep breath. "I'm moving in."

He blew out his breath as a sigh of relief. "About time."

"Are we still waiting out the week?"

"Yeah." He paused. "But I'm not opposed to engaging in the loophole, though."

"What looph—" I paused. "Oh."

"Come on in the shower," he said, "and we'll get the sweat off of you and the dust off of me. But no touching."

"Okay," I said. "Just like when we first met."

He grinned.

37

SPILL

"WHAT DO YOU THINK of your experiment, Marie? Your two-week sexual hiatus?" asked Will.

"We still have a week to go," I answered, snuggling into him, front to front, my head in his bare chest, in his antique bed that night. I felt comfy in my light pink tank top and blue plaid pajama shorts. We were both peaceful now, having picked enough fights with each other for the time being. "It's too early to tell. So far so good. You're overwhelming, big guy. The sex is too good." I looked up and could see the smirk on his face. "I needed to take a break to sort out my head. But it seemed to work."

He leaned over and kissed me. "Yeah," he said. "You did. You finally get your shit together?"

I nodded. "I think so. I've never been like this. I've never allowed a guy in or anyone, really. I don't know, I just somehow got the idea that I needed to be fun all the time. But if you're fun all the time, you don't get to the deeper stuff. It's like all desserts and no vegetables. I'd never really let myself be open with another person, except for Amelia, and that's different. Sure, I had crushes, and sure I had liked guys and had sex—"

"Not sure I wanna hear this part," he complained, eyes amused.

"But no one, ever, has made me feel the way you do. I dated a lot. I partied a lot. I laughed and drank and had fun. It was all light, though. There was no depth to it. I never fell. Not for real, in a sense that was open and honest. No one ever showed me the stars like you do."

He squeezed me. "I get it, darlin'."

"So we're going to keep this moratorium up for another week?" I asked.

"Yeah." He lazed a hand down my arm.

"Why?"

"I think we agreed on it so we should do it," he responded, his eyes liquid. "I want us to keep our promises to each other."

I liked that answer. Still. "Did we cheat in the shower?"

He grinned his half-smile. "I didn't fuck you, so no." And he kissed me. When we broke apart, I had to find my breath.

"Okay," I agreed.

In the shower, he hadn't touched me and I didn't touch him, but it was hot. Seeing him take care of himself while I took care of myself? Erotic as hell. Both of us looking into each other's eyes, the water flowing around us, the need there, but no touching each other. It felt intimate in a way I'd never been intimate before. That was definitely part of the reason why we were both so relaxed right now. That, and finally confessing our feelings for each other.

Now that I realized it, I'd felt my extraordinary feelings for him all along. I was just a dumb shit for not identifying them and for thinking of reasons to not let them in.

So where would we go from here?

Curiosity came over me. "Are you going to tell me what you are going to do to me on Friday? What is the anything?"

He kissed me softly, ran his finger down my cheek, and said with his lowest voice, "If I had to pick right now? Making love to you, very slowly, taking my time, exploring your body with my mouth and my fingers and then my cock, making you hum, then making you come. Games can wait."

Fuck me. "That'd work," I muttered, nonchalantly, and totally faking it. Then I snuggled into him again. "But no. I want to see you kinky. You've held back with me. I want to see it."

He buried his nose in my hair and said, "You want it, you got it. I'll have to go to the store. Need supplies. But I'm not telling. Man's gotta have some secrets."

"No he doesn't. Spill."

"Nope."

Shit.

Cuddling with my cowboy, I took a moment to acknowledge how good it felt to be in the arms of this good man that I loved— yes, loved, but who also could work my body the way he did.

It felt like I had completely shed myself of a layer of old, dead skin that didn't fit me anymore. Sure, there were more layers underneath, but it felt like I had unburdened myself from some of my crap. And to know that he loved me back, and had been showing it practically since we met? Awesome.

And I was thrilled beyond belief to find out what he planned next. We went to sleep and when we woke up, we spent most of the rest of the weekend together. He did the rounds of the ranch Saturday morning, and we both checked on Happy, for whom the crisis had passed, although we were still on alert.

Saturday afternoon, after lunch with his parents, he took me for a walk along the beach with Trixie. He brought a tennis ball with him and threw it for Trixie to catch. At one point, he threw it, and Trixie ran in the water on her way to catch it and got totally wet, coming back and shaking all over us. We kept our hands off of each other, but I'll admit that it was harder than usual to do so, seeing him all wet in a white t-shirt sticking to his farm boy sculpted torso.

Later on, we drove to Ryan's beach house to join him and Amelia for dinner, taking advantage of the classic California summer evening, clear and comfortable at the beach, with a slight breeze. I didn't know how Amelia hooked one who could cook and liked to do so, but Ryan cooked for all of us while Amelia and I sat outside on the deck, gossiping, catching up, watching the surf and surfers, and drinking chilled white wine. Ryan cooked barbecued chicken. He was so sweet, though, because the rest of the meal was vegan, with a lentil salad, herbed rice, a huge green salad, and a vegan cake from Trader Joe's, a place that was apparently an obsession of his. He also refused help from anyone. While the girls were outside, Trixie curled up at Will's feet, who sat on a bar stool inside, drinking beer and talking to Ryan about farming.

Amelia went on for at least twenty minutes about the table settings for her wedding, but she didn't seem to care too much about the dress, cake, guest list, or anything else. That was my girl.

"So you're going to be my maid of honor, right?" she finally asked me.

"Girl? I thought you'd never ask. Although that's not really asking, that's telling. You've been hanging around a bossy guy too long."

She laughed. "Bossy guys can be hot if they love you." Then she continued. "I'm so glad you got your head out of your ass, girl. What the fuck? How come you took so long to get it about your cowboy god? I knew it when we visited."

"At first I didn't want to because he can be such an asshole. And then I didn't want to because he's a Republican asshole, and that's worse. And then I didn't want to because, well, I didn't. I don't know. I started thinking that if I really liked him, I had to leave at the end of summer and I didn't want to fall for someone that hard if it's just a summer thing."

"Ever since I've known you," she said, "you've been the crazy party girl that everyone adored, but no one really knew. I got in there early and I've stayed there. No one else that I know of has. I'm glad that Will broke through. He's a keeper."

I nodded. He was.

38

TRUST

"JUST FIVE MORE DAYS," I whispered Sunday night, lying in bed, leaning up against Will. "The kids leave after breakfast on Friday."

"Yeah," he answered, in his low rumble, against my neck, as he sucked on it, gliding his fingers up and down my bare arm. Letting out a sigh, he wrapped his arms around me in a big bear hug. "They gotta get here first, though." He squeezed me tight. "We got this." I relaxed and enjoyed his comforting warmth, trying to not think any more about the self-imposed sexual moratorium, and then drifted to sleep.

The next morning, a group of kids arrived at Headlands. They were entirely different than any previous group. This time we had twenty-five twelve and thirteen year olds from a Boys and Girls Club in East Los Angeles. Given the demographics of the area, I expected that they would all be Hispanic like me, and they were.

When the bus arrived, the children and leaders spilled out and I repeated the drill that I had done with the other groups, waving and enthusiastically greeting them. I noticed, immediately, that this group seemed quieter than the group from

Oakland, the kids keeping amongst themselves, not chattering as much, and giving each other space, rather than mingling together.

One nervous-looking girl came up to me in the bunkhouse hall after she had set her duffle bag, sleeping bag, and pillow on a bottom bunk in the room. "I don't want to leave my things here. The door to the room doesn't lock."

"It'll be safe, don't worry," I said.

She just looked at me. "Don't you have someplace, you know, safe, I can put them?"

"They'll be safe here," I repeated, and she looked at me skeptically and took off back down to the room. But she made me think. What would it be like if I didn't feel safe? If I didn't trust? Like how I trusted Will?

When they finished we went outside.

"Okay, guys," I said. "We are going to play a name game so that I can know who you are and what you like to do." I explained the game. We would go around in a circle and take turns saying our name and our favorite hobby. "I'm Marie and I like to eat vegan food."

The girl next to me, pretty, with shoulder length dark hair and glasses, said, "I'm Josephine and I like to listen to music, and this is Marie and she likes to eat vegan food." Then we continued with the next child, and so on.

Once we had gotten most of the way around the circle, the kids were starting to giggle at everyone's hobbies: "I like to eat gummy bears," "I like to play video games," "I like to watch YouTube," "I like to sleep in." Will walked by toward the end and I invited him to join us. Because he came in late to the game, he didn't have the advantage of hearing everyone repeating all the names twenty times. He tried to remember the children's names and failed miserably. "This is, uh, Danny—"

"David!" piped up a tiny boy in a Dodger t-shirt.

"Yeah, David, and he likes to play baseball—"

"No, play football."

I could see Will trying not to swear.

But he played along, asking David why he wore a baseball shirt if he liked football.

"Because it's baseball season."

God, I loved my cowboy.

When we were done, I strode over to Will and whispered in his ear, "I think that participation in a name game earns you an extra treat on Friday."

"Holdin' you to that one," he responded, looking me in the eye, making me shiver even though it was hot out, and then sauntering to his truck.

"FOUR DAYS, DARLIN'," Will whispered in my ear that night as he spooned behind me. His breath against my neck set off a chain reaction of sensations in my body that wound up making me tense between my legs. "Nice work with the campfire tonight."

"Thanks," I whispered back. I flopped over and ran my fingers over his nipples and his pecs. But then he kissed me and that got a little out of control, tongues touching tongues, and we both had to pull back, breathing heavy.

We looked at each other.

"Night," I said hastily, at the same time that he said, "Night." He tucked me into him to go to sleep, both of us ignoring the feelings that were building: I had a wet throbbing between my legs and my breasts were heavy, and I could feel him poking me in the back, poor guy. I sighed and went to sleep.

The next day after breakfast, I took the kids to the corrals and they rode the horses under the watch of the wranglers.

I needed a break, so I ran into the ranch house, wandered

down the hall, and opened the bathroom door to use it and collided into a naked, wet, William Charles Thrash III, owner of Headlands Ranch, standing, dripping shower water on a bath mat.

Figured.

He took one look at me, and his immediate pissed off look morphed into a full-on, out of control, male laugh, making him hold his toned tummy.

"You ever gonna learn to fucking knock?" he finally managed, wrapping a towel around his pelvis and then pulling me close to him. "Shit."

I'd lost control laughing, too, and hugged him back, probably drying him off in the process. "I don't think so. Especially not if these are the goodies I'm gonna get. Just lock the door if you don't want me barging in."

"Wish I could lock the door right now."

I had received a good eyeful of Mr. Will and I could tell that he was starting to get ideas. Or he had them already. It wasn't getting any easier to stay away from him. So I kissed him quickly, wriggled out of his grasp, and hightailed it out of there, finding the other bathroom.

On Wednesday morning, I sat next to Will in the chow hall for breakfast, Josephine sitting across from me and David sitting next to her. They were chattering about their favorite horses. As usual, Will pressed his leg against mine the entire meal, although he did glance disgustedly at my muesli and soy milk, shaking his head.

The schedule was horses in the morning, lunch, and then a group games session. "Alright everyone, gather around," I called to the kids. "We're going to do something called a trust fall."

Grouping the children and leaders into two units, I instructed them. "We are going to take turns experiencing what it feels like to fall and have someone catch you. You are going to close your eyes, cross your arms over your chest, and fall backwards, trusting that everyone will keep you from falling. Have any of you ever done that before?"

I received some blank stares and a few heads shaking.

"It will be a new experience, then, but I think it's important to try it. And it's important to know that everyone here will support everyone else. Josephine, if David asked you if you would let him fall, would you?"

"No," she answered. "I would catch him if I could."

"Good," I said. "You will have help. You don't have to do it alone. Now, this is scary. It is normal for it to feel scary. It will feel like you are free falling. You have to trust. But I want everyone to tell me, individually, that you will catch whoever is going to fall."

"David, would you catch whoever is going to fall?"

"Yes."

We did it. The feeling of having to trust, having to close your eyes, and just fall—I figured that these kids had never experienced that before. I did it too, going into one group, and falling backwards, feeling a dozen pairs of hands hold me up.

Hands held every individual up.

Exactly the way Will held me up.

Exactly the way we all need to hold each other up and learn to trust. Learn to earn that trust and learn to accept that trust.

When the hands returned a person gently to a standing position, almost everyone had a look of delight on his or her face.

Awesomesauce. They were starting to bond.

By Thursday afternoon, the kids were grooming horses, feeding chickens, mucking out stalls, and running free. They laughed, told stories, teased each other, made tie-dyes, and helped. It was a good week.

But I couldn't wait for it to be over.

On Friday morning, everyone packed up, and they left after breakfast, smiling and waving goodbye.

Then the staff who had days off took off. All I could think about was my cowboy.

And then I went to find Will over by the barns, my heart rate elevated, my panties wet, from thinking all morning about what he was going to do. He wasn't in the barn when I called, so I went over to the tack room, but he wasn't in there either. As I went to leave, I saw him standing in the doorway, a look on his face that I could only describe as desire.

Our two weeks were up.

39

KINKY

"WHAT THE HELL DO you have there?" I cried, staring at Will, who stood in the doorway of the tack room.

Bridles and reins hung on hooks all around the large tack room, which was sparsely furnished with a table, chair, and a few sawhorses. Extra bales of hay sat in a corner. Now that the kids were gone, most of the staff had taken off, we were alone in the tack room, and we had the ranch to ourselves.

We'd made it the two weeks. Sleeping together every night, I felt closer to him than I'd felt to another human being, ever; we'd kissed, we'd hugged, we'd caressed. But despite our insistent mutual attraction, there'd been no sex, no fucking, no making love.

And we were ready to explode.

Will had on a tight, dark blue, faded t-shirt, jeans, belt, boots, and a Justin trucker hat that crushed his unruly hair. He held a plastic bag from a drug store, a blanket, and something that looked like a dead animal. He turned around and closed and locked the door.

Oh, shit.

"Deal was," he said, stalking over to me, "we went two weeks without fucking, I get to do anything I want to you, except hurt you."

"Uh-huh," I managed.

"It's been two weeks. You up for it?"

I nodded. He'd stunned me into silence. I'd been turned on for days. I had been wet for the past hour. I wanted him and I wanted him now.

"Now's the time for kinky. Take your clothes off, Marie," he commanded. "Now."

He took a Pendleton blanket and spread it out on the ground. "Stand on this. You should know. If you want me to make love to you, right now, I will, wherever you want. But you wanted to see kinky. So, this is what is kinky to me."

He continued. "Gonna tie you up. Wanna take you to the edge, a time or two, but not let you come. But you gotta trust me that I'm gonna let you, eventually, after I play with you for a bit, and it will be massive."

I looked him in his gentle, chocolate brown eyes, trusting him with everything. Trusting him with me. I wanted him to feel like he could show me all parts of him, even those secret parts about what turned him on, what made him crazy. I loved all of him and I wanted to see all of him.

"Let's do it," I said. *Show me what turns you on.*

He smiled warmly and then his features changed and he looked at me fixedly.

Then, not breaking my gaze, I licked my lips.

I reached down and unbuttoned the buttons on my western-style shirt, one at a time, slowly, watching him the entire time. I eased my shirt off of one arm, then another, and I set it gently on a nearby table. Then I shuffled out of my vegan boots and socks, and onto the blanket. I unbuttoned my tight Wrangler jeans—the ones from high school, unzipped them, and eased them down over my hips and down my long legs.

I stood there, looking at him, bleached hair over my shoulders, wearing a fuchsia pink demi-bra and matching Brazilian cut panties, dying for him to touch me.

He stood there, looking back at me, eyes wide.

Then he took the furry thing, some sort of animal hide, and spread it on the nearby bales of hay.

"Is that a dead animal?"

"Relax. It's fake. Feel it."

I leaned over and felt the velvety blanket. I could deal with faux fur.

"Are you going to put on a cowboy hat?" I teased him. "Because if you're going for a weird dom/sub fantasy thing, I want you in a cowboy hat and no shirt."

"'Kay," he said, and strode over to another part of the tack room. He came back, holding a black cowboy hat. He set it down, took off his trucker hat, shrugged off his t-shirt, and put the cowboy hat on, low down on his face. In a trucker hat, he just looked like a hot guy. But in a cowboy hat? He looked dangerous. So heavenly tall, so muscular, in jeans, boots, and a black cowboy hat, his beautiful torso on display, his face a combination of turned on and amused, his dark eyes intense. All I could think was holy shit, my cowboy in all of his glory.

"I said clothes off, but I think I'll help you with this," he said. And then he pulled a folded dark blue bandanna out of the back of his pocket. "Think you need to have some sensory deprivation. You trust me?"

"I do," I said. "You know I do. I'm just fucking turned on."

"Good. Me too. Now I'm not gonna let you come right now. But I promise I will and it'll be really good."

"And then?"

"Fuck you 'til you scream," he answered, huskily, in my ear, as he tied the bandanna around my eyes, and my legs almost buckled.

I nodded, unable to process, unable to do anything else. I managed out a whisper, "What's in the bag?"

"Lube and a remote control vibrator from Rite Aid. And extra batteries."

"They sell vibrators?"

"You'd be amazed what you can get at a drug store these days."

Standing in the tack room, in my bra and panties, on a summer day, with no one around, felt incredibly naughty, mostly because it was a public place where any of the wranglers could walk in. But with the door locked, we should be fine. I hoped. It still felt like it heightened the anticipation, like we could get caught.

My pulse started to race and my breathing got shallow.

I didn't know where he was at first, he didn't make a sound. I suppose he just stood there, gazing at me, and the thought made my nipples pucker. I fidgeted and let out a breath.

Then I felt him behind me, and his hand pushed aside my hair and I felt his lips on the back of my neck, a wet kiss. His hands traveled down my arms lightly, making me have goosebumps.

"Can smell you," he said. "It's fantastic. How long have you been wet?"

"All day," I admitted.

"Wanted to be balls deep inside you for two weeks now and fighting off being hard for an hour. So fucking turned on." Without any trouble, he unhooked my bra and released my heavy breasts, pulling the straps down one arm, and then the other. Then I could feel his rugged hands on my side, tracing my tattoo, going down, down, down, lower, and hooking into the sides of my panties and taking them off as I shifted to help him.

So now I was naked and blindfolded in a barn, with Will shirtless, wearing a cowboy hat.

The goosebumps increased.

"Spread your legs," he said and I felt him behind me, the presence of his body brushing against mine. With one hand, he started kneading my breast, teasing the nipple, caressing it, as he stood behind me and started sucking on my neck—deep, warm kisses. Then his other hand snaked around my other side and made its way down the middle of my torso, until he reached my pussy, kissing my neck the whole time, his bicep muscles holding me still.

"Goddamn," he said against the skin right below my ear, "you are so wet." And he started rolling a finger around my clit, against it, teasing it, reaching around and working on the other breast as he attended to the sensitive skin on my neck with his lush mouth, pressing his erection into my back. I kept wriggling and collapsing into him, my pussy starting to spasm, it felt so good all over. Each kiss from him was a sensuous attack, an assault on my senses, and I couldn't stay still to take it. I had to move. But it felt so exquisite to be touched by him after we'd been hands off for two weeks, and I let out an involuntary moan.

"Wanna try something," he whispered, and came around my front. Since I lost his lips on my neck and his fingers on my clit, I whimpered. But then he stepped forward and crashed his lips into mine, one hand on my ass, one hand pulling me to him. Both of my hands shot up into his thick hair, knocking his hat off of him. I let one hand stay there, at the nape of his neck, holding him to me; the other went down his broad back to his ass, and lingered there and I pressed him into me, feeling his hard ass, pressing his cock into my stomach.

Then he broke apart from my lips, nibbled his way down my jaw and neck and bit me very gently where my neck met my shoulder.

Oh!

He made his way with his mouth down the middle of my torso, stopping to lick and suck on each nipple in turn, making them hard, leaving them wet and glistening. Then he kept going down my middle, inserting his tongue in my belly button. His tongue kept going, down, down, and he pushed my legs farther apart, using his fingers to spread my pussy, tonguing me as far as he could go.

But then I lost his tongue, and he walked around behind me. "Bend over, darlin'" and then he licked my pussy starting from where he had stopped on the other side, continuing between my ass, all the way up my spine to my neck.

Holy shit.

"Needed a taste of you all over. You opposed to getting tied up?"

I shook my head.

"I'll guide you. C'mere." And he picked me up behind my knees and my shoulders, and laid me gently down on the squashy fur blanket on the hay. "Hands together, baby," he said, and I put my wrists together in front of my belly. He took them, gently, and wrapped something around it, by the smell it must have been leather.

"What is that?"

"Reins."

He wrapped the leather around my hands gently, but firmly, and then hoisted my hands over my head. "Keep 'em here for now," he said. "Need a pillow?"

I was actually comfortable on the blanket and I shook my head.

Then I could feel him taking my ankle and wrapping something around it. A rope? He slipped a knot around it and then left. "Tying you to the hook on the wall," he informed me.

He repeated this with the other ankle, apparently tying me to the adjacent wall.

So now I lay there spread out in Will's tack room, bound with ropes and reins, blindfolded, covered in his saliva.

My stomach went up and down as I tried to breathe.

I heard the bag rustle.

"You're so wet, you don't need the lube, but you're gonna have to guide me here on where it feels best."

I heard a small buzzing, and then a vibration against my pussy. He gently skipped it around, looking, I think, for the right place to put it. Some places he put it, I swear, if he'd kept it there for five seconds, I'd've come. Others simply felt good. The only way I communicated this to him was by moaning when it was in the extraordinary places. But then he took it and slipped it inside me, saying, "We'll keep this on the lowest setting for now."

Oh, my.

I could feel my muscles massaged by the vibrator, the clenching of my pussy, the pleasure starting to build.

"This is a little buddy with a remote control," he said, "and I can make it stronger if I want," and he did something to make it vibrate harder and faster.

Uh, uh, uh, uh, uh. I was starting to forget how to think. I was starting to do nothing but concentrate on the feelings in my pussy. I couldn't see anything, I couldn't move, all I could do was feel.

But then the vibrations went back down to a dull roar, with him controlling the setting and lowering the pressure.

And then his tongue landed on my clit.

And then he set off a chain reaction of all-consuming pleasure in my body.

I couldn't wiggle, I couldn't really move, my legs were strung up like some sort of weird trussed animal, I could only move my arms up and down, so I left them up over my head, and I struggled with the restraints.

Holy shit.

I was going to blow over big.

My body trembled, the muscles in my stomach tensed, my shoulders pressed into the fur, my triceps died for relief.

And Will licking my pussy with the vibrator inside was just too much, and then . . .

He stopped and pulled the vibrator out.

"You fucker, that was gonna be good."

"I know. Wait." My pussy felt cool and wet, and he blew on it.

Then he inserted a finger in me, gently exploring, gently massaging, gently rolling around, and his tongue teased me again, building me up, and I wiggled, shaking in the restraints.

And then he stopped.

"AAAAAAHHHH!" I yelled.

He chuckled.

"Will, you asshole, you better let me come."

"I will, darlin'." And he leaned over and licked my pussy again, this time long, laving strokes of his tongue, all broad and covering the territory. Ohmigod. This could make me come. And he did it repeatedly. And then—

No.

He stopped.

"Bastard!"

He pulled back and then I heard him walk away, rustle the bag, and come back.

My body jerked, the need for release real, palpable.

This sucked.

And it was also sublime.

And then I felt the ropes slacken on my legs and he pulled my legs together, tying my ankles to each other.

Sitting next to me, he gathered me up in his arms when he

finished, my legs in his lap, my breathing restored, and said, "Can you sit?"

"Yeah."

"I'm gonna put lube on your beautiful tits. And put the little buddy back in."

I sat on the fur on the hay bale, ankles tied together, and spread my knees so that he could put the vibrator back in me, which he did on a slightly higher speed than before, setting the remote control next to my hip.

I felt the preorgasm blossoming again. Oh, God, I needed it.

"Want the blindfold off?"

I nodded. I liked it, but I wanted to see him.

He reached around me, and took it off, and the first thing I saw was his face right in front of mine, those handsome brown eyes, those cheekbones, those lips, that jaw, that hair, right there.

And he kissed me, licking my tongue, wet meeting wet, the taste of me on him. Then he bit my lower lip gently.

The stronger setting on the vibrator brought me close to a real, fucking hard orgasm yet again.

He stepped back, still in his jeans, still in his boots, K-Y in his hands. "Gonna lube you up," he said, and squirted a little in his fingers. Then he rubbed it between my breasts.

"Will, I want to help you out of your pants, but I can't," I complained.

"Don't need help with that. Just keep your hands in your lap and squeeze your hot as fuck tits together with your arms."

The vibrator kept going. My pelvic muscles shaking. My shoulders danced.

He walked over and put the cowboy hat back on. Then he stood in front of me, unhooked his belt buckle, unbuttoned his pants, and slid down his jeans. He shucked off his boots and his socks, and took everything off, and walked toward me, kissing me deeply again.

"How you doin' with our little buddy? Okay?"

I nodded.

"Gonna titty fuck you then bend you over."

"Whatever you say," I gasped.

He stood before me, and then leaned over and put his cock between my breasts. I squeezed them together with my arms, unable to touch him, unable to feel him, my hands tied together with the reins still, and he let out a groan.

"Fuck yeah, baby," he growled, as he went faster and faster between my breasts. His cock hit my mouth and I opened it, to lick the tip, to let him in as he rubbed himself against me up and down, the vibrator in me pulsing.

And then, after a few more thrusts, he stepped away, turned me around, still bound, held my hands over my head, bent me over the blanket on the hay, popped out the vibrator, spread my knees, and thrust in.

There was no other way to describe it—he was banging me in the tack room.

After thrusting hard for a while, he slowed his pace, snaking a finger down to my clit. "I could go on, but I think I'll let you come now."

He rubbed me on the outside of my pussy, while filling me from within, and the tension built up, and oh, oh, oh, finally, finally, a release. I screamed, my body vibrating, my pussy vibrating, my hips raised and pressed against him, riding out the biggest orgasm in the history of the planet. It tilted the galaxies.

I saw stars.

But he didn't let go, and another one was on its heels and holy shit, I came again, not as big but sweet and beautiful, and I screamed again.

After all this time, after this wait, after all the tension that we felt over the past two weeks, having him inside me was so heavenly, hitting the right parts, repeatedly, over and over, as he fucked me against the hay.

Fucking brilliant.

He didn't last long, slippery from my juices and the lube, and hard for days. He increased his thrusting into me at a serious, marked pace, all the feelings, all the nerves tingling, and then he released in a huge shudder, collapsing into my back, pushing me into the blanket.

We breathed together, his flat belly going into my butt, his chest on my back, his mouth on my neck.

After a bit, he pulled out and ran his hands down my sides.

Then he untied my wrists, massaging them gently. And then he untied my ankles, doing the same. And then he gathered me, naked, into his lap as he sat down on the hay, my arms wrapped around him, my legs across his lap. I snuggled into his neck and kissed it, knocking his hat off again.

"That wasn't all that kinky, Will."

He smiled. "I know. I was breaking you in. That was only the first round."

40

EQUAL

WILL STOOD NAKED IN my room in the bunkhouse, his toned torso glistening from the warmth of a summer's day and the activities from earlier, his hands tied to the top bunk, his cock hard, a satisfied growl emanating from his throat.

To rewind.

After the trussed chicken routine in the tack room, we both felt much more relaxed than we had been for two weeks. I also felt really close to him. We'd made it through our initial attraction, the questioning because of our beliefs, the passion of getting together, but also the reevaluation of whether we should be together. It felt like we had shown each other ourselves and both of us liked the other. Loved the other. It felt like we were unafraid to be who we really were with each other, because we trusted that the other one would accept us for who we are. Will didn't care that I cussed at him all the time or got mad at him for his politics. He wasn't going to change them for me, but he also didn't make me change for him. And despite neither of us asking the other to change, both of us had changed for the other.

As silent as he was, he had a way of showing me that he had the biggest heart of anyone I had ever met. He didn't brag about it, he barely talked about what he did, but his actions spoke volumes.

Oh, and he took care of my body like no one ever had before.

I had sat, nude, snuggled in his lap on the hay bale, tracing his arms, tracing his side, tracing his face with my fingertips. He put his chin on the top of my head and said, "God, you're spectacular. You're the whole thing, Marie. The whole thing."

This just made me snuggle into him more, which was barely possible. I pressed my eyes shut to keep any tears from forming.

"I love you too," I whispered, and he squeezed me tight.

I heard his heartbeat against my ear, felt his arms around me, and clung to him, my ark, for a long time. I had never felt safer with another person. After we'd settled down from the intensity of our sex, I kissed him, long and wet, then I climbed up, and started getting dressed, stepping into my panties and pulling them up, then my jeans. He watched me for a moment, then arose to get dressed himself.

As I slid my bra straps up my arms, I informed him, "You know, I have a kinky side too."

He let out a chuckle and grabbed his jeans, putting them on.

"Yeah? You gonna show me?"

I buttoned up my shirt and smoothed out my hair. "What I need to figure out is how much *I* can push *you*?"

He leaned over, hands buttoning his fly, and kissed me gently. "Pretty far, I'd say."

"I bought you a present," I told him slyly.

"Yeah?" He pulled on his t-shirt.

"A sexual present." He got his head through the neck hole of his shirt and stopped, an eyebrow raised.

"Now I'm really interested."

I smiled at him. "It's in my room."

He nodded and looked thoughtful.

We finished getting dressed. Will hung up the reins, I folded the blanket and grabbed the items he had bought, and together, we put the tack room back together. Then, hand in hand, carrying the blanket and bag and faux fur, we strolled over to the bunkhouse.

"We should move you in with me," he mused, as he glanced around my room with all of the bunk beds, "'specially now that we gotta week off before the next set of kids come."

My stomach got all nervous and tingly and butterfly-ey. Moving in with Will. Letting go of my studio in Santa Barbara. Commuting to my master's program. All of it. Stomach freaking out. I aimed for cool, but probably failed miserably. "We're gonna do this?"

"You don't wanna?"

I let out my breath. It was a big step, but yeah, I wanted to stay with him. Forever. So, I smiled, and said bravely, with as much nonchalance as I could muster, "Fine by me." Then I thought of something. "We didn't get to christen this room."

He leaned over and spoke low in my ear. "No one's around."

God, he always could make me shiver. Then I looked at him and smiled. "Okay. Do you want to get cleaned up first?"

"I'll go get a washcloth. We can shower after." He purloined one of mine, went down the hall, and came back with it, dampened. "Strip," he ordered.

I smiled at him. "Not so fast, Mister. This is my turf. I'm in charge now." That eyebrow of his got raised, with amusement. "This is the way you're going to try out being a feminist, Will. Let me try something on you that I think you've never done before. Equal play, bub. If you don't like it, fine. We'll stop," and I opened up the brown package and took out the tiny, purple plastic toy, putting it in his hand.

Chuckling, he said, "A butt plug?"

"Have you ever used one?"

"Sure." Interesting.

"On you?"

He looked taken aback. "Uh, no."

"This one is for you."

He looked at me incredulously. Then he burst out laughing, the big, full-on male laugh that I'd only heard a few times.

I pushed him in the chest. Hmm. Yum. His chest. "Try it. You're sexually adventuresome. You're open in bed. Try it. No one has to know. This one is supposed to be for guys."

He shoved his hands in his pockets, scuffed his boots on the floor, and looked up at the ceiling.

I kept going. "I'd never been tied up before like that. No one had ever tried to *not* give me an orgasm before. This isn't going to suddenly make you not you, it's just an experi—"

"Shit. Okay," he interrupted.

"Okay?"

"Yeah. Just don't fuckin' emasculate me."

I looked him straight in the eye. "That will never happen. This is the type of feminism where you get a blow job, which I'll admit is kind of strange, but it's because I want to do it, not because you're telling me to do it."

"Darlin'?"

"Yes?"

"Sign me up."

But I was serious about this issue. Will had said that he wasn't a feminist, but he never did anything to make me feel lesser than him. He was just all dude, all man, all guy, and he liked to drive. I think he just had a problem with the label, but not the concept. I felt like I had plenty of say around him. Sex and politics could get messy, and Will and I lived in that messy world, and I didn't know if we would ever leave it, or indeed, agree on everything. But I didn't care anymore. He was a loving, caring soul, and generous and gentle. The label that he liked didn't matter, just as the labels I liked didn't matter.

Well, they mattered less to me than they did before.

What this meant was simple: I wanted the chance to be in charge. I knew what I liked, sexually, and I let him push me on all fronts and I liked it when he took control. It was fucking hot. But now I wanted the chance to push him, to see how he would take it.

"Strip, cowboy," I ordered.

"Shit, is it gonna be like that?" he muttered. But he said it with a smile and started taking off his boots.

"Yep. Now, gorgeous."

His shoes shucked off, his shirt, gone, his pants a distant memory, he stood before me, all brawny guy, and my own personal sexual playground.

God, this was fun.

"I want to tie you up."

He snorted. "Seriously?"

"Yep," I said, and I pulled out a cotton, woven belt of mine, with rings for a closure, from the chest of drawers.

"Now how ya gonna do that, darlin'?" he asked, teasing me.

"Hands together." And he put his wrists together in front of him. I wrapped the belt around his wrists, and then fastened it to the top bunk behind his head. "You okay?" I asked.

"I think so, yeah," he said. "This is fucking weird."

Using the washcloth he'd dampened, I cleaned him off, which had the added bonus of making him fully aroused. I washed him and stroked him.

All clean and wet, I licked the tip of his cock, and he let out a groan. I let my lips go all over the place, tonguing his balls, licking the entire length, getting his taste in my mouth. I played with him, teasing him. His hands over his head, he leaned away from them and toward me, letting me love him up.

But then I took the lube out of my back pocket, and he looked down at me, heated, but leery.

"If you don't like it, you don't have to do it, and I'll never tell a soul."

He nodded.

I reached between his legs, with my fingers, and explored. When I got to the right spot with my finger, he hissed at me, but didn't object. I put even more lube on my hand and played with him, while I sucked on his cock, and he moaned in pleasure.

Then I got out his little toy, lubed it up, and carefully reached around and inserted it.

"*Fuck*," he said loudly.

"You okay?" I asked.

"Yeah," he said. "More than."

"It feel good?"

"Yeah," he answered. "Different sensation. Fucking hell."

"Okay, darlin', here we go for reals," I said, and I started sucking on him in earnest. I kept going and going, using my hands, using my tongue, using my lips, using my throat, until he came, shuddering, into my mouth, and collapsed, leaning against the restraints, my shoulders holding him up.

I carefully removed the plug and wiped my hands off on the washcloth. Then I stood up and untied him.

And then he grabbed me in the biggest hug I'd ever received from him, his eyes gratified, his voice low, saying, "That was phenomenal, babe. I've never come so hard. Fuck, I love you."

We got him dressed again and lay down on my bunk for a while, just holding each other.

And then he helped me pack up and move into his house for real.

41

I JUST WANT TO DANCE WITH YOU

A S I TRUDGED THE last suitcase into Will's house, I started, "Now for that next kinky round—" but he interrupted me.

"Christ, give me a Gatorade," he groaned. "I have stamina, but shit, a man needs recovery time. I'm not fifteen."

I giggled. "We could go to a health food store and get you ginseng." He raised an eyebrow. "What were you planning before I hijacked your kinky?"

"No plans." He paused, giving me a heated look. "A lot of ideas, though."

"Ideas?"

"How 'bout I take you out to dinner tonight, and dancin', and tell you 'bout 'em?"

That evening, I put on a butter yellow, smocked sundress and my espadrilles and drove with Will, who had on a crisp, plaid, short sleeve shirt and jeans, to an Italian restaurant he liked. His hair was still wet and wavy from the shower, and he smelled utterly yummy. And the restaurant? Vegan paradise. Over my pasta primavera, he proceeded to tell me, in exquisite detail, the sexual things that he liked. Thank God we were squirreled away in a dark corner. My panties barely survived.

"Like that part of your neck, Marie, the part where your neck meets your shoulder. Good for bitin'." He reached over and traced his hand along my bare shoulder in my sun dress. He lowered his voice. "Like the taste of you in my mouth. Like it when you squirm when you're tied up. Like it when you come— any time, but especially when you beg for it, when you're pissed off about not getting it. Love your tits. I wanna eat every part of you. I wanna have some fun with whipped cream—"

"That's not vegan," I interrupted, as my stomach fluttered with the thought, and he grinned, reaching for a bite of his dinner.

"You're not the one eating it," he argued, fork held high.

Will's tongue all over my body.

Yeah, fuck vegan. At least for ice cream, whipped cream, and Will's red meat. Another exception to my rule.

After dinner, he drove me to the same country steakhouse as before, but tonight it was filled with an after-dinner bar crowd, rather than restaurant diners. I noticed the dim light and country music playing, and as we walked in, Will held out his arm. "Dance with me."

He took me out to the dance floor and gave me a spin and I laughed and giggled as my skirt spun around. Then he took me in his arms and danced with me all around, totally in control. The song came to an end and he whispered in my ear, as the next song began, "This is George Strait, baby. Good song. 'I Just Wanna Dance With You.' How I feel." Feeling his muscles under his clothes, smelling his clean smell, holding him, I was in bliss. Then he leaned down and kissed me on the dance floor, soft tongue darting against mine, and I was done for.

"Let's get out of here," I whispered.

"Yeah," he agreed quickly.

We arrived home—my home now—and tumbled out of our clothes and into bed. No kinky this time. No games, no tricks. Just fingers, hands, touch, sensation, tongues, and lips all over. He traced my star tattoos on my hips with his fingers and gave each of them wet kisses. Then, when I was primed, he entered me, his cock filling me, giving me pleasure, connecting us together. After we both had climaxed, he fell onto me, his weight feeling secure, and then lifted himself off and gave me a sweet kiss. "Love you," he said. "Let's go outside, it's a nice night."

We slowly got dressed in sweatpants. He handed me his tie-dye and I put it on without a bra, giggling, and we walked down the stairs, Will whistling for Trixie to join us.

Hand in hand, we walked to the bluff, stopping every once in a while to look up at the vast majesty of the sky. Out here, there was no light pollution, no street lights to dim the stars, no sound but the ocean.

We're all part of something universal. What we call it doesn't matter. There's not much separating us, We're all connected. And it's the most apparent under the night sky, where we look at the specks out there, and know that we are just specks on a blue marble looking back.

After a while, not saying much, he squeezed my hand, and we walked back to the ranch house, tucked in, and went to sleep.

> I've moved in, officially, with Will,

I texted Amelia two days later.

> Gave up my studio. Changed addresses. All my shit's in his house. It's gonna look like the Grateful Dead meets Little House on the Prairie.

Wow. That's . . . something. It might work out as a decorating style.

> We're working out too. Amelia, I'm in love. Out of control, my whole heart, never to return, in love with Will Thrash.

<Sobs into her coffee>

On Thursday night, Will and I strolled, hand in hand, down San Luis Obispo's Higuera Street, enjoying the busy Farmer's Market. Table after table overflowed with fresh, local produce: shiny, plump, red tomatoes, piles of orange and purple carrots, green lettuce stacked high. An Andes band with those flutes played along a side street. Other booths advertised political causes, massages, crafts, and just about everything else you could imagine.

I looked up at my tall, divine cowboy, wearing a dark blue western-style shirt, and his Wranglers and boots. He looked like a lot of people here. I was dressed in a long, hippie skirt that went down to my toes, and a white tank top that showed off my tats. I looked like a lot of people here too.

Oh, but he wore his cowboy hat instead of his trucker hat, and I positively swooned the second he put it on. I don't know what it was. I never had a thing for cowboys before. But Will was so authentically country, that it just fit him, fit his personality, and because he was so tall, it made him look, if possible, like he was even more in charge. I ate it up.

We stopped to buy street corn—no butter—for me, and a tri-tip sandwich for him, and he traced his fingers down the "*Omnia causa fiunt*" tattoo on my arm.

"Everything happens for a reason?" he asked. "You believe that?"

I nodded. "I'm sure I was meant to take the job at Head-lands so that I could meet you. And get my head out of my ass."

"Same," he said, and kissed the top of my head and we watched the people walk by.

As we waited, a group of people came up to him, all of them about his age and country-looking like him in Wranglers, boots, and baseball caps. The women were in flashy, rhinestone cowgirl jeans.

"Well if it isn't Will Thrash?" said a stocky guy in the country boy uniform, modified with a Nascar baseball hat, stepping forward to shake his hand.

"Phil," Will replied, "good to see you, man." He nodded to everyone else. "This is my girlfriend, Marie."

I felt like all eyes were on me. This was the moment that I'd been scared of ever since we got together. The judging. The "What is an edgy weirdo like her doing with a guy like that?" The looks of disapproval from people who knew Will and thought that we didn't belong together. The comments that we didn't match.

I didn't get it.

"Congratulations!" said one of the women, a pretty brunette in really awesome heeled boots.

"Nice one," said another guy to Will. "Good to meet you, Marie," he said to me.

They all smiled and were genuinely polite. I felt relieved, like I had passed a test that I had been worried about.

Maybe we matched after all.

No.

I knew we matched after all.

EPILOGUE: TATTOOS

TWO *YEARS LATER*

Will lay back in the saran wrap-covered chair, his Wrangler jeans unbuttoned and pulled down to an indecent level. The gloved tattoo artist had his head bent, working on the design on Will's hipbone, a tattoo machine in his hand, permanently inking the purple pattern.

Stars to match mine.

One was already done; we had returned for his second, matching star.

My lover. My soul mate.

My husband.

I sat in a chair to the side, my legs tucked under me, my arms resting on my swelling belly, my fingers playing with my ring, twirling it around. In about five months, there'd be a new Thrash child. We had decided not to find out if it was a boy or a girl, but to be surprised.

Since I met Will, I'd finished up my degree at UCSB and opened a small therapy office in a downstairs room of the ranch house. I had patients come from miles away for counseling, mostly children, and I think that the relaxed air of Headlands Ranch aided in their recovery.

The avocados came in really well last year, with the lucky coincidence of prices going sky high, and he was able to make a sizable down payment on the neighbor's property. We were in escrow to close, and the acreage would ensure that the area would remain rural, without the development. These days, since he wasn't getting development pressure, he was a lot more relaxed.

Will had proposed to me a year ago, while we were out riding Thor.

It was a summer's day and the first time that I'd ridden bareback. He was teaching me how. Once you got the feel for it, bareback riding wasn't that hard. But it was fun to go riding together, me in the front and Will behind, holding my waist.

We ambled through the orchards and took a ride through the vineyards, back around, and then went out to our favorite bluff overlooking the beach. There, looking out at the ocean, the sun shining, and the air sultry, he pulled an antique filigree diamond ring out of his pocket and slipped it on my hand while we had stopped to look at the view.

Startled, I looked down at my hand, and then turned around on the horse to look at him.

"Want to be with you forever," he told me, sincerely. "I've loved you since I met you and always will. This was my grand-mother's ring. Asked my dad for it. Want you to wear it. Marry me, Marie."

Overcome, unable to form words, I simply nodded, and burst into tears, and he wrapped me in an enthusiastic hug and then kissed me.

"Tonight. I don't want to wait anymore."

"Tonight?" I answered, startled. He smiled.

"Do you want a big wedding?"

No. I didn't. "No."

"Then tonight, baby. Pack a suitcase. Tell the Fieldings to meet us in Vegas."

I burst out laughing, and he pulled out a printout of the plane tickets from his pocket.

"You're serious?" I asked, astonished.

"Yep." His brown eyes were amused, but completely serious.

"What if I'd said no?" I asked him, unable to stop challenging him.

"You haven't said yes yet," he retorted.

Giddy with excitement, I burst out, "Yes, you crazy cowboy, Okay, yes, today." I paused. And it hit me. "Ohmigod, we're getting married today." And I totally squealed.

He dug his heels into Thor and we galloped back to the stables, put the tack away and settled him in, cleaned off, and were in his truck, headed to the Santa Barbara airport within an hour and a half. I shook, trembling with excitement, and could barely keep my hands off of him.

Even Will kept laughing, happy.

Ryan and Amelia met us at the airport. I shrieked when I saw her and almost bowled her over with a hug. Ryan gave Will one of those dude handshake, half hug, back slap things, and then wrapped me in a big hug, too. Will had apparently tipped them off to our trip. Actually, not just that, because Amelia had packed up a special suitcase with a new dress for me. She remembered my favorite one, she said, from going shopping with her for her wedding, and she went ahead and bought it for me.

We were all wired with excitement and could barely sit still in the small charter plane. Ryan had hired one as a wedding present.

It felt like we were barely up in the air and then we touched down in Las Vegas. When we pulled up to the Wynn, Amelia and I squealed yet again, and the guys looked amused. I was joyous and ridiculous, and I didn't care who knew it. Courtesy of Mr. Fielding, we were booked into two over-the-top luxurious suites, and I couldn't stop pacing around, checking it out. The guys took over one to watch television while Amelia and I used the other to get ready.

Amelia had bought me a bias cut slip dress, very 1930s Jean Harlow, in an off-white silk satin. She helped me wrap my hair up in a chignon and tucked a huge red rose behind my ear. While the dress was old-fashioned, my tattoos made it edgy and I loved it. Amelia, who thought of everything, even remembered to pack a pretty strapless bra. She'd brought me strappy stilettos and handed me a bouquet of dark red roses, so dark they were almost black.

An hour and a half later, we sent the guys off in a limo because I wanted to be at least marginally traditional and not let Will see me. The limo came back, picked us up, and we met the guys at the Chapel of the Flowers. When we arrived, Amelia got out first, wearing a tight, knee length, red strapless dress. She scoped out where the guys were, and made sure the coast was clear and that the chapel was ready for us.

Then I walked in, and walked down the aisle, holding her arm, trembling from excitement, but completely ecstatic to be marrying my guy.

Will stood at the end of the aisle in black pants, a white shirt with a bolero tie, a black western jacket, and boots. Fuck me, cowboy. The white shirt contrasted with his tan skin, and his hair was a mop of dark lusciousness. Ryan, stunning as always, wore slacks, a jacket, and a shirt and tie. They both had red roses in their lapels. Amelia to the rescue.

I turned to Amelia. "Is this heaven?"

She laughed.

When I arrived at the end of the short aisle, Will held my

hand, and looked down at me, his brown eyes loving. "You okay?" he whispered.

"Never better," I whispered back and squeezed his hand.

"You look so beautiful," he whispered, "Can't wait until you're mine."

"I've been yours since I met you," I whispered back and he smiled.

And then it was "I do," and "I do," and when it was time, he dipped me back and kissed me so that the entire outside world dropped away. Then I noticed Amelia whooping next to me.

When he finished, I put my hand over my mouth and giggled.

Mrs. William C. Thrash III.

I felt like I'd come home at last.

When we were outside, giddy still, Ryan asked what we wanted to do next.

Did he need to ask? Vegas is my kind of place. The party girl in her element.

Let's just say we had fun that night.

Now, a year later, as the tattoo artist wiped up the blood, I asked Will, "You're seriously going to vote no on that proposition?"

"It's gonna cost the taxpayers money," he responded.

"Well, I'm voting yes, so it's gonna cancel yours out. We might as well not vote."

He laughed.

I turned to the tattoo artist. "This is the way we are. Fight and then makeup sex and then fight and then, well, you get the idea."

The tattoo artist looked up at Will, who shrugged, and then said, "Better to argue about something than to argue about nothing. It means you care what the other one thinks."

Will and I looked at each other and burst out laughing.

"Yep," said Will. "We do." And he motioned for me to come close, and gave me a wet kiss.

That night, in the ranch house, a dressing on his hipbone, the stars on his hips united with mine for the first time.

And definitely not the last.

BONUS: WILL'S "BACK STORY"

Author's Note

A friend asked me to write one of Will's threesomes for her. I did it, although I was concerned about taking away from his love for Marie by describing sex with someone else. Or two someones.

Still, I wrote it. Because I write porn, I mean erotica, for my friends.

So here's a twenty-three-year-old Will's first threesome. Don't read it if you can't imagine him being with anyone but Marie.

~

Eleven years earlier
Santa Maria, California

"MGD," I told the bartender, a tough broad. She leaned over the bar in a pink v-neck t-shirt that showed too much of her tan, wrinkled, sagging jugs. Her overly bleached blonde hair looked like it'd fall out of her head if you touched it.

She was nice to me, though, calling me hun, and making

sure I didn't have to wait too long for a beer. I was on beer number two. Still early.

Slapping down a coaster, she took off the cap and handed me the bottle.

I took a pull, my back to the counter, and surveyed the crowd, hooking a heel of my boot to the rung towards the bottom of the bar.

The dive played Brooks and Dunn, always a good sign. I hated it when they played this other, newer country shit that was coming out. Garth Brooks started it, and he's okay, but I'm a traditional guy. George Strait. This new shit's not real country with any real emotion; it's just manufactured pop. Makes me disgusted.

To my right, sitting at the bar stools, lurked a big bear of a guy with a beard and a gut barely covered by his Harley t-shirt and his woman, prettier than he deserved, both drinking whiskey and laughing. To my left, an older, skinny cowboy, clothes hanging off of his frame, sitting alone nursing a Coors. There were plenty of people here tonight, Friday night, after work, wanting to blow off steam: College students, ranchers, farmers, and country folk.

I sure needed to cut loose. It'd been a long week of water pumps going out on the ranch, cattle getting loose, fences needing fixing, and my ma having an episode. I needed a release and I needed it now. The beer helped. But, no way around it, I needed to get laid and my hand wasn't going to do the job.

As I drank my beer, a big group of college girls walked in, followed by a couple of cowgirls, who looked older than me, but not by much. One was a blonde, with long, wavy hair and a pretty face. The other was a sultry Latina, all curves, in a tiny jean skirt and white boots. They stopped as they walked in, the blonde turning to whisper something in the Latina's ear. She had on Rocky Mountain jeans, the high waisted, not fashionable kind, but I love 'em because there's no back pockets so there's nothing to obscure the view of pure ass. Definite prospects.

But which one?

They came over to the bar and sidled up next to me, the blonde ordering a Bud Light and the Latina a Jack and Coke. I raised an eyebrow to the blonde, who giggled and said, "Hi, I'm Patty. This is Luz. What's your name?"

I told them, shook their hands, and pulled a sip of my beer. "You all go to school here?" I asked.

"No. We're not from around here. I went to community college ages ago, but never finished," said the blonde. Patty. Patty. Remember that. "I work as a dental assistant. Luz is getting her teaching credential."

"Cool."

The song changed to George Strait's "All My Ex's Live in Texas." Yeah, that fits. Didn't wanna think about her. "Wanna dance?" I asked the blonde.

She giggled, looked at her friend, and said, "Sure."

After my mom had that car accident when I was a baby, she could never walk again. But as a young woman, she'd really loved to dance. So she made sure that I had lessons when I was a kid. I could do it and I liked to. Not much to it, really, you just gotta lead the way.

Patty smelled good, very pretty, and once I got my hands on her, I could tell that she was all soft and sweet.

"How old are you, handsome?" she asked, looking up at me. Her eyes were light blue, very clear.

"Twenty-three."

"You're just a baby," she said, laughing.

"Man's not supposed to ask, but you?"

"Twenty-seven. Luz is twenty-eight." Older women. I like 'em.

"What brings you out tonight?"

"We needed to get a little crazy," she said. "We've been working too hard."

I nodded.

The song ended, but another one started, just as good but a little faster, so I spun her around and she laughed. Then she pulled me a little tighter to her, and I breathed in the scent of her shampoo. A good, clean girl. I don't know if she would be the one for tonight. She seemed experienced, but she also seemed too innocent. Maybe it was the blue eyes. When the song ended, we went back over to her friend, Luz, who babysat the beers. "Thanks for watching my drink," I said.

"Don't mention it," she said.

"You wanna dance too?"

She brightened up a little bit. "Yeah. You seem to know what you're doing out there."

Dancing, sure, I can do. Fucking, sure. But figuring out how to juggle flirting with two women at once? Dunno.

The Latina smelled good too. Like fancy perfume, but the good kind. Her dark, thick hair hung over her shoulders and it spun around when I turned her. The blonde was good to dance with but the Latina really knew how to dance, moving with me well.

Then she leaned up in my ear and said, "You think you can take us both on, cowboy?"

Fuck me.

I looked down at her, all pretty in her boots and mini skirt and I furrowed my eyebrows together.

"What are you . . . you saying what I think you're sayin'?"

"Patty and me made a deal," she replied. "We were going to go out tonight and pick up the most handsome cowboy we could find. If we could find two, fine, but we were going to take him to a hotel and fuck his brains out."

Shit.

"Shit." My dick stirred. "That's kinda forward," I said. Couldn't help it. It was.

"You think?" she answered, sarcastically. "You don't get anything in life unless you ask for it. The second we saw you, Patty and I agreed that you're the one. So, you up for it? Two at once?"

She didn't have to ask me twice. This was what I had come out for, although I wasn't anticipating two. I'd never had two girls at once. Since she broke off the engagement, I'd picked up plenty of women from bars, been to their houses, fucked them, and left them. But this way, with them picking me up? Didn't happen that much.

Still, I was up for it.

I nodded. "Where to?"

"We drove out from Fresno because it was too damn hot and we wanted to go to the beach. So we have a hotel in Pismo. Wanna join us?"

"Tell me which one and I'll follow you in my truck."

I was glad that none of us had too much to drink so we could leave immediately, horny as hell. I followed Patty and Luz in their big ol' white truck with mud on the tires to Pismo Beach, met them in the parking lot, and followed them up the elevator to their room, which looked over the beach. Pretty nice place.

They pulled out a bottle of Jack, a Diet Coke, and I went down the hall for some ice.

When they let me in, I asked, "Have you gals done this before?"

"Nope," said Patty, at the same time Luz said, "Yes."

Interesting.

"I'm bi, and she's open," said Luz. "Have a drink," and she handed me a Jack and Diet Coke.

I downed it, needing the liquor to take away the awkwardness. The Jack warmed my throat and belly and I poured another one. I needed it.

"Alright girls, what are you thinking?"

They each sipped on their drinks, Patty giggling and Luz looking thoughtful.

"Strip poker," Luz announced.

I wasn't bad at poker. Luz went over to a suitcase and pulled out a deck of cards and she and I sat on the little light green hotel couch, Patty on an armchair. I stretched out my legs, still wearing my boots. At least they didn't have too much mud on them.

Luz dealt the cards and I turned them over. Pair of twos and a pair of Jacks.

We went around and bet, and I picked up a card. Another two. Full house. Lady Luck was with me tonight.

When it was time to show our cards, I won. Both Luz and Patty folded and took off their shoes.

I took another shot of Jack. I'd better watch it.

We played another few rounds. Eventually, I lost my boots, my socks, my belt, and my shirt. Luz had only her bra and a mini skirt. Patty down to just her satin, light blue panties, her perky little tits on display, her hair brushing her shoulders. The bottle of Jack Daniels was low, though by this point I'd quit the shots and just drank the soda.

I was fucking hard.

Especially looking at Patty's pretty tits.

"So what do we do when we lose?" asked Patty. "Since I'm the one who's lost the most hands?"

"The two winners fuck the loser," said Luz.

I laughed. "That doesn't make sense."

She shrugged. "Motivation to get your clothes off."

We played another round, and I lost the hand. This meant

my jeans had to go. But since I hadn't worn anything underneath, I'd be the first to get naked.

I lost the game.

I stood up.

One minute, I wore my jeans.

The next, they were around my ankles.

And the next, the girls were on me, Luz on her knees in front of me, sucking me off.

"Fuck yeah, baby," I groaned, as she licked the length and then tongued my balls. After some god-fucking-awesomeness, I pulled out because I didn't want to go just yet. "Clothes off, Luz. You won. Patty, you too. We're gonna try something."

Patty giggled and shimmied out of her panties, revealing a pussy with almost no hair. She was so downy, it was like there was nothing there.

Luz stared up at me, then stood up, took off her mini skirt, standing in a black bra and black panties. She slowly took off the bra, one snap at a time, then her panties. She was bare. Fuckin' awesome.

"Here's what we're gonna do," I said. "First, I'm gonna get you both off. Then one of you is gonna ride my face and the other is gonna ride my cock."

Patty giggled and Luz looked pleased.

"Think I gotta loosen you up a bit," I said, and I started ordering them around. "Patty, on the bed. Legs spread. Luz, darlin', right here next to us. Now finger yourself."

"No," she said, "I'm going to help you with Patty."

And fuck me, she leaned over and gave Patty a scorching hot, wet kiss with lots of tongue.

Shit.

I bent down between Patty's legs and smelled her sweet womanly smell. God, I love the smell of pussy. It smells like sex, like I'm gonna get some. The best thing in the world.

Licking her up one side of her thigh and then the other, I paused to see what Luz was doing. She sucked on Patty's tits like there was nothing else to do, fondling one, kissing the other. Patty let out a moan of pleasure as I tongued her clit, then I put one finger in her hole, then two, and rubbed inside her, while I licked and sucked on her clit.

I could feel her get wetter, I could feel her tense up, I kept going, finger fucking her, eating her, until she came on my face, fuck yeah, shuddering all over me.

When she came back down, I leaned back, hard-on hurting, and looked at Luz, who smiled at me.

"Your turn, darlin'," I said to Luz.

"I think you can take both of us on at once, handsome," she replied.

What a crazy night. But I was up for the challenge. I got up, went to my wallet, and pulled out a condom. Then I got on my back on the bed, and bunched a couple of pillows under my head.

"Luz, you pick, where do you want to be. My cock or my face."

She smiled wickedly. "Face."

"Then, Patty, c'mon, darlin." She climbed over, and lowered herself on my cock, fuck yeah, that felt good, and Luz straddled my head, holding herself above me, facing Patty. "Let me see you kiss again," I moaned, and the girls leaned over and met mouth to mouth, tonguing each other.

Fuck, this was the most erotic thing I had ever seen, experienced, felt, thought of.

Patty started riding me, going up and down my cock, slowly, and Luz lowered herself on my face. Her bare pussy was so magnificent. I reached a finger up her pussy, and a finger up her ass, and held her to my mouth, licking and sucking her, as she kissed Patty, feeling up Patty's breasts.

I'd no idea how we were all gonna come at once but I was enjoying the ride.

I could feel Luz building up, so I kept going, licking, sucking, into it, and she came in a burst of juice on my face. Loved it.

One down. She moved, and rolled over to the side, and started fingering herself next to me. God, I loved that too.

"Patty, darlin'," I managed, "you gonna come?"

"Maybe," she said.

"Let's do this," I said. "Luz, I'm gonna take you from behind. You wanna eat her?"

Her eyes lit up.

Patty spread her legs on the bed, and Luz immediately lowered her face to Patty's pussy. I almost shot my load from that. I got a new condom, put it on, and positioned myself behind Luz, entering her, mounting her.

Now this was even better. I watched Luz's back, her head giving Patty everything she had. Patty writhed and struggled on the bed, ready to let out another orgasm. And I fucked Luz hard from behind, spanking her sweet ass.

Then, when I was about to come, I fingered her clit, and she shuddered around my cock, making me come, hard and long, yeah, in warm spurts. Luz kept going on Patty's pussy, I don't know how, but Patty came again, and we all collapsed onto each other.

Most incredible Friday night ever.

I kissed the back of Luz's neck, pulled out of her, then leaned over and kissed Patty. Then I went to the bathroom and threw away the condom.

Standing there in the doorway of the bathroom, the two girls snuggling into each other, I thought, hot damn, I'm a lucky man.

ACKNOWLEDGMENTS

I wish to express my appreciation to those who specifically helped with this book, including: Heather "Here, have a dick pic" Roberts; Maxine "I want to read Will's threesome" Donner; Meghan "I really think there should be bug zappers on the ranch" Clark; Little ":]" Dude; Summer "Write a story about a girl named Summer" Graystone; Mary "Will you be my beta forever?" Carr (of Romazing Reader); Jerica "No commas for you" MacMillan; Kristy Lin "Marie sounds like a twelve-year-old boy, oh and by the way my wife likes to look over my shoulder at the hot men on your Facebook page" Billuni (of www.sexygrammar.com); Cassy "Goddess" Roop (of Pink Ink Designs); Michele "Also Goddess" Catalano (of Michele Catalano Creative); Cory "I like to throw you off your game" Stierley; Mitchell "I'm serious about the McLaren, dude" Wick; and the team at Social Butterfly PR.

I am so grateful to my family and friends for support, whether I sit down with you for lunch or connect with you online.

I love you all.

EXCERPT FROM ALL THE WATERS OF THE EARTH

Jake Slausen, hottie workaholic lawyer, is married to his job. Lucy Figueroa, a five foot nothing, sassy romance novelist, thinks she met her fictional hunk come to life when he moves in next door to her. But since he's never lived, he doesn't know how to be a romance hero.

She'll help him figure it out.

ROMANCE WRITER'S PROBLEMS

My fingers hovered over the keyboard of my computer. I kept typing.

. . . and he shifted, pressing his full male heat into her petals.

Delete.

. . . and he gently slid his member into her secret center.

No. Delete.

. . . and he impaled her on his straining shaft.

Ugh. Delete.

I rapped my fingers on the side of my desk.

What's on Facebook?

No. No distractions. Keep writing.

Or . . . take a break.

I got my ample booty out of my chair and walked into the kitchen of my duplex to pour a glass of water. Today's writing was not going very well. Romance novel number sixteen, I feared, was falling into the pitfalls of **cliché** and drivel. I needed something new. My hero was not making me wet. At all. I tired of typing and deleting, typing and deleting, not getting anywhere.

The thing was, I loved being a romance novelist. I loved everything about it: inventing cute ways to make the characters meet, describing the hot men and women, making up a secret, tragic past, and the sex. Oh, the sex. I loved all of it.

My fictional guys tended to have a few things in common. They were all tall. They had chiseled good looks: high cheekbones, strong jaws, full heads of hair, and gorgeous bodies. They were uniformly Alpha males, the type who would fuck you hard against a wall and make you moan in pleasure. The type to order you around and then show you their soft underbelly. Ooh, baby, make me shiver. I liked them to be men, you know, not wishy-washy, but I liked them to have a soul, too.

For some reason, though, I was having trouble with this book. I always started with the sex, but if I couldn't get that right, then I knew the rest of it wouldn't work either.

I needed inspiration.

Given my profession, I had this habit of always looking for the real life versions of my heroes. I couldn't stop doing it. That sexy-ass DILF in line at Target, with broad shoulders and a beard, balancing a tiny baby girl on his impressive bicep? He looked like Zack from my fourth book. That tattooed masterpiece at Home Depot, all jeans and legs and boots and body? If you grew his dark hair a little shaggier, he kind of looked like Clint in book twelve. And that artsy hottie standing by the bar with the Smith and Wesson belt and what had to be a giant cock? I was going to have to write a book about him next. He was first on my list of heroes after this one.

The thing was, I'd banged out fifteen romance novels in seven years and I wasn't stopping anytime soon. Normally, it was pretty easy for me to do; just not this day, for some reason. I'd done this long enough that I knew the secret to finishing a novel: keep at it. And I kept at it, almost every day, all day. I was not one of those OCD people who has to write every day at the same time and have the same music on and wear the same clothes.

Well, most of the time I wore yoga pants and a cami but they were clean and rotated.

But still, I wasn't really a girl for routine. No manky old college sweatshirt for me to write in, sitting slovenly around the house. A girl had to show some pride. You would never find me without full makeup on every day and a Brazilian blowout for my naturally frizzy hair. I had to look good to take my kid to school.

I was no writer recluse either. I got out of the house, often, going for drinks. Life was too short not to play. I liked to go out with my friends and made sure to get babysitters even though I had a kid when I was seventeen. But I also liked to write, and I did it almost daily. And I was glad to make a living at it, although I had to supplement my income in other ways: I got child support from my ex, Carlos. And, whether you believe it or not, I also posed as a nude model at an art school.

No judgies.

My body was womanly and I flaunted it.

The nude model gig brought in a little bit of dough to spend on high heels and video games for Rob.

There was no way that I could be a regular five foot ten, one hundred twenty-five pound model. No way. I was what you would call fun-sized. Five foot nothin', baby. I never really took off my high heels, except in art class. Short girl problems.

And you know those magazine articles about how to dress for your type and they are all, like, are you an apple or a carrot or something? Me? Pear shaped. And how.

I defined the term "junk in the trunk." My booty entered the room thirty seconds after I did. My waist? Nothing there. It was tiny. My boobs? Small, but perky. My legs? Short and strong.

When I bought pants, they never fit because they were too big in the waist and too long in the legs.

But you know what? That was the problem of the clothing manufacturers, not me.

Though my body was not made for high fashion modeling, it was ideal for modeling for art classes, where they celebrated shapes and curves. I had decided a long time ago not to waste precious brain space wishing I had a different body. This was the one I was born with and I accepted my looks. This was how tall I was, and I was not getting any taller. This was how long my legs were, and they weren't getting any longer. And my booty? Yeah, I showed it off sometimes in a tight mini skirt and heels when I went out dancing.

As I drank my water, I looked around my nice Santa Barbara duplex. A royalty check for my fourth novel made for the down payment. Royalty checks on the fifth and sixth helped to pay the mortgage. The rest of the books paid for food for me and my twelve year old son, Rob, as well as clothes, taxes, insurance, and all of the other grown up things in this life.

I must say, though, I was really not a fan of the grown up things in life. I'd rather be a romantic. Who had any use for the real world? That was why we have books.

My home felt cozy and lived-in. Rob had his Xbox and games out, but other than that, we kept it neat. There was a small kitchen, a large great room that was both a dining room and a living room, three bedrooms, one of which I used as an office, and two bathrooms, all in a square. I would call the style early Target, with a dash of Restoration Hardware, meets Dia de los Muertos.

The duplex was part of a larger complex that had a home-owner's association and we had a pool and a tennis court and everything. My unit shared a wall and a laundry room with the unit next door, which was a rental. Someone had moved in over the weekend but I hadn't seen them yet. We had adjoining patios that looked out over the pool. I loved to swim and used the pool often. We were lucky in California that the time of year did not hamper the ability to go swimming and I could go now even though it was nearing Thanksgiving.

Maybe I just needed to get out of the house for a while and take a break. Rob wouldn't be back from school for a while. Sometimes doing things like laundry or driving or swimming or walking helped with the writing.

Downing the last of my water, I went into the bedroom and put on a pink string bikini. I was a girlie girl. I did not do utilitarian. Since I was so close to the pool, I rarely took much down there: just a towel and my oversized sunglasses.

Grabbing my keys, I slipped on my high heeled sandals, threw open the door, and there was a man standing there, with his hand raised to knock on my door.

A very handsome man.

The most handsome man that I had ever seen.

Thick, ebony hair. Sapphire blue eyes. His face had the curves and the edges of a romance hero, with high cheek bones, the hollows in his cheeks, and a shapely jaw.

He was dressed in Mr. Business Man attire: a crisp white shirt, perfect, thick, and lush; a gray and blue silk tie that matched his eyes, not too shiny, not too matte; and a dark gray suit that enhanced his frame. He was tall, but of course everyone was tall next to me. That said, he was probably a foot taller than me, or more, with muscular legs, a flat waist, and broad shoulders.

For a second, I couldn't believe it. There was no fucking way this man was on my front porch. He was the kind of man I wrote about in my books. But those men did not really exist. Those men were just figments of my imagination. Real men have bellies and are too short or too lanky and wear cargo shorts and

Star Wars t-shirts and need to manscape. They don't show up at your door looking like Gideon Cross.

He looked at me, equally startled, and then his eyes went up and down my body, taking in my tiny pink bikini and high-heeled sandals. Then he seemed to recover and took a step back and started talking.

"Hi, I'm Jake Slausen. I moved in next door. I'm staying here for a while because I'm remodeling my place. So, I guess I'm your neighbor. Nice to meet you." He had a deep, melodious voice, which was very attractive. But boy, he was a chatterbox. He held out his hand.

"Lucy Figueroa," I said, shaking his hand. His hand was warm, firm, and strong.

I wondered what it would feel like between my legs.

Probably pretty damn fine.

I continued, "I was just heading for the pool. Have you been down there yet?"

"Not yet. I have to get back to work. I stopped by here because I forgot something, and then I went to check in the laundry room—I guess we share the laundry room, right?" I nodded. "Well, I went to check it, and I figured that this was yours."

And he held out his other hand and there, dangling, were my red, lace, thong panties.

I grabbed my undergarment. "Thanks," I said, mustering up as much dignity that I could under the circumstances, my cheeks burning red.

Then we stared at each other. I bit my lip. He ran his fingers under his jaw and then behind his neck.

"Well, it's nice to meet you, Lucy. I work a lot but I'm sure to see you around here."

"I'll have to bring you some tamales," I said, trying to think of an excuse to see him again. "Christmas is coming and we do that around here."

"That sounds good," he said absently, still looking up and down my body. And then he took a step backwards and brushed up against the large potted ficus that sat on my front porch, tripping slightly. Pushing it aside, he turned to leave, and said, "Well, I'll be seeing you. I have to go back to the office." And then he turned and left.

I stared at him as he left and then I closed my door slowly, depositing my panties in my bedroom.

A shiver of excitement ran through my body from top to toe. Of course I was short so this didn't take too long. But this thrill that I felt? I had not felt it in a long time.

And this guy was my new *neighbor*?

Life was about to get more interesting.

I needed to cook up a plan to get to know him better. He seemed just perfect - perfect looks, perfect manners, perfect voice. I wonder if he was perfect in bed, too.

Retracing my steps to my front door, I took my towel, sunglasses, and keys, now on a mission to think about not only my new book, but also this new romance hero, living next to me.

ALSO BY LESLIE MCADAM

Sarina Bowen's World of True North (m/m)

Undone (audio narrated by Iggy Toma and Tim Paige)

Unmanageable (audio narrated by Jacob Morgan and Teddy Hamilton)

IOU Series (m/m)

Ambiguous (audio narrated by Hamish Long and Kirt Graves)

Studious

Oblivious (coming soon)

Contemporary Romance (m/f)

All American Boy Series

Boy on a Train (audio narrated by Desiree Ketchum and James Cavenaugh)

Romantic comedies with Lex Martin

All About the D (audio narrated by Stephen Dexter and Ava Erickson)

Surprise, Baby! (audio narrated by Jacob Morgan and Muffy Newton)

The Giving You ... series

The Sun and the Moon (audio narrated by Tor Thom and Charley Ongel)

The Stars in the Sky

All the Waters of the Earth

The Ground Beneath Our Feet (audio narrated by Tor Thom and Charley Ongel)

Love in Translation series

Sol

Sombra

Standalone novella

Lumbersexual (audio narrated by Tor Thom and Charley Ongel)

ABOUT THE AUTHOR

Leslie McAdam is a California girl who loves romance and well-defined abs. She lives in a drafty old farmhouse on a small orange tree farm in Southern California with her husband and two children. Leslie's first published book, *The Sun and the Moon*, won a 2015 Watty, which is the world's largest online writing competition. She's gone on to receive additional literary awards and has been featured in multiple publications, including Cosmopolitan.com. Her books have been Top 100 Bestsellers on both Amazon and Apple Books. Leslie is employed by day but spends her nights writing about the men of your fantasies.

Website: https://www.lesliemcadamauthor.com

M/M-only newsletter: http://eepurl.com/hD9a4r